DEATH OF AN INNOCENT

Recent Titles by Sally Spencer from Severn House

THE DARK LADY
DEAD ON CUE
DEATH OF A CAVE DWELLER
GOLDEN MILE TO MURDER
MURDER AT SWANN'S LAKE
THE PARADISE JOB
THE RED HERRING
THE SALTON KILLINGS

DEATH OF AN INNOCENT

A Chief Inspector Woodend Novel

Sally Spencer

This first world edition published in Great Britain 2002 by
SEVERN HOUSE PUBLISHERS LTD of
9–15 High Street, Sutton, Surrey SM1 1DF.
This first world edition published in the USA 2003 by
SEVERN HOUSE PUBLISHERS INC of
595 Madison Avenue, New York, N.Y. 10022.

British Library Cataloguing in Publication Data

Spencer, Sally, 1949-
    Death of an innocent
    1. Woodend, Chief Inspector (Fictitious character) - Fiction
    2. Police - England - Fiction
    3. Detective and mystery stories
    I. Title
    823.9'14 [F]

    ISBN 0-7278-5708-8

Typeset by Palimpsest Book Production Ltd.,
Polmont, Stirlingshire, Scotland.
Printed and bound in Great Britain by
MPG Books Ltd., Bodmin, Cornwall.

One

The first flakes of snow had made their appearance in the middle of the night, floating gently down to earth like mellow kamikaze pilots and melting wistfully away almost as soon as they made contact. The ones which followed were better organized, tighter packed and more determined, and by the time dawn finally broke, the moors were covered with a thick white blanket.

It was still snowing as Detective Sergeant Monika Paniatowski coaxed her seven-year-old MGA down the rutted track which led to the hand-loom weaver's cottage that her boss, Charlie Woodend, had bought when Scotland Yard had exiled him to the North of his youth.

Paniatowski checked her watch. Woodend himself wouldn't mind being disturbed at this ungodly time on a Sunday morning, she thought, but she didn't imagine for a moment that Joan, his wife, would be best pleased.

She eased her car round a bend in the lane and brought it to a halt in front of the stone cottage. Woodend, who must have heard the MGA's tortuous progress – and understood immediately what it signified – was already standing by the front door, dressed in a shabby overcoat and inhaling energetically on a Capstan Full Strength cigarette.

Paniatowski wound down her window just in time to hear his parting words to his wife.

'Don't be daft, lass. You'll never get a taxi in this weather,' the big man said. 'Besides, I'm not havin' some stranger seein' you off. You're my missis, an' *I'll* take you down to the station.'

He closed the door, and walked down the steps to the car. 'If you're draggin' me out on a mornin' like this for anythin' less than the wholesale massacre of the Whitebridge Boy Scouts, you're in big trouble, Monika,' he growled.

'It's not quite as spectacular as that, sir – but we have got two dead bodies on our hands. I tried to ring you about it, but all I got was the engaged signal.'

Woodend walked round to the passenger side and opened the door. 'Telephone line's probably down. It happens a lot with the snow. Still, it won't bother Joan. She's goin' to Altrincham.'

'I don't quite follow you, sir.'

Woodend looked at her almost pityingly. 'It won't be snowin' in Altrincham, because they're too posh there to have the same weather as everybody else,' he explained.

'Family visit?' Paniatowski asked.

'Aye,' Woodend agreed. 'She'll be stayin' with her sister – the one who was smart enough to marry a bank manager rather than a policeman.' He opened the passenger door, and squeezed inside. 'I wish you'd get a bigger car, Monika.'

'I wish you'd get a better road, sir,' his sergeant told him.

'So what's it all about this time?' Woodend asked, as Paniatowski began to execute a three-point turn on the slippery snow.

'I haven't got all the details yet,' the sergeant said. 'All I know is that a reporter from the BBC rang the station and said he'd found two bodies – a man and a woman – at a farmhouse out on the moors.'

'Probably hypothermia,' Woodend pronounced. 'You get a lot of that with the cold weather. Why aren't the uniforms handlin' it?'

'Because these two didn't freeze to death. They were both

shot – at close range. It's all very messy, apparently. Which makes it sound like a job for us, doesn't it?'

'Oh aye,' Woodend agreed. 'That sounds just up our street.'

The snowploughs would probably turn out later in the day to cut a swathe through the snow, but for the moment it was nature, not man, that was in control. These were the real moors they were crossing now – not the half-civilized moors which existed on the edge of the villages, but the brooding expanses of untamed land which had not changed for five thousand years. The few farmhouses they passed were squat, stone buildings, hunkered down against the wind and the rain, and the folk who lived behind the thick walls could go for days without seeing even their nearest neighbours. It took a special kind of person to farm out on the proper moors, Woodend thought. Special – and bloody weird!

'You say it was a reporter from the BBC who phoned this case in?' he asked, as Paniatowski did her best to keep the MGA travelling in a straight line.

'That's right, sir.'

'An' what the bloody hell was a reporter doin' out on the moors before the crack of dawn?'

'Beats me,' Paniatowski admitted.

A large building site, surrounded by a chain-link fence, loomed incongruously up in front of them. Woodend looked at the huge billboard picture of neat, detached houses and read the banner which proclaimed, 'The Moorland Village – a new concept in rural living from T. A. Taylor and Associates!'

'Bollocks!' he said.

'I take it from that you're not very keen on housing estates, sir,' Monika Paniatowski observed.

'Housin' estates are all very well in their place – an' their

3

place is the towns,' Woodend told her. 'If you want to live in the countryside, then bloody live in it properly.'

It was another four miles beyond the building site before Paniatowski pointed ahead and said, 'I think that's the place, sir.'

The farmhouse was located about two hundred yards from the main road. It was similar to the other farms they passed on the way, except that there were at least six vehicles parked in its yard.

'Jesus Christ!' Woodend exploded. 'What the bloody hell did they think they were doin', drivin' right up to the place like that? Which soft bugger's in charge of the team? Mickey Mouse?'

'DI Harris was on duty at the time when the call came in,' Paniatowski said flatly.

'Well, there's no bloody wonder this has happened then, is there?' Woodend demanded angrily. 'Harris needs a map to find his way to his own office.'

'Should we park here and walk the rest of the way?' Monika Paniatowski suggested.

Woodend looked again at the caravan of vehicles parked in front of the farmhouse.

'That'd be like puttin' a French letter on *after* you've had your end away,' he growled.

'Pardon, sir?'

'It's a bit too late to start takin' precautions now, isn't it?'

Paniatowski turned on to the narrow lane, and dropped into a lower gear. The MGA bumped and scraped against the ruts in the track. Woodend studied the vehicles which had already arrived at the scene. There were two family saloons which he recognized as belonging to a couple of his detective constables, two patrol cars, an ambulance, the Humber Super Snipe which Dr Pierson, the police surgeon, had recently acquired, a Triumph Spitfire he didn't recognize at all – and a big green Volvo.

4

'Bloody hell, Dick the Prick's here!' Woodend exclaimed. 'Now that's really *all* I needed!'

Paniatowski nodded sympathetically. The enmity which existed between Chief Inspector Charlie Woodend and Deputy Chief Constable Richard Ainsworth was almost legendary in the Central Lancashire Police. Ainsworth disliked many things about Woodend, including his general attitude to authority, his total lack of dress sense, and the fact that instead of staying at the command centre – as a senior office, in Ainsworth's opinion, should – the bloody man would insist on rooting around at the scene of the crime like a truffle pig. As for Woodend's opinion of Ainsworth, it could not properly be expressed in language he would use in front of a woman – even if that woman were his hardboiled bagman, Monika Paniatowski.

'I can't work out why Dick's here at all,' Woodend mused, as Paniatowski manoeuvred the MGA carefully around the side of the ambulance. 'It's just not like him. Durin' normal workin' hours it's well known his arse is firmly glued to his seat, an' *outside* workin' hours the idle sod probably likes to pretend he's a country gentleman rather than a bobby.'

Paniatowski parked. Woodend heaved himself out of the cramped passenger seat, and took in the scene. The ambulance driver and his mate were sitting in the cab of their vehicle, smoking and reading the Sunday papers. In the distance, a couple of uniformed constables were inspecting one of the outbuildings. And one of Woodend's own regular team, the burly DC Hardcastle, stood on duty by the farmhouse's front door.

As he reached in his overcoat pocket for his cigarettes, Woodend saw DCC Ainsworth emerge from the farmhouse. Ainsworth noticed *him*, too, and made a beeline for him.

'It's extremely kind of you to have finally turned up, Charlie,' the DCC said.

5

'I got here as soon as I could, sir, given the conditions,' Woodend replied evenly. 'Have you been here long yourself?'

'Apart from that reporter from the BBC who discovered the bodies, I was the first one on the scene.'

'Is that right?' Woodend asked quizzically. 'That was fortunate for us, wasn't it?'

'As it happens, it was more by luck than judgement,' Ainsworth conceded. 'I've a busy day ahead of me, so I got up especially early to take one of the dogs over to the kennels in Skelton. We breed and show beagles, you know. We've won prizes for it.'

'No, oddly enough, I didn't know that.'

'Anyway, my errand took me along the Tops Road, and I couldn't have been more than three or four miles from here when I heard about this incident on the police band. So I came straight over.'

'An' did you find anythin' useful, sir?'

'Nothing of note. I just established that the victims were the only people in the house, and then, since I'm not the kind of man who's constantly looking over his subordinates' shoulders, I decided to leave the rest up to you.'

'That was very thoughtful of you, sir.'

If Ainsworth noticed the irony, he showed no sign of it. Instead, he glanced down at his watch.

'My God, how time flies,' he said. 'You don't mind if I go now, do you? I'm expecting some rather important people round for luncheon in just over three hours time.'

An' you wouldn't like to let a simple thing like a double murder get in the way of that, now would you? Woodend thought.

But aloud all he said was, 'If I should happen to need to consult you about anythin', you wouldn't object to me ringin' you at home, would you, sir?'

'Not at all,' Ainsworth said, without much conviction. 'Carry on, Chief Inspector.'

Then he turned and walked back towards his Volvo.

Paniatowski had been tactfully hanging back during the conversation, but now she joined Woodend.

'What did the Old Man have to say for himself?' she asked.

'He said he's got some rather important people comin' round for "luncheon" – which, in case you don't know, is a fancy way of sayin' "Sunday dinner" – so he's had to dash off. You've not got any very important people comin' round for luncheon yourself, have you?'

'Let me think,' Paniatowski said. 'No, I don't think I have, sir.'

'Well, that's a blessin',' Woodend said. 'So, since you don't seem to have anythin' better to do with your time at the moment, let's you an' me go an' look at the scene of the crime, shall we, lass?'

It was as they approached the farmhouse that Woodend first noticed that something was not quite right about the man standing on duty by the door. DC Hardcastle was a stolid and dependable – if uninspired – officer, as well as a pillar of the police rugby team. His face normally glowed with health and vigour, but now he seemed as pale as a ghost.

'Are you all right, Hardie?' Woodend asked solicitously.

The detective constable nodded. 'Yes, sir.'

'Well, I have to say that you don't look it. What's upset you, lad?' He pointed into the farmhouse. 'Was it somethin' you saw in there?'

Hardcastle nodded again, but said nothing.

Woodend frowned. Hardcastle, he knew from experience, was not the kind of man to go into a near faint at the sight of blood.

'Is it somethin' that I should know about before I go in there myself?' he asked.

DC Hardcastle's eyes clouded over and his lips began to tremble like a landed fish's.

'It's . . . it's not somethin' I can tell you about, sir,' he gasped. 'You . . . you won't know . . . you won't understand . . . until you've seen it for yourself.'

Then his broad shoulders shook, and he began to sob uncontrollably.

Two

There was no entrance hall to the farmhouse, and stepping through the front door Woodend found himself in the living room. It was a large, square room, of the sort in which the moorland farmers of a previous generation – and possibly a few of those still around – would cook, eat, repair their equipment, and even tend to sick animals. But it had never been intended to be turned into the slaughterhouse it had become that cold winter morning.

The closest victim to the door – the male – was lying on his back. The front of his white shirt was shredded, revealing a chest which was pitted with scores of small wounds. The man's face was a pulp, with bits of brain, bone and muscle forming an obscene corona around the upper part of the head. The second victim – the female – was bunched up in the far corner of the room, and for the moment was partly obscured by Dr Pierson, who was bending over her body.

There were two other men in the room, one dusting the sideboard with powder, the other standing self-importantly next to the large stone fireplace.

'Found anythin' useful yet, Battersby?' Woodend asked the man by the sideboard.

Constable Clive Battersby turned round to face his boss. 'It's a bit early to say, sir. But there's certainly plenty of prints.'

Woodend nodded. Battersby didn't impress most people

at first sight, he thought – and there was good reason
for it. The detective constable was rapidly running to fat,
and the shiny blue suit he was wearing should have been
thrown out long ago. Yet there was no doubt that he'd
performed very well on the Home Office courses he'd
attended, and when DCC Ainsworth had once referred to
him at a press conference as 'one of our highly trained team
of site-evaluation experts', he'd probably come closer to the
truth than he usually did when he opened his mouth.

The Chief Inspector turned his attention to the other man.
Like Battersby, he was in his early thirties, but showed none
of the constable's inclination to put on weight. His body was
lean, and his face bore those signs of insecurity which can
sometimes manifest themselves equally as arrogance and
extreme sensitivity. There were those who said that DI
Harris had been promoted too soon – and those who said
that he should not have been promoted at all, Woodend
reminded himself. Looking at Harris now, he could not
help wishing that, for a case as serious this one, he had
had Bob Rutter, his old bagman, as his Number Two. But
that was not to be. Rutter was down at the police college
in Hendon, on a course which had been specially designed
for highflying young detective inspectors like him.

'Any leads, Vic?' Woodend asked Harris.

'The farm's owned by a man called Wilfred Dugdale,'
the DI replied.

'That's probably why it says Dugdale's Farm on the
gate,' Woodend said dryly. He pointed to the male corpse.
'Is that him?'

Harris shook his head. 'Dugdale's got white hair and is
in his early sixties. It's hard to be completely accurate about
the victim's age, what with half his face being blown away,
but I wouldn't put him at any more than late forties. And
his hair is mousy brown.'

'So if this isn't Mr Dugdale, where is he?'

'We've no idea. We've searched all the outbuildings, and there's no sign of him.'

'Is there any indication that he was here at the time of the murders?'

'Nothing conclusive, one way or the other.'

Woodend sighed, and wished he didn't have to drag every last piece of information out of this bugger.

'Assumin', for the moment, that he was here at the time of the murders, how would he have left? Do you think he could have *driven* away?' he asked.

'There's a Land Rover parked in one of the outhouses.'

It was like pulling teeth. 'And does Mr Dugdale own any other vehicle?'

'We'll have to check on that.'

You should *already* have checked on it, Woodend thought.

Of course, life would have been a lot easier but for bloody DCC Ainsworth. If Dick the Prick hadn't driven straight up to the farm, none of the other vehicles would have followed him, and it might have been possible to find some tyre tracks in the snow leading away from it. But there was no chance of that now.

If anybody else had made a cock-up like that, I'd have had his balls on a platter, Woodend thought. But Ainsworth wasn't anybody else – and officers of his rank didn't make cock-ups, they were just prone to errors of judgement.

'What else have you got?' Woodend asked Harris.

'We're almost certain that the murder weapon was Dugdale's personal property.'

'Oh aye? An' why's that?'

'We found a shotgun lying on the floor. It had recently been fired. It was registered to Wilfred Dugdale.'

'So you've already put out the word that you want him picked up, have you?'

'No, I . . . should I have done?'

'It might have been an idea.' Woodend turned to

Paniatowski. 'Radio the station. I want roadblocks in place everywhere within a twenty-mile radius of the farm. Anybody with white hair is to be stopped an' questioned. An' if we find out that Dugdale *does* have a second vehicle, I want all cars of a similar make an' model stopped as well.'

'Got it,' the sergeant said.

Woodend looked down at the male corpse again. Harris was probably right about his age – well, Harris had to be right about *something*. The victim was wearing a suit which had seen better days, and had hardly been impressive when new. It was obvious from the position in which the dead man was lying that he'd been standing up when he was shot in the chest, which meant that the second cartridge had been emptied into his face when he was already on the ground.

Now why had the killer done that? Woodend wondered. Because he was so panicked that he hadn't realized his victim was already dead? Or because, on the contrary, he'd remained cool enough after the first discharge to decide it would be to his advantage to make identifying the victim difficult.

Or was there even a third possibility? Could he have hated the other man so much that even killing him was not enough – he'd felt the urge to mutilate him as well?

Doc Pierson had finished examining the female victim, and walked across the room to join Woodend. The doctor was in his late forties, and had distinguished grey hair. He usually moved with the grace of a natural sportsman, but there was none of the normal spring to his step now. Not only that, but his eyes were red, and his face was drawn.

'Rough night?' Woodend asked.

The doctor looked as if he were about to nod his head, then thought better of doing anything so vigorous.

'If I'd known I was going to be here at this godawful hour

of the morning, I'd never have had those last two whiskies,' he said.

'So what can you tell me about the stiffs?'

'Cause of death is self-evident, I'd have thought. Shotgun wounds at close range.'

'Did they die at the same time?'

'Pretty much.'

'And when would that be?'

'Going by the extent of the rigor mortis, I'd say they died somewhere between three o'clock and five o'clock this morning.'

Woodend looked down at the male victim. He was wearing a cheap Timex watch, and the glass had been smashed, probably when he put his hand across his chest in a futile attempt to protect himself.

The Chief Inspector crouched down to take a closer look. The watch face was dented, and the hands twisted, but the small hand was clearly very close to eight and the big one on nine.

'The watch seems to have stopped at a quarter to eight,' he said. 'Which would indicate that's when the gun was fired. Unless, of course, the pellet knocked the hands out of place. Or the man was in the habit of always keeping his watch a couple of hours fast.'

He stood up again and waited for the doctor to comment, but Pierson appeared to be too wrapped up in his own thoughts.

'So what do you think?' Woodend asked.

Pierson shrugged, and then winced at the effect that even such a mild action was having on his body.

'It's possible they were killed later than I said,' he admitted. 'I haven't taken the temperature in here, and I've no idea how long it is since the fire went out.' He paused. 'And to be honest with you, Charlie, my own judgement's not all it might be right now. It's taking me all my effort to even see straight, but give me a couple of hours to get over this hangover and I'll be able to give you a much more accurate assessment.'

Woodend nodded, understandingly. Though he himself could knock back ten pints of best bitter during an evening and wake up fresh as a lark the following morning, he'd long ago accepted the fact that drink could take other men in other ways.

'Do you feel up to talkin' me through the second stiff?' he asked.

'Just about, I suppose,' the doctor said grudgingly.

They walked over to the corner of the room. The victim looked almost too small to be a full-grown woman, Woodend thought, though perhaps, cramped up as she was, that was merely a trick of perspective.

It was possible, even with part of her skull missing, to see that she had long blonde hair. She was wearing a blouse, and a skirt that came to just below her knees. Woodend did not know a great deal about clothes, but he was prepared to bet that the skirt alone had cost considerably more than the dead man's entire outfit.

He let his eyes travel below the skirt. Her legs were slim, and her feet were so small they were almost tiny. The shoes, as with the rest of the outfit, looked expensive.

'Just one wound,' Dr Pierson said, 'though it was probably from both barrels.' His voice cracked. 'It should never have happened, Charlie. It should simply never have happened.'

Woodend shifted to one side, to examine the corpse from another angle. It didn't make any difference. He understood now why DC Hardcastle, who had three daughters of his own, had broken down in tears. He almost felt like following suit himself. He'd been thinking of her up to that point merely as a female corpse – as a dead *woman*. But she wasn't a woman at all – she was no more than a *girl*.

'How old was she?' he asked, feeling a lump in his throat.

'Difficult to say exactly, without a closer examination. Kids grow at different rates. But if I had to make a guess, I'd say she was around fifteen.'

Fifteen! Jesus Christ! Less than two years younger than his beloved Annie, the apple of his eye who had just begun a nursing course in Manchester.

'She's a child!' he said. 'She'd hardly started livin'!'

'I know,' Pierson agreed, sombrely.

Paniatowski came in from the yard. 'The roadblocks should be in place within the next few minutes, sir,' she said. Then she noticed the expression on Woodend's face. 'Are you all right, sir?'

'I'm . . . I'm fine.'

'Do you want me for anything else at the moment, Charlie?' Dr Pierson asked.

'What? Do I . . . ? No, I don't think so.'

'In that case I think I'll go home. Have a few black coffees – and maybe a hair of the dog – before I begin the PMs.'

'Yes, that's a good idea,' Woodend said abstractly.

A kid! he was thinking. A child! Only a few years beyond the dolls and teddy bear stages – yet lying there with her face spattered all over a cold flagstone floor. She would never feel butterflies in her stomach when the boy she'd been mooning after for weeks finally invited her out on a date. She'd never know what it was like to get married and have kids of her own. It was all wrong!

'You're sure you're OK, sir?' Paniatowski asked.

Woodend took a deep breath. 'I told you, I'm fine. Let's see what else we've got here.'

His attention had been focused entirely on the victims before, but now that he had seen enough of them – perhaps more than enough, in the case of the girl – he took in the room. Structurally, it had been probably been unchanged

15

since the day it was built, a couple of hundred years earlier. The walls were dressed stone, the beams of blackened oak. There was the large fireplace in the middle of the side wall, and narrow mullion windows which looked out on to the moor in the front wall.

All perfectly normal – all just as he might have expected.

The furniture – on the other hand – took him completely by surprise.

Harris came back into the room. 'I've just checked with headquarters. The only vehicle registered to Wilfred Dugdale is the Land Rover, sir.'

'So assumin' he was here when the murders were committed – an' it's more than likely that he was – how did he get away?'

'He could have walked, couldn't he?'

'If he'd gone off on foot along the road he'd have been spotted by one of our cars.'

'Perhaps he cut across the moors, then.'

Woodend went over to the window. It was snowing harder out there on the tops than it had been in his village. The snow would be probably at least two feet thick in most places. And where it had drifted, it would be even deeper. Walking across the moors would be very arduous work, even for a man much younger and fitter than Dugdale. Probably dangerous, too. And an old farmer, brought up on the moors, would be bound to know that.

'Wherever he is, I want him found,' Woodend told Harris. 'See to it, will you, Inspector?'

'Yes, sir.'

Woodend turned his attention back to Paniatowski. 'Does anythin' strike you as odd about the furniture in this place, Monika?'

Paniatowski looked around her. The dining table and chairs were polished hardwood, as was the sideboard and corner unit. There were two sofas and three easy chairs, all

in soft white leather. And a rocking chair which looked as
if it had been expensive.

'Too much – and too posh,' she said.

Which was just what Woodend had been thinking. 'Talk
me through it,' he suggested.

'I've been to three or four of these farms during my time
on the force,' Paniatowski said. 'There's not much of a living
to be made out here any more, and anyway, most of these
old farmers are too canny to go spending their cash when
there's no need to.'

'So?'

'So the typical farmhouse is furnished with the heavy old
furniture – Victorian mostly – which the farmer's parents
or grandparents bought. It might be ugly, but I doubt if
they even notice that, and they see no point in throwing
out things that are still perfectly serviceable. And even if
they do replace it, it's normally with modern, factory-made
tat, whereas there's real craftsmanship in the stuff Dugdale's
bought.'

'You said "too much" as well as "too posh". Why's that?
The room doesn't feel cramped, does it?'

'Far from it,' Paniatowski agreed. 'But another thing
about these old farmers is that they tend to keep pretty
much to themselves. If they come into town once a week
to do their shopping, it's a social event. So why does he
need all these easy chairs?'

'True,' Woodend agreed. 'Unless he's the exception
which proves the rule, there's no need for it at all.' He
checked his watch. 'I have to pop back to take Joan to the
station. Can I borrow your car?'

Paniatowski smiled. 'Think you can handle it, sir?'

'Yes, I can handle it, you cheeky young madam,'
Woodend said.

Paniatowski handed him the keys. 'Are you leaving
right now?'

'No,' Woodend decided. 'I've still got a few minutes to spare. I think I'll go an' have a talk with this journalist feller, to see if I can find out just what he was doin' out at a desolate place like this so early on a Sunday mornin'.'

3217351

Three

Woodend gazed pensively across the moors towards Whitebridge. The sun had reluctantly emerged from behind the heavy banks of clouds, and the snow glistened under its pale light as if it were made up of a million tiny diamonds. The view could almost have come off a Christmas card – except that the backs of Christmas cards did not contain grisly scenes like the one he would see if he turned around again and re-entered the farmhouse.

A detective constable approached him. 'Hardcastle was in a bit of a state, so I've told him to go an' sit in the car for a while, sir,' he said. 'I hope that's all right with you.'

Woodend nodded. A good bobby should always look after his partner, and Woodend thought that DC Barney Duxbury was a *very* good bobby. He'd put Duxbury's name forward for promotion a few months earlier. And he'd been surprised that the promotion had been turned down, until, that was, he'd learned that Duxbury's son had been made his school's Sportsman of the Year, and that his only serious competition for the title had been Peter Ainsworth – DCC Ainsworth's son and heir.

'I'm goin' to have a word with this reporter feller,' Woodend said. 'Where will I find him?'

'Over there,' Duxbury said, pointing to the sleek, new Triumph Spitfire which was parked close to the barn.

'Nice set of wheels,' Woodend said. 'Very nice. Obviously, workin' for the BBC pays better than I'd thought it did.'

19

The Chief Inspector made his way over to the Spitfire.
The man sitting behind the wheel could not have more than
twenty-five or twenty-six, he noted, as he got closer. The
reporter had taken off his overcoat and – apparently unconcerned about the price of petrol – had left the engine running
in order to heat the car. He was wearing a suede jacket with
knitted sleeves and pockets, which Woodend assumed was
fashionable, and probably hadn't been bought locally.

The Chief Inspector tapped on the side window. As
the reporter wound the window down, a blast of hot air
rushed from the car into the chilled atmosphere which
surrounded it.

'Mr Bennett?' Woodend asked.

'That's right.'

'If you don't mind, sir, I'd like to ask you some questions.'

Bennett ran his eyes quickly over Woodend's shabby
overcoat. 'And if *you* don't mind, I'd prefer to wait until
your boss gets here, Sergeant.'

'Chief Inspector.'

'I beg your pardon?'

'I'm Chief Inspector Woodend. An' the last time I checked
on it, I *was* the boss.'

Bennett grinned. 'My mistake,' he said easily, and without any hint of apology. 'Would you like to get into
the car?'

Woodend shook his head. 'Nay, lad. It looks a bit too
cramped for my legs. Why don't you get out?'

Bennett sighed, as if he considered that an unreasonable
imposition, but then he reached for his overcoat and stepped
out of the Spitfire.

'The first thing I'd like to know is how you came to
be here at this godawful time on a Sunday morning,'
Woodend said, as the reporter slipped into his expensive
camelhair coat.

'I got a phone call at about half past seven suggesting that I should come up here.'

'Who was this phone call from?'

'He didn't give his name.'

'Do you often get anonymous phone calls?'

'They're not uncommon. I work for both regional radio *and* regional television. *Bennett's Beat*, my television programme's called. If anybody thinks they've been badly done by, they call me to investigate. I create quite a stir sometimes – uncovering wrongs which would probably have gone totally unnoticed otherwise. But surely, I don't need to tell you that. You must have seen the programme yourself, mustn't you?'

Yes, now Bennett mentioned it, his face was starting to look vaguely familiar, Woodend thought. But he was buggered if he was going to give the smug young sod the satisfaction of hearing him admit it.

'Can't say I watch much television,' he said aloud. 'An' when I do, it's usually the national news. I find that much more professional.'

'You'd be surprised just how professional some of us can be,' Bennett said, clearly stung. 'Anyway, as I was saying, since I'm something of a local celebrity, it's to me that most people turn to when they have a good story to tell.'

'So you weren't surprised to get the call. An' what did this particular caller have to say for himself?'

'That if I didn't want to miss the biggest story of my career, I should get out to Dugdale's Farm as quickly as I could.'

'So let me see if I've got this straight,' Woodend said sceptically. 'It's early on Sunday mornin', an' you get this phone call which, for all you know, could be from a complete bloody nutter. Yet you still jump out of your bed an' drive twenty-odd miles to see if there's anythin' to the story.'

'I was already up – I like to rise early. And I didn't have to

drive twenty-odd miles, as you put it, because I live locally.
Not more than five miles from here, as a matter of fact.'

'Alone?'

Bennett shrugged awkwardly. 'With my parents, actually,' he confessed. 'But that's only a temporary meas-
ure – until the house I've bought in Moorland Village is
finished.'

The BBC *did* pay well, Woodend thought. 'Tell me
about the man who called you,' he said. 'It was a man,
wasn't it?'

'Yes, it was a man. I'd guess from his voice that he was
middle-aged. And from his accent,' Bennett continued, with
all the flourish of a magician pulling a rabbit out of his hat,
'I'd say he was from Manchester rather than Whitebridge –
and not particularly well-educated, either.'

Woodend took out his Capstan Full Strengths and offered
the packet to the reporter. Bennett shook his head and
produced a packet of thin, black cigarettes with a gold
band round each one.

'So you decided to follow the lead, an' drove up here,'
Woodend said. 'Did you see much traffic on the way?'

'There was some in Whitebridge – the normal Sunday
morning stuff – but it wasn't until I was up here on the
moors that I saw any vehicle which I would have described
as suspicious.'

The bugger was milking his story for all it was worth,
Woodend thought. Maybe he *always* behaved as if the
television cameras were on him. Still, in the long run the
quickest thing would probably be to play along with him.

'A vehicle which you would have described as suspicious?' the Chief Inspector said.

'That's right. It was a rather beaten-up yellow Austin
A40, and it was going hell-for-leather towards Whitebridge.'
Bennett paused, and gave Woodend a Spitfire-owner's
superior smile. 'When I say hell-for-leather, of course,

I mean it was going as fast as a wreck like that possibly could.'

'So, as you say, it aroused your suspicions?'

'Yes, in my business you soon learn to—'

'An' naturally, you made a note of the number plate.'

'Well . . . not exactly,' Bennett confessed.

'Meanin'?'

'Meaning, I suppose, that I didn't get the number. As I mentioned, it was travellin' rather quickly—'

'For a wreck.'

'– and by the time I'd realized there was something not quite right about it, it was gone.'

'Did you happen to notice who was inside this suspicious vehicle?'

'Two men. Both in the front.'

'An' did either of these men have white hair?'

'The driver was wearing a trilby, and the passenger had a flat cap on. I suppose one of them might have had white hair, but I certainly couldn't see it.'

Woodend shook his head despairingly. 'The reporter's trained eye,' he said. 'There's nothin' like it, is there?'

'Now, hold on a minute,' Bennett protested. 'It was snowing rather heavily and I—'

'What time did you finally get to the farm?' Woodend interrupted.

'I think it must have been at about five minutes to eight.'

'An' what did you do once you'd parked?'

'I couldn't see anybody around, so I knocked on the front door. When there was no answer, I tried the latch. The door wasn't locked, so I pushed it open and stepped inside. That's when I saw the bodies. I'm not a man who's easily shocked, but I have to admit I was definitely shaken at that particular moment.'

'You didn't go into the farmhouse, did you?'

'Of course not,' the reporter said, rather too quickly.

'You're lyin'!' Woodend told him.

'How dare you suggest—?'

'An' I'll tell you *how* I know you're lyin'. Standin' in the doorway, you could have seen both the bodies – you'd probably have seen the blood – but you'd have to have got close to the victims to establish the exact cause of death.'

'Perhaps so, but I was still close enough to see they were dead, so I phoned the police,' Bennett said defensively.

'You didn't just say they were dead when you phoned – you said they'd been *shot*.'

'Then perhaps I did go a little way into the farmhouse,' Bennett agreed reluctantly. 'That's not a crime, is it?'

'It might be,' Woodend said, noncommittally. 'It very well might be. So, once you'd established that they'd been murdered, did you phone Whitebridge police station immediately?'

'Absolutely.'

'Did you use the phone in the house?'

Bennett gave him a superior chuckle. 'No, of course I didn't use the phone in the house. I told you, I'm an experienced reporter. I know enough not to mess up the scene of the crime by doing that.'

But not enough to stop you from trailin' all over the bloody living room, Woodend thought.

'So where *did* you ring from?' he asked.

'There's a phone box just about a mile back down the road. I called from there.'

The farmhouse door burst open, and Monika Paniatowski strode angrily out into the farmyard.

'Is there a problem, Sergeant?' Woodend asked.

'You could say that, sir. I've just had Whitebridge HQ on the radio. The duty sergeant had his wireless tuned into the BBC Home Service. There was a newsflash he thought we might like to know about.'

24

'What kind of newsflash?'

'What kind do you think, sir? A report on the double murder at Dugdale's Farm. It gave all the details! Cause of death! Ages of the victims! Every-bloody-thing! It even mentioned that a yellow Austin A40 had been spotted close to the farm. Do you know anything about that?'

'I've just been told,' Woodend said. With rising fury, he swung back towards Bennett. 'You didn't just ring the police, did you? You also rang the BBC.'

'I'm a reporter,' Bennett said, unconcerned. 'If I come across a good story, I phone it in.'

'Don't you know that you're supposed to get clearance from us before you release any details of a crime?'

'If there'd been any of you people around, that's exactly what I would have done. But you *weren't* around, and if I'd waited until later I would have lost my exclusive. Anyway, it seemed to me that since I discovered the bodies – and saved you hours, or even days – an exclusive was what I was entitled to.'

Woodend threw his cigarette butt on to the ground and stamped on it viciously. 'Get one of the lads to drive Mr Bennett down to headquarters, Monika,' he told Paniatowski.

'Drive me?' Bennett repeated, mystified. 'I'm perfectly capable of driving myself.'

'Do it, Sergeant,' Woodend said, ignoring the reporter.

Paniatowski nodded, and walked back towards the farm-house.

The implications of what the policeman had said were just starting to hit the reporter, and his mouth dropped open in amazement.

'You're not suggesting that I'm under arrest, are you, Chief Inspector?' he asked.

'I'm doin' more than suggest it. I'm tellin' you that you're bloody-well nicked.'

'On what charge?'

'I'm so spoiled for choice that I haven't quite decided on that yet. Let's start with obstructin' a police investigation, an' conspiracy to pervert the course of justice, shall we?'

Not to mention wearing a poncy suede jacket better suited to swinging London than the middle of sensible Lancashire, he added mentally. That *isn't* actually a crime – but it certainly should be!

'Do you have any idea at all who you're dealing with here?' Bennett demanded.

'Aye. I'm dealin' with just the kind of bloody nuisance we don't need on a case like this.'

Paniatowski emerged from the farmhouse again with Duxbury at her side. As the DC approached Bennett, the reporter gestured angrily with his arm that Duxbury should not come any closer.

'Oh, do resist arrest, Mr Bennett,' Woodend cajoled. 'I really would like that.'

For a moment it seemed as if resist was just what the journalist was intending to do, then he shrugged again and said, 'You're making a big mistake, you know, Chief Inspector.'

'Maybe I am, at that,' Woodend agreed, 'but I don't half feel better for makin' it.'

Duxbury came to a halt several feet away from the journalist. 'If you'd like to follow me, sir,' he said.

With a show of reluctance, Bennett did as he'd been instructed. Woodend turned back towards the moors. It had started to snow again – a light, fluffy snow which would probably not have stuck as a first fall, but would have no trouble adhering to what was already on the ground.

The Chief Inspector wondered if Dugdale was out there, somewhere – up to his knees in drifting snow, yet still struggling to put as many miles between himself and the farmhouse as possible.

Common sense said that he was the murderer. It was, after all, his house in which the crime had been committed, and his gun which had done the deed. Yet the common-sense answer just didn't seem to be the right one this time. It was true that some of these old moorland farmers could be a bit trigger-happy – Woodend had dealt with complaints about them before – but there was a big difference between loosing off the odd barrel at a trespasser somewhere in the distance and deliberately shooting two people – one of them a kid – full in the face at close range.

Still, if Wilfred Dugdale *wasn't* the killer, why had he gone and done a runner?

Four

Driving Joan to the railway station should have been no more than a brief interlude away from the case. But the weather conditions had worsened, adding time to the journey and delaying the train, so it was a fretful Charlie Woodend who found himself standing on the platform and looking hopefully up the track.

'I'll be all right now,' Joan assured him, seeing through the veneer of patience he had clumsily attempted to wrap himself in. 'You can go back to the station, if you want to.'

'No need,' Woodend said – sounding slightly guilty because that was exactly what he *did* want to do. 'Monika can handle the preliminaries.'

It was true, he told himself. Paniatowski was shaping up very well, and the experience would be good for her. Besides, leaving a woman standing alone at a railway station was not something he'd find easy to do, given the way he'd been brought up.

'You won't work too hard while I'm away, will you?' Joan asked. 'You'll make sure you get regular meals?'

'Yes.'

'And cut down a bit on the beer and cigarettes – like the doctor's told you to?'

Woodend grinned. Northern wives – at least northern wives of Joan's generation, saw it as their duty to mither their husbands to death. And husbands of his generation accepted it without protest. It seemed to be the natural order of things in Lancashire that no sooner had you escaped from your own mother than you'd find yourself falling into the arms of another woman who'd treat you just as if you were a little kid again.

'Are you listenin' to me, Charlie?' Joan asked sharply.

'I'll take it easy,' Woodend said, knowing as he spoke the words that he was making a promise he would never keep.

The train – one of those blasted soulless diesels which seemed to be taking over from steam everywhere – rattled into the station. Woodend hefted Joan's heavy case into the air, placed it in the nearest carriage, and pecked his wife on the cheek. Joan climbed on to the train, and Woodend forced himself to remain on the platform as it chugged out of the station. The moment it had rounded the bend, however, he made his way hurriedly back to the car park.

It was a short drive to police headquarters, and soon he could see the red sandstone edifice in front of him. He felt great affection for the old place. The headquarters had been built when Whitebridge was still a thriving cotton mill town, and during his childhood its classical frontage had blended in perfectly with the grave civic buildings which surrounded it.

The whole town centre, back then, had reflected both the affluence and the pomposity of the cotton millionaires who had effectively run Whitebridge. But times had changed, as they always did. Cotton was no longer king, and urban redevelopment was in vogue. The city fathers had thrown Whitebridge to the planners with as little thought as if they were throwing a dead deer to a pack of starving dogs. And the planners, just like starving dogs, had acted on blind instinct. The historic market hall had been demolished without a second thought. The buildings between Prince Albert Road and Blackberry Lane had been bulldozed, so that instead of there being two narrow streets down which shoppers could take a leisurely stroll, there was a dual carriageway which cut the town effectively in two. The town hall had soon gone the same way as the market, and in place of granite and dignity these new developers had constructed a concrete and glass monstrosity which towered malevolently over the surrounding area.

Whitebridge had never been a pretty place, Woodend accepted that, but it had had a certain anarchic charm which was all its own. Now, with the new shopping precinct lined with national chain stores, it had become a place without a history, indistinguishable from hundreds of other small towns up and down the country, and only the police station, which had somehow escaped the developers' demolition hammers, stood as a reminder of the past.

The lines which marked out the parking places in the police station yard were buried under a layer of snow, and Woodend was forced to make a rough guess at where his own spot was. He ran his eyes over the cars already parked there . . . an Austin 1100, one of the new Mini Minors, Monika Paniatowski's MGA, Ainsworth's Volvo . . .

Ainsworth's Volvo!

Again!

First the DCC had turned up – totally uncharacteristically – at Dugdale's Farm, and now, even though he'd clearly said he was having some very important people round to luncheon, he was at the station.

Woodend entered the building through the back door, and made his way along the wide corridor which lead to the basement where the Major Incident Room was being set up.

On the whole, Woodend didn't like working out of what Ainsworth relished calling the 'M.I.R.' In his opinion, a crime should be investigated from close to where it happened, and his habit of running his investigation from a pub, club or school had irritated any number of his bosses, long before Dick the Prick had ever appeared on the scene.

This time, however, it was different. There was little point in setting up shop in a farmhouse stuck in the middle of nowhere, so, for once, he could both do the job as he thought it should be done *and* please his superiors.

As he reached the basement, he saw that Monika Paniatowski had, as he'd expected she would, got things pretty well under control.

A large blackboard had been erected at the front of the room. Desks had been placed in a horseshoe formation for easy communication during barnstorming sessions. A couple of post office engineers were busy installing extra phone lines and several detective constables were using the lines which were already working. Paniatowski herself was standing in front of a large-scale Ordnance Survey map which had been pinned to the wall.

'Found Dugdale yet?' Woodend asked her.

Paniatowski shook her head. 'He has to be somewhere within that area,' she said, running her index finger across the map and tracing a circle which was centred on the farm. 'There's really nowhere else he could be – so that's where we're concentrating the search.'

Woodend's eyes narrowed. 'Why do I get the distinct impression that you're not happy with the way things are goin'?'

'Maybe because I'm not. The area should be easy to search because it's all open moorland. If the snow does anything at all, it helps rather than hinders us. So it ought to be a doddle to spot Dugdale, and if we haven't done it by now – which we haven't – then I don't think we ever will.'

'Of course, we don't actually know he was at the farm at the time of the murders,' Woodend pointed out.

'But we do know he was there just a few hours before,' his sergeant countered.

'Do we? How?'

'While you were seeing Joan off, one of the lads found a witness who saw him last night.'

'Go on,' Woodend said.

'It was a neighbour of his – or at least, what passes for a neighbour out on the moors. He was driving back from Whitebridge at about eight o'clock last night when he saw Dugdale's Land Rover broken down by the side of the road. He pulled over and helped Dugdale to get it started again. But it still wasn't running very well, so he followed it all the way back to the farm, just to make sure that it didn't break down a second time.'

So Wilfred Dugdale had been at the farm somewhere between six and eleven hours before the murders, depending on whether they accepted Doc Pierson's estimate of the time of death or relied on the evidence of the smashed watch on the dead man's wrist.

Woodend lit up a cigarette. He was starting to share his sergeant's unease about the search.

'You're sure Dugdale didn't have another vehicle?' he asked.

'Positive.'

'Then he just has to be somewhere out there.'

Paniatowski glanced up at the window which was set high in the basement wall. The pavement it looked out on to was already covered with a good three inches of snow.

'He's an old man,' she pointed out. 'Say crossing the moors in this weather was all too much of an effort for him, and he collapsed. He'll be covered with snow by now. The search parties could walk within a couple of feet of him and still not see him.'

If that was what had happened, then the old farmer would be dead by the time they *did* find him, Woodend thought. And then what conclusion would they probably be forced to draw? That Dugdale had suddenly gone berserk, killed the two guests at his farmhouse, and died trying to escape.

It would certainly be a neat and tidy way to wrap things up, but Woodend had long ago come to distrust neat and tidy solutions where murder was concerned.

'What else have you been doin' while I've been at the railway station?' he asked.

'Following the usual procedures. Contacting all the other police stations in the immediate area to see if anybody's been reported missing. Co-ordinating with Traffic and—'

'That reporter . . . what's his name . . . ?'

'Bennett.'

'Bennett said that the man who phoned him up early this morning had a definite Manchester accent, an' since he works there, I suppose we should take his word for it. See if Manchester Police can tell us anythin' useful.'

'Will do.'

'What about fingerprints?'

'According to DC Battersby, there were loads of latents. I think we might strike it lucky and get a match with our records.'

'What makes you say that?' Woodend wondered.

'I've just got the feeling that there are criminals involved.'

Woodend smiled. 'Generally speaking, murder *is* regarded as a crime,' he said – but still, he knew exactly what she meant.

'Take the male victim,' Paniatowski said earnestly. 'He looks as if he was undernourished as a kid, but then lots of kids were undernourished thirty or forty years ago. His clothes were cheap, but again, lots of perfectly innocent people buy cheap clothes. I can't even say he's got a criminal face – because most of his face was blown away. And yet . . .'

'An' yet?'

'There's something about him which makes me think he's no stranger to the inside of a prison.'

'I wouldn't dismiss that as a possibility, either.'

33

Sally Spencer

'And then there's the actual murders themselves. Again, I've no grounds for saying this, but I got the impression that they were a professional job.'

'So Dugdale's not the man we're really looking for?'

'No. I don't think he is.'

'You're telling me this was a contract killin'?'

'Not even that,' Paniatowski admitted, frowning. 'If it had been planned in advance, it probably wouldn't have been so messy, and we wouldn't have found the bodies so easily. But I still get the sense that whoever fired the shotgun had killed before.'

I know what you mean, Monika, Woodend thought. I know *exactly* what you mean.

A young uniformed constable appeared in the doorway and walked straight over to the Chief Inspector and his sergeant.

'The DCC says he wants to see you immediately, sir,' the constable announced.

Immediately?

That was a bit strong, even coming from Dick the Prick. Being a deputy chief constable might have convinced Ainsworth, as it had convinced others before him, that he had the right to have his senior staff jump through the hoops occasionally – but it certainly wasn't the form to let the lower ranks see them doing it.

'You sure that's what Mr Ainsworth said?' Woodend asked. 'He wants to see me *immediately*.'

The constable blushed. 'He . . . he . . .'

'Spit it out, lad.'

'Yes, sir, that's what he said. He was quite clear about it.'

Woodend and Paniatowski exchanged questioning glances.

'Can you manage on your own for a while down here, Monika?' Woodend asked.

The sergeant nodded. 'We're making so little progress

34

at the moment that I could manage this operation *and* knit myself a woolly jumper at the same time.'

'If you knew how to knit, that is,' Woodend said, forcing a smile to his face.

'If I knew how to knit,' Paniatowski agreed, matching his smile with a forced one of her own.

'Right,' Woodend said. 'I suppose I'd better go and see what Mr Ainsworth wants. I shouldn't be long.'

But as he left the basement, he wondered if his last statement had been quite accurate.

DCC Ainsworth sat at his desk, the phone jammed hard against his right ear.

'Yes, sir,' he said to whoever was on the other end of the line. 'Yes, that's exactly the situation. No, he didn't . . . I agree with you on that . . .'

Woodend – who had not been invited to sit down and hence was standing like an errant cadet before his boss's desk – raised his eyes to the wall above Ainsworth's head, and found himself examining a gallery of exhibits which portrayed the DCC's public life. There were framed certificates from courses he'd attended, and commendations he'd been awarded. There were photographs of him with the police rugby team he'd once played in, and of tables in restaurants where he sat eating with the top brass. There were even a couple of letters from members of the general public – 'the little people' he claimed not to have lost touch with – praising the way he had conducted an investigation.

All show, Woodend thought – all bloody show.

'Yes, sir,' Ainsworth continued. 'Yes, that's what I think. Thank you for giving me your backing – I'll see to it right away.'

He slammed the receiver violently back on its cradle and glared up at Woodend.

'There was a time when I thought you were only being

an awkward bastard because – as an old mate of our late, lamented chief constable – you thought you could get away with it,' Ainsworth said. 'But the sainted Jack Dinnage is long gone now, and you're still as obstreperous as you ever were. So I can only assume it's part of your nature.'

'What's this all about, sir?' Woodend asked levelly.

'What's this all about?' Ainsworth repeated. 'It's about you arresting journalists – *BBC* journalists – when what you were supposed to be doing was chasing murderers.'

'As far as I can recall, I've only actually arrested the *one* journalist,' Woodend pointed out.

'Yes, you're quite right – it was only one. But one who was guaranteed to make waves.'

'I beg your pardon, sir?'

'Peter Bennett's not just some hack working for the local rag. As I've already pointed out, he works for *the BBC*.'

'I don't see it makes any difference who he's working for, sir,' Woodend said stubbornly.

'Don't you?' Ainsworth countered. 'Well, consider this, then? As you were making your ill-considered arrest, didn't the name "Bennett" ring any bells with you? Even *faint* bells?'

'It's a common enough name. There's a fair amount of Bennetts livin' around the Whitebridge area.'

'But as far as I know, there's only one *Harold* Bennett.'

'Are you talkin' about *Councillor* Bennett?'

'That's right. *Councillor* Bennett. The owner of Bennett's Foundry, the chairman of the Whitebridge Police Watch Committee – and the father of young Peter. How do you think he's going to feel about having his son banged up like a common criminal?'

'Not too pleased,' Woodend admitted. 'But that's neither here nor there, is it? Peter Bennett got in the way of my investigation – got *seriously* in the way – an' even if we don't actually charge him with anythin', it'll do him no harm to cool his heels in the cells for a few hours.'

Ainsworth smiled unpleasantly. 'He isn't in the cells, Chief Inspector. I've let him go.'

'You've done *what*?'

'You heard me. I've let him go.'

'That's the second time you've screwed up my investigation in one mornin',' Woodend said hotly.

'And what exactly do you mean by that?'

'First you drive that bloody big Volvo of yours over the tyre tracks in the snow at the farm—'

'Do you take me for a complete bloody fool, Chief Inspector?' Ainsworth interrupted.

Yes, I certainly bloody do, Woodend thought.

'Of course not, sir,' he said aloud.

'If there had *been* tyre tracks in the snow, I'd have parked on the road and walked the rest of the way, but since it was quite evident that there weren't any, I saw no harm in driving right up to the farmhouse. I'm sure that, in the interest of speed, you've have done the same thing.'

He might be telling the truth, Woodend thought. Then again – and not for the first time – he might be lying through his teeth. But whichever was the case, what was done was done, and there was no point in having a shouting match about what *could have* been.

'I'm sorry, sir,' he said. 'I didn't mean to suggest that—'

'You did more than simply suggest! You accused me outright of incompetence. Your insubordination has been noted, and will go down on your record in good time, but for the moment I'm more concerned with the case of this journalist. I consider your actions in regard to him to be hasty and ill judged – and the Chief Constable agrees with me wholeheartedly.'

That came as no surprise at all, Woodend told himself, not when you knew the Chief Constable as well as he did.

'Excuse me, sir, but if I'm to get a bollockin' for this, wouldn't it be more appropriate comin' from my immediate superior, DCS Whittle?' he asked.

'If a reprimand were *all* you were getting, it would indeed be coming from DCS Whittle. But this particular incident is serious enough to have gone beyond a simple reprimand, and I have to inform you, here and now, that you are being suspended on full pay, pending a full investigation into your conduct.'

'What!' Woodend said.

'I think you heard me the first time.'

This couldn't be happening, Woodend told himself. At the start of an important murder hunt, it simply *couldn't* be happening!

'Even if I have made an error of judgement, it doesn't merit a suspension,' he said.

'That is my decision to make, not yours.'

'Couldn't you defer the suspension until the case is closed?'

'No, I couldn't. And I must warn you that you're bordering on insubordination again.'

Woodend took a deep breath. His own situation could be dealt with later – what mattered at the moment was that there was a proper investigation of the case of the poor bloody girl who'd been murdered out at Dugdale's Farm.

'Will Mr Whittle be bringin' someone in from outside the area to take over from me, sir?' he asked, knowing full well that the decision would not rest with Whittle himself, but the man who pulled Whittle's strings and was sitting opposite him now. 'Because if we are gettin' outside help, could you suggest to him that he tries to get—?'

'He won't be bringing anyone in from outside.'

'Then he's goin' to be handlin' it himself?'

'No, although both DCS Whittle and I will, of course, take a close personal interest in the case.'

'So who's—?'

'DI Harris will be taking over the investigation.'

DI Harris! Sweet Jesus!

'With respect, sir, DI Harris couldn't find his own arse-hole if he used both hands,' Woodend said.

Ainsworth frowned his heavy disapproval. 'No doubt using that kind of language makes you feel like you're still one of the boys, but while the members of your team may have to tolerate your coarseness, I certainly do not, and will not,' he said.

'If you're goin' to take me off the case, at least make sure I'm replaced by somebody who can—'

'I have always found your arrogance one of the least attractive of your many unattractive characteristics,' Ainsworth said. 'We work as a team here in Whitebridge, and DI Harris is an effective and efficient part of that team. You will not question my judgement – DCS Whittle's judgement, I should say – in assigning the case to Harris. Is that clearly understood?'

'Yes, sir.'

Ainsworth held out his hand. 'You will give me your warrant card now, and then I will arrange for you to be accompanied to your office, from where you will be allowed to remove any articles of a purely personal nature.'

'I'd like to ask you to reconsider your decision,' Woodend said. 'If not for my benefit, then at least for the good of the force.'

The fingers of Ainsworth's outstretched waiting hand twitched impatiently. 'I *am* thinking of the good of the force,' he said. 'That's why I want you out of the building as soon as possible.'

Five

The White Swan – known locally as the Dirty Duck – was situated on the corner of Prince Albert Street and the Boulevard. It had once been a lively pub, then some bright young spark at the brewery had come up with the idea of tearing out its organically developed heart and replacing it with one made of chrome and smoked glass. Now, Woodend thought – as he sat in the corner of what had been the public bar in the days before all the internal walls had been knocked down – it was less a pub than a drinking shop, dispensing alcohol much as the grocer's dispensed pounds of cheese.

The Chief Inspector glanced idly around the barn of a room. A young couple sat by the window, having the kind of whispered conversation that people indulge in when they're arguing in a public place. At the bar, a group of men in chunky sweaters were talking loudly about millions of pounds and buying each other halves of bitter. A pensioner dozed fitfully over his bottle of Guinness. And a youth who probably couldn't afford it was feeding sixpenny piece after sixpenny piece into the one-armed bandit.

Everything looked so *normal*, Woodend thought – and wondered how that could possibly be, when his own world was crumbling in front of his eyes. He'd given nearly twenty years of his life to the police force. It was almost inconceivable to him that he should have been suspended. Yet unless he was losing his mind, that was exactly what *had* happened. And there might be worse to come. Though he personally didn't take the charge levelled against him seriously, it was always possible that the disciplinary board just might. And then what would happen? The force was his anchor – he knew no other kind of work, nor did he have the desire to learn any. If he lost his job, it would be like losing a major part of himself.

He checked his watch. Monika Paniatowski had promised that she'd be there by half past one at the latest. And now it was nearly a quarter to two. Where the hell was she?

The young couple seemed to have settled their argument, the men in chunky sweaters were still talking loudly about high finance, the pensioner had woken up and the young gambler had finally run out of funds. Woodend resisted the temptation to look at his watch again, and lit another cigarette instead.

It was five minutes to two – almost afternoon closing time – when Monika Paniatowski finally entered the Dirty Duck, brushing snow from her shoulders as she stepped through the door. The sergeant went over to the bar and ordered a vodka from the bottle which the landlord kept especially for her use. Then, instead of going straight over to where her boss was sitting – as he'd expected her to – she glanced around the pub.

She's checkin' to see if there's anybody she knows in here, Woodend thought – anybody she might not want to see her talkin' to me.

And suddenly he felt very alone.

Apparently satisfied that it was safe to do so, Monika walked over to the table and sat down.

'Sorry I took so long,' she said, 'but with DI Harris strutting around the basement like the cock of the walk, it was difficult for me to get away from there at all.'

'What developments have there been in the case, Monika?' Woodend asked anxiously.

'None. We still haven't found Wilfred Dugdale, and there's no match on our records from any of the finger-prints that DC Battersby lifted from the surfaces at the farmhouse.'

'No match at all?'

'That's what I've been told.'

'Not even the dead man's?'

'Not even his.'

But both he and Paniatowski had been so *sure* there'd be at least one match, Woodend thought. And they weren't amateurs – they knew when their instincts were on track!

'What about the yellow Austin A40 that Bennett claims to have seen comin' from the direction of the farmhouse?' Woodend asked.

'Four A40s have been stopped at the roadblocks. One was being driven by an old vicar on his way to church, another belonged to a mill worker who had his wife and four kids with him. I can't remember the exact details of the other two, but they didn't look very promising, either. Of course, we'll do follow-up investigations on all of them, but I'm not really expecting it to lead any-where.'

'Aren't there *any* other leads?'

Paniatowski shook her head. 'Nobody's been reported missing, and nobody in the immediate neighbourhood – if that's what you want to call a big stretch of open moors – saw anything that could be of the slightest use to us.' She looked deep into Woodend's eyes. 'Let's forget the investigation for a minute, shall we? How are *you* feeling, sir?'

'How do you think I'm feelin'? How would you feel if you'd been suspended on some trumped-up excuse?'

'I'd feel like hell,' Paniatowski admitted.

'What I don't understand – *really* don't understand – is *why* I've been fitted up.'

'Mr Ainsworth's not exactly the biggest fan you've got in Whitebridge, you know, sir.'

'Mr Ainsworth hates my guts with a passion – he has done from the very first moment I walked into the station. But even if he wanted to shaft me good and proper, why do it now?'

'Maybe he just saw his opportunity and—'

'Look, this murder case is the most important one to break in Whitebridge since the war. Maybe even before that. The pressure will be on the force for a quick result, an' I'm the best person to deliver that result, aren't I?'

'Undoubtedly.'

'An' Ainsworth knows that as well as you do. Besides, if the case *isn't* solved, the press will be lookin' for somebody to crucify. Up until a couple of hours ago, that person was me. But by suspendin' me, Ainsworth's put himself straight into the hot seat. An' that's not like him at all. So I say again, Monika, why try to shaft me *now*?'

'Could it be that he thinks that if you *did* solve the case, your position would be unassailable?' Paniatowski wondered.

'Now there's a possibility I hadn't considered,' Woodend conceded. He stubbed his cigarette out forcefully in the ashtray. 'But I'm not the main issue here, anyway. What's really got me worried is that whoever murdered that poor bloody kiddie might just get away with it.'

Paniatowski took a sip of her vodka. 'There's nothing *you* can do about that now,' she said, with a warning edge to her voice.

'Isn't there?'

Paniatowski sighed heavily. 'I really hope you're not thinking what I think you're thinking.'

'On the one hand you've got you an' me – a good team. An' on the other hand, you've got DI Harris – an idiot. Who do you think is more likely to solve the case?' Woodend asked – trying not to sound desperate, and knowing he wasn't *quite* making it. 'We can crack this together, Monika.'

'Or we could give Mr Ainsworth a *real* reason to bury you,' Paniatowski pointed out. 'And me along with you.'

'Nobody need ever know.'

'They'll find out. They always do.'

'You're probably right, lass,' Woodend agreed. 'No, I'm *sure* you're right. An' you've worked far too hard – put too much of yourself into the job – to be dragged down with me.' He rose heavily to his feet. 'Best of luck with the case, lass. I'll see you around.'

He walked over to the door. The argumentative courting couple had left. The boy who'd been gambling fruitlessly on the one-armed bandit had gone, too. And a few new customers – eager to get a last drink before closing time was called – had taken their place. That was how things went.

Times changed. Situations changed. The formidable sergeant who he'd lived in terror of when he'd first joined the force was probably now nothing more than a doddering old man who didn't even scare the little kids rampaging over his allotment. So why should he ever have imagined that he was any different? Why shouldn't he accept that his time had come, just as it came for everybody?

'Because I can still do the job!' he told himself angrily, as he stepped out on to the street.

He was *not* fooling himself – *not* overlooking weaknesses and failings which had sneaked up on him unawares. He was still the best senior detective in Central Lancashire, and if anybody could get to the bottom of the murders at Dugdale's Farm, it was him.

He turned the corner on to the Boulevard. The bus queues were longer than usual, not – he suspected – because more people were travelling on this particular Sunday, but because

with the snow, the buses were finding it impossible to keep
to their schedule.

Where the bloody hell was Dugdale? he asked himself.

Had an old farmer, who'd known the moors like the
back of his hand for most of his life, really thought that
he could cross them under these conditions? It didn't seem
at all likely.

He heard a click-click of hurrying high-heeled shoes
behind him, and wondered why – when there were no buses
leaving the station at that moment – the woman should be
in such a rush to get there.

'Sir!' said a voice.

He stopped, and turned round. 'Did I forget somethin' in
the pub, Monika?' he asked.

'No, *I* forgot something,' Paniatowski told him. 'I forgot
how much I owe you. And I forgot why I joined the force
in the first place. You're right about DI Harris. And you're
right about us! You're needed on this case, and if the only
information you get is the second-hand stuff that I can feed
you, well, I suppose that's better than nothing.'

Woodend had not expected that if his persuasion worked,
he would feel guilty – but he did.

'You're takin' a big chance,' he warned his sergeant.

'As long as we're careful, it won't be *that* big a chance,'
Paniatowski replied, unconvincingly.

'So how do we handle it?'

Monika Paniatowski glanced nervously around her, as
if she suspected informers lurking behind every lamp-
post.

'Don't phone me – ever,' she said. 'Not even at home.'

'Then how will we—?'

'We'll arrange in advance where we're to meet. And it
had better not be a place anywhere near as public as the
Boulevard.'

Woodend nodded. 'So where will our next meetin' be?'

Paniatowski thought for a moment. 'You know that build-ing site – the one on the way out to Dugdale's Farm?'

'The new estate Taylor's are buildin'?'

'That's right. Be there at noon tomorrow.'

'You want to leave it that long?' Woodend asked disap-pointedly.

'Of course I don't. I'd like you to be with me every inch of the way. But we've got to be practical. I want your help, but I can't be consulting you every five minutes. As little as we may like it, we've got to keep some distance between you and the investigation.'

Yes, Woodend thought gloomily. Yes, he supposed they had.

Six

Investigations had moods, just like people did. They could be up on top of the world, buoyed by the feeling that even if things hadn't quite gone right yet, they would soon start to. Or they could be down – wallowing in a swamp of lethargy – going through the motions, but with very little expectation that it would ever lead anywhere. As DS Monika Paniatowski entered the basement the next morning, after snatching a few hours' sleep, she immediately sensed that the mood of *this* investigation was far closer to down than it was to up.

She stopped and looked around her. The phones were being manned, statements were being re-checked, just as they should have been. Yet already, just over twenty-four hours after the bodies had been discovered, the atmosphere was thick with failure.

Charlie Woodend would never have allowed this, she thought. Charlie Woodend, unlike DI Harris, understood that getting control into his own hands wasn't important – that it was only how he *used* that control which mattered.

She was walking over to her desk when a voice said, 'DS Monika Paniatowski, is it?'

She stopped and turned. The man who'd addressed her was around forty-five, she guessed. He had a bullet-shaped head, and quick, darting eyes. Between his large nose and thin-lipped mouth, he had a well-clipped moustache. Even

47

in a crowd, Monika would have picked him out as some kind of hatchet man.

'Yes, I'm Paniatowski,' she said.

The man held out his hand to her. 'DCI Evans. I've been seconded from Preston.'

So Ainsworth had come to his senses, Paniatowski thought. After wasting the first day of the investigation, he had realized that Harris couldn't cope, and had brought in somebody from outside. She could only hope that Evans would move quickly to undo the damage which had already been done.

'Have you officially taken charge yet, sir?' she asked.

'Taken charge?' Evans repeated, mystified.

'Of the case?'

'I'm afraid you're labouring under some misapprehension, Sergeant. I'm not here to assist with your murder investigation.'

'You're not?'

'No. My brief is to investigate the charges which have been brought against DCI Woodend.'

This was bloody unbelievable, Paniatowski thought. It was bad enough that they were trying to shaft Cloggin'-it Charlie at all – it was insane that they should have chosen to do it at this crucial stage in the investigation.

'I don't really see how I can assist you, sir,' she said.

'Don't you?' Evans asked. 'Well, from your perspective, you probably don't. But it's my perspective which matters here, and *I* think we need to have a serious talk.'

Phones were ringing all around them. Fresh information was being chalked up on the blackboard.

'I can probably squeeze a few minutes for you round about lunchtime,' Paniatowski said.

'You'll give me as much time as I need,' Evans said coldly. 'And you'll give it to me now!'

'But, sir—' Paniatowski protested.

'It's not a request,' Evans told her. 'It's an order. Is there a room we could use where we might have a bit more privacy?'

'There's probably an office free upstairs.'

'Then take me to it.'

Paniatowski led Evans up the basement stairs to the ground floor. The second office she tried was free. Evans walked round the desk, sat down behind it as if it were his own, and signalled the sergeant to take one of the visitors' chairs.

'A suspension is a very serious matter,' he said heavily. 'As Mr Woodend's sergeant, I would expect your natural inclination to be one of loyalty, but I must ask you to clear such tendencies from your mind, and do all you can to help me to establish the facts.'

'The reporter from the BBC was completely in the wrong,' Paniatowski said. 'You know yourself that the facts we choose to hold back from the general public can be as important as the ones we reveal, especially in the early stages of an investigation, and besides—'

'Have you ever been to Chief Inspector Woodend's house?' Evans interrupted her.

'Yes,' Paniatowski replied, puzzled.

'Socially?'

'*Mrs* Woodend has invited me round for a meal a few times.'

'And were you the only guest?'

'No, I—'

'Who else was there?'

'What has this got to do with—?'

'*Who else was there?*'

'The first time there was Detective Inspector Rutter and his wife. I think Mr Woodend was hoping that if DI Rutter and I got to know each other better outside work, we might—'

'And the second time?'

'A couple called Jackson. Mr Jackson's an old friend of Mr Woodend's. They've known each other since elementary school.'

'That would Mortimor Jackson? Of Jackson's Transport?'

'I believe Mr Jackson does own some lorries.'

'A large number of lorries,' Evans said ominously. 'But to get back to Mr Woodend. He lives in an old hand-loom weaver's cottage, just outside Whitebridge, doesn't he?'

'That's right.'

'Well, that certainly seems modest enough.' Evans took a notebook out of his pocket and wrote something down. 'What did you have to eat when you went to Mr Woodend's house?'

'I don't see how this—'

'Just answer the question, Sergeant!'

'On one occasion, we had roast beef and Yorkshire pudding. Another time, I think it was Lancashire hot-pot.'

'Again, modest enough,' Evans mused. 'But then a clever man knows better than to be ostentatious. Was there wine with the meal?'

'Mr Woodend doesn't drink wine. He's strictly a pint of best bitter man, and—'

'That wasn't what I asked.'

'Yes, there was wine for those who wanted it,' Paniatowski admitted.

'What kind of wine? Cheap Portuguese muck? Or was it something more expensive? French, perhaps?'

'I'm no expert on the subject, but I believe it was French.'

'I see,' Evans said, making another note in his book. 'Do you happen to know where Mr Woodend goes for his holidays?'

'With respect, sir, could I know what this has to do with the investigation in hand?'

'You're here to answer my questions, not to put forward any of your own,' Evans said firmly. 'Where does Mr Woodend go for his holidays?'

'He doesn't take many holidays. There isn't time.'

'But he does take *some*?'

'Yes.'

'And where does he go, when he *does* find the time?'

'Mr Woodend likes to visit the Lake District. He's a great walker, and he says the Lakes are just the place to—'

'And does he have what I suppose you might call "a little place" up in the Lakes.'

'I beg your pardon, sir?'

'Does Mr Woodend own any property up in the Lakes?'

'Not as far as I know.'

Evans nodded. 'Not as far as you *know*. That's significant.'

'Mr Woodend and I work together, but we don't live in each other's pockets,' Paniatowski said. 'I don't think he has a house in the Lakes, but I couldn't say for sure.'

Evans nodded again. 'I think you're being wise.'

'I'm sorry, sir?'

'In any investigation, there's always a danger that the people close to the subject of it will be suspected of guilt by association. You're wise to start distancing yourself now.'

'I wasn't aware that I was distancing myself.'

'That's exactly the line to take,' Evans said, as if he were agreeing with something Paniatowski was sure she'd never said. 'Circumstances forced you into the company of Mr Woodend, but that was as far as it went.' He paused. 'If you play your cards right, Sergeant, you could walk away from this whole affair with a completely unblemished record.'

'What whole affair?'

'There's nothing else you'd care to tell me about Mr Woodend's private life, is there?' Evans said, as if she

51

hadn't spoken. 'Nothing you might have heard? Nothing he could have let slip at an unguarded moment?'

'Mr Woodend is the best boss I've ever worked for,' Paniatowski said passionately. 'He's very good at his job, is straight with the team working under him, and is as honest as they come.'

'As far as you know.'

'As far as anyone can ever really know anything.'

'But everyone is capable of making a mistake about the people they work with. And if I were you, Sergeant, I really would keep that in mind from now on. In other words, what I'm saying is that there's a distinction between being *wrong* and being *rotten*, and if you have to choose between them, it's always better to be seen as wrong. Do you understand what I'm telling you here, Sergeant?'

'No, sir,' Paniatowski said. 'No, I'm not sure that I do.'

Evans' sigh had just a hint of exasperation in it. 'Give it a little time to settle, and I'm sure you'll get the point, Sergeant,' he said. 'All right, you can go now.'

Monika stood and walked towards the door. It was only as she reaching for the handle that she realized she was trembling.

Seven

The barking of the dogs cut through the empty moorland air like the wail of a demented banshee. There was nothing warm or welcoming about it. It was not even a fair warning that the animals would defend their territory if they were forced to. It was, instead, a declaration of war – a solemn promise that if they once escaped from behind the high chain-linked fence, they would wreak a terrible destruction on any living thing they could find.

As Woodend parked his ten-year-old Wolseley in the shadow of the Moorland Village, the dogs came loping purposefully toward the fence. There were four of them. All Dobermanns. All with powerful shoulders and thin, half-starved bodies. As he stepped out of his car, the Chief Inspector was more than conscious of the fact that their wild eyes were fixed so intently on him that they almost seemed to be burning their way into his skin.

Woodend lit up a cigarette, and returned their gaze. The dogs had come to a halt a few feet from the fence, and their lips were curled back to reveal their razor-sharp teeth. The leader of the pack tensed, then took a flying leap at the wire. Several feet away – and knowing logically that he was perfectly safe – Woodend felt himself flinch and take a sudden step backwards.

The dog hit the wire with a force which would have knocked even a heavy man like him to the ground. The wire bulged dangerously outwards for a split second, then sprang back, catapulting the dog to the ground. A second dog, undeterred by his leader's failure, flung himself at the wire with the same determination, and with the same result. The remaining two, seeing the pointlessness of their repeating the attack, contented themselves with adopting a menacing crouch from which it would be possible to spring should the fence miraculously disappear.

The barking all but stopped, and was replaced now by low growls, primeval enough to turn the blood cold. Woodend took a drag on his cigarette. The Dobermanns were not so much animals as trained killing-machines, he decided, and, given the opportunity, they would rip out his throat – or anybody else's – without a second's hesitation.

He turned to look at the scene behind him. The council snowploughs had been out working since first light, and now the snow itself was banked up at the sides of the road, forming a cold, glistening palisade which separated the civilized man-made world of the asphalt from the savage beauty of the moors.

The dogs were still emitting their low growl, but there was no accompanying noise of machinery. The weather had put a temporary stop to work on 'the excitingly original concept in rural living from T. A. Taylor and Associates'.

And a good thing, too! the Chief Inspector thought. The countryside was not meant to be tamed, and true country-dwellers knew it. They understood that *it* didn't bend to *you*. No, *you* bent to *it* – accepting it for the way it was and building your life around its natural rhythms. Then people like T. A. Taylor and Associates came along – churning up a landscape which had taken thousands of years to evolve, and putting in its place a safe, sanitized community which gave people who were brought up as townees the illusion of living a rural existence. It should never have been allowed. In fact, now he came to think about it, he wondered how, given the existing planning regulations, it ever *had* been allowed.

There was a low rumble in the distance which heralded the imminent arrival of another car. Woodend looked up and saw Monika Paniatowski's MGA. The dogs, poised only a few feet from him, heard it too, and their snarls deepened as they expressed their anger at the approach of yet another enemy.

Paniatowski pulled her MGA up next to Woodend's Wolseley and climbed out. She looked grim.

'What's the matter, lass?' Woodend asked.

'There's something I need to know,' the sergeant said. 'A question I need an answer to right now.'

'An' what question might that be?'

Paniatowski took a deep breath. 'Have you ever done anybody a favour in return for them doing one for you? Have you ever taken a bribe – or accepted a present which might possibly be construed as a bribe?'

Woodend felt as if he had suddenly been doused in icy water. 'You shouldn't even need to ask that,' he said bitterly.

'I know I bloody shouldn't. But when things happen which start to make you question your own judgement, you *have* to ask. So what's the answer? Have you ever taken any bribes?'

'Get back to the station, Sergeant,' Woodend said coldly. 'Get back right now, before your new boss – the excellent Inspector Harris – starts wonderin' where you are.'

'I need to know,' Paniatowski persisted, anguishedly. 'If I'm going to put my own career on the line, I need a straight answer. Give it to me now, and I promise I'll never ask again.'

'If you don't know me by now—'

'*Please*! Please tell me, just this once, *Charlie*!'

'I've never taken a bribe in my life,' Woodend said. 'An' if I've done anybody favours – which I have when justice has needed temperin' with a bit common humanity – it's never been in the hope of gettin' anythin' in return. Does that answer your question?'

Paniatowski let out a gasp of relief, and then was instantly businesslike again. 'You're in big trouble.'

'I know that.'

'No, you don't. At least, you don't know quite *how* big it is. Have you ever heard of a bobby called Stan Evans?'

'DCI Evans, do you mean? Bullet-head Evans. Based in Preston?'

'That's the man,' Paniatowski agreed. 'I met himself this morning. Mr Evans is the one who's been called in to investigate the case against you.'

'Shit!' Woodend said.

'Shit is right,' Paniatowski agreed. 'He's only been on the job for a few hours, and he's already started to turn the station inside out.'

'What the hell for?' Woodend demanded. 'The complaint's a simple one. He doesn't even need to be in the station at all.'

'You still don't get it, do you?' Paniatowski asked, almost pityingly. 'Evans isn't just interested in what you did to that reporter. He wants a lot more than that.'

'More of what?'

'More evidence. Evidence that you're dirty.'

'He'll not find any,' Woodend said firmly.

'Are you sure?'

'Haven't I just told you that I'm not bent?' Woodend exploded.

'And I believed you when you said it. But that doesn't mean that, if Evans digs long enough, he won't be able to come up with something that makes you *look* bent.'

She was right, Woodend thought. There were cases in his past which had not been solved. There'd been criminals he'd arrested who'd escaped custodial sentences because the evidence hadn't been *quite* strong enough to convince a jury.

Who was to say, with absolute certainty, that these failures had been no more than bad luck? Who could claim, with complete conviction, that when the guilty went unpunished it wasn't because Charlie Woodend had been pulling the strings behind the scenes, in return for a thick wad of cash?

He pictured himself defending his career in front of a committee of cold-eyed men bent on his destruction, and knew that no man's record was protection against organized malevolence. Then, in a sudden burst of irritation, he pushed the image to the back of his mind.

Whatever the future held in store for him, there was nothing he could do about it now, he told himself. So there was really no point in dwelling on it, was there? Especially when there were more pressing matters to be dealt with.

'Tell me about how the case is goin',' he said. 'What new leads have you got?'

'None,' Paniatowski said. 'And, as much as I'd like to, I can't really blame all of it on DI Harris. Whichever way we turn, we seem to be running into dead ends.'

'You must have done *somethin'* constructive since the last time we spoke,' Woodend persisted.

'We've asked Battersby do a second comparison between the prints he lifted at the farm and the ones we've already got on record.'

We've asked, Woodend noted. She was speaking about a team of which he was no longer a part.

'With what result?' he asked.

'There were no matches.'

'Not a single one?'

'That's what I said.'

'An' you've just left it at that, have you?'

Paniatowski sighed. 'No, of course, we haven't just left it at that. We've sent the prints down to London, so that Scotland Yard can check them against the national records – but that kind of thing all takes time.'

She was starting to talk to him as if he were an outsider, Woodend thought – starting to regard him as a civilian who couldn't even begin to appreciate the pressures and complexities which came from being involved in this particular investigation. In a way, he supposed, she was right to think like that – because even after less than twenty-four hours off the case, he could feel himself starting to lose touch with it. And the feeling would only get worse as time went by, unless he could find a way to plug himself firmly back into the case – unless he could find a way to convince Paniatowski that she really needed him. If there was ever a time for him to pull a rabbit out of the hat, that time was now.

'How many sets of prints did Battersby manage to lift from the farmhouse?' he asked.

'Without more detailed study – and that takes time as well – it's difficult to say with any degree of accuracy.'

I *know* it takes time, Woodend thought. Stop treating me like an idiot.

'Doesn't Battersby even have a rough idea?' he asked.

'He thinks there may be around twenty sets of prints,' Paniatowski admitted.

'An' has anybody bothered to ask themselves *why* there are so many sets?'

'I don't think I'm following you, sir.'

'If you dusted my house down, you'd find my prints, Joan's, Annie's, a couple of the neighbours, three or four friends and maybe the ones left by the man who came to read the electricity meter. That wouldn't come to anythin' like twenty sets. Yet we're a fairly sociable family. So how did a lonely old farmer livin' out on the moors end up with so many visitors? What possible reason could twenty people have *had* for goin' to Dugdale's Farm?'

Paniatowski grinned. 'I've only been without you for a day, and I'm missing you already,' she said.

Woodend felt a surge of relief run through him, but was well aware that he could not afford to relax yet.

'So who are all these people?' he asked. 'Does Wilfred Dugdale have a large family?'

'Not as far as we've been able to establish. He was an only child. His parents are long dead, and he doesn't seem to have any cousins in the area.'

'Friends, then? Did he belong to any particular organization? The Lions or the Rotary, for example?'

'No. He seems to have kept pretty much to himself. Apart from the occasional shopping expedition into Whitebridge, he hardly ever left the farm.'

'An' yet nearly two dozen people came to visit him. He had a lot of visitors – an' now he's vanished into thin air. What do you make of that, Sergeant?'

'If he's not lying under a couple of feet of snow somewhere, maybe one of those visitors is hiding him?' Paniatowski suggested.

'Who would *you* hide?'

'How do you mean?'

'What would it take for you to agree to hide someone the police were looking for? Who would you run the risk of goin' to jail for?'

Paniatowski thought about it for a second. 'Close family. Close friends,' she said finally.

'But we've already established that Dugdale had neither close friends nor family. So where does that leave us?'

'Completely mystified?'

'Aye, it does that,' Woodend agreed. 'So what else has DI Harris been up to?'

'Well, he's working on identifying the victims.'

'An' how's he going about it?'

'He's trying to trace the shops where the girl's clothes were purchased.'

'But not the man's?'

59

'There wouldn't be much point in that. His clothes were all bought from Marks and Spencer's or C & A, and they're from the bottom of the range. They must have sold thousands of suits just like the one he was wearing.'

'But the girl's clothes are different?'

'Oh yes. You noticed that yourself, at the time. She was wearing some very pricy labels. I don't think you could even have found half the stuff she had on in Whitebridge.'

'So you're sayin' that they must have been bought in a big city?'

'That's the thinking at the moment.'

'Bennett – that reporter from BBC Manchester – said whoever phoned him early on Sunday mornin' had a Manchester accent. Maybe that's where the girl's from.'

'Or Liverpool,' Paniatowski countered. 'Or London, Birmingham, Glasgow or Leeds.'

True, Woodend thought. Assuming that she came from Manchester was clutching at a straw – and he wasn't *quite* ready to go in for any straw-clutching yet.

'Has there been an autopsy?' he asked.

'Doc Pierson put both the victims under the knife early yesterday afternoon.' Paniatowski smiled slightly. 'Which means that he must have been over his hangover by then, don't you think?'

'I imagine so,' Woodend agreed. 'An' has the Doc been able to tell you anythin' useful?'

'Nothing we hadn't deduced for ourselves, just from looking at the bodies. The male victim was in his early forties. The female was somewhere between thirteen and fifteen. Cause of death in both cases was shotgun pellets – him to the chest, her to the face. Approximate time of death: eight o'clock yesterday morning – which probably means *after* Bennett got his mysterious phone call.'

'No other findin's? Was there any evidence that the girl had been interfered with?'

'Sexually, you mean?'

'Yes.'

'Not even a hint of it.' Paniatowski looked around her and, as if gaining inspiration from her surroundings, she added, 'Dr Pierson said she was as pure as the driven snow.'

Doc Pierson was not a man to make mistakes, Woodend thought. True, he'd slipped up on the time of death at the farmhouse, but as he pointed out at the time, he was feeling rough. And even if there hadn't been the evidence of the broken wristwatch to make him question his initial estimate, he'd probably have amended it anyway, once he'd had the victims on the table.

'I'd better be getting back before I'm missed,' Paniatowski said.

'As bad as that, is it?'

'Worse. DI Harris doesn't work like you, sir. He's not content to let his team follow their instincts and report back to him when they've got something solid to contribute. He wants to know where we are every hour of the day.'

A real paper-pusher and rubber-band counter, Woodend thought. Just like dear old Deputy Chief Constable Ainsworth. But it wasn't the Harrises and Ainsworths of this world who came up with the solutions to serious crimes – it was the men like him, men who weren't afraid to get their hands dirty when the situation called for it.

'When can we meet again?' he asked.

'I don't know,' Paniatowski said awkwardly. 'It's difficult to fix a definite time.'

Was that another way of saying that she'd rather they *didn't* meet again? Woodend wondered – a gentle way of breaking it to him that things were getting too hot for her, and she'd rather pull out while she had the chance?

'Let's make some kind of arrangement,' he suggested. 'If it doesn't work out, you can always cancel or simply not turn up.'

Sally Spencer

'I don't want to waste your time,' Paniatowski said.

'Time seems to be all I've got plenty of at the moment. I can afford to waste hours of it.'

'The best thing you could do would be to go home and wait for me to ring you,' Paniatowski said.

Or to put it another way, 'Don't call me, I'll call you,' Woodend thought.

He didn't *want* to go home. He dreaded the idea of sitting around in an empty house, twiddling his thumbs while others did the work. But what other choice did he have?

'You *will* ring me, won't you?' he said.

'When I can,' Paniatowski replied evasively.

She got back into her MGA and fired up the engine. The dogs behind the chain-linked fence had been relatively quiet for a while, but now, with these new signs of activity, they pressed their muzzles fiercely through the wire.

Woodend watched Paniatowski's MGA disappear down the road – and tried to tell himself that his hopes were not disappearing with it. Then, when the MGA was finally out of sight, he turned back to contemplate the moors.

In the distance, well beyond the other side of the road, he saw two small brown shapes scurrying across the snow.

Rabbits!

He wondered what it would be like to have a life as simple as theirs – a life driven only by the primeval desires for food, sex and shelter.

An ominous black shadow glided across the snow and, looking up, he saw a large kestrel hawk. He had been wrong about the rabbits, he decided. Their lives weren't so simple after all – other creatures, with different needs to their own, had ensured that.

He thought about his own, personal predator, DCI Stanley Evans, who had swooped down from Preston that morning, and was already hovering over his career, waiting to strike.

Death of an Innocent

'You won't get *me*, Evans,' he said loudly, to the empty moors. 'I swear you bloody won't.'

He took his packet of Capstan Full Strengths out of his overcoat pocket and, cupping his hand, lit one. When he looked up again, there was no sign of either of the rabbits or the hawk.

Had the furry little animals escaped the feathered killer? he found himself wondering. Or had the hawk soared off in triumph, a trembling rabbit held tightly in its cruel claws?

If he'd been watching, he'd have had an answer to that question. But he hadn't been watching, and now he would never know whether there had been yet another unwitnessed murder on the moors.

He glanced down at his wristwatch. It was only half past twelve, which meant that most of the day was still ahead of him. Unless something really dramatic broke in the investigation, it was unlikely that Monika Paniatowski would ring him again until the following morning. How the hell was he going to fill in the time until then?

He sighed heavily, and reached into his pocket for his car keys.

63

Eight

It was just after the grandfather clock had struck nine when Woodend realized that though he'd been staring at the television screen since the evening news came on three hours earlier, he had not even the vaguest idea what programmes he'd sat through.

Well, it was pointless being there any longer, he decided, hauling himself off the sofa and reaching for his coat. Even if he couldn't do much about his mind, he could at least treat his body to a few pints of best bitter.

It had been years since he'd gone out drinking on his own, he thought as he headed up the lane towards the Victoria Hotel. But that was because it was years since he'd *needed* to. At that end of any normal day, there was always an ongoing case to discuss with his team – and where else but in the pub would he have chosen to discuss it? There was a case that wanted talking over that night, too, but he had neither the information which would make his own contribution worthwhile, nor the available subordinates to bounce his ideas off.

Poor old Charlie, he mocked himself. Has that nasty Mr Ainsworth taken all your toys away from you? Won't he even let you play with your little friends any more?

There were a number of cars parked in front of the pub, but two of them stood out clearly from the rest. One was a Jaguar 'E' type – a car which was still uncommon enough in Whitebridge for it to turn the envious heads of drivers of more humble vehicles The second was a Mercedes Benz 300S, an even rarer sight in the town. But it was not so much the vehicles themselves which caught his attention as the colour schemes their owners had chosen.

The Jag's owner had selected a deep, muted blue, whereas the Merc was painted in a vivid red which, it seemed to him, served to rob it of some of its inherent dignity. Parked as they were, side by side, they presented a bizarre contrast, and the detective who was deeply ingrained inside Woodend decided that while both the owners of the Jag and the Merc undoubtedly had plenty of money, only one of them really knew how to use it.

He entered the bar, walked up to the counter, and looked around him. There were some familiar faces there, but also quite a number of customers who were unknown to him.

Even *local* pubs had stopped *really* being local, he thought. The days when everyone had walked to the boozer, as he had done himself that night, were gone forever. Now that so many people had cars, they were travelling further afield for their entertainment, often abandoning the town centre altogether, and making country pubs like this one their chosen destination. It was, he supposed, just another example of the townees' yearning for the country – just one more example of the trend which had allowed places like Moorland Village to come into existence.

'Well, speak of the devil!' he exclaimed.

He hadn't meant to say the words out loud, but from the reaction of the drinkers standing on either side of him, he realized that he must have done.

'Are you, by any chance, referrin' to me when you mention the devil?' asked a voice from the other side of the bar.

Woodend turned to the red-faced man who was standing beside the till and grinning at him.

'No, not you, Arthur,' he admitted, returning the landlord's grin. 'I was meanin' that feller over there.'

He pointed to a man dressed in an expensive blue suit, sitting at one of the tables in the corner and looking so self-absorbed that he seemed barely aware of the world around him.

'Should I know him?' the landlord asked.

'A good landlord should be like a good bobby,' Woodend said, as a surge of jocularity temporarily dampened down the feelings of depression which had been flaring up in him all day. 'He should make it his business to know *everybody* on his patch who's important.'

'An' is yon bugger important, then?'

'Most people around here seem to think he is. It's Terry Taylor.'

'Of Taylor's Caterin'?'

'Aye,' Woodend agreed. 'Not to mention Taylor's Department Store, Taylor's Bookmakers an' T. A. Taylor an' Associates, builders of this parish. I've just been up near his latest project – the Moorland Village. That's why it was a bit of a surprise to see him.'

'So you're involved in this latest murder, are you?' the landlord asked. 'I thought it said in the paper that a feller called Harris was in charge.'

It would no doubt also soon say in the papers that he himself had been suspended – and was under investigation, Woodend thought. But he didn't feel like going into the details with the landlord just at that moment.

'Aye, Harris is in charge of the inquiry,' he said, 'but we're all . . . you know . . . part of the same team.'

As soon as the words were out of his mouth, he cursed himself for being so cowardly and evasive. A man should never be ashamed of the truth of his situation – because it was only one step from that to being ashamed of himself. And what was the point in lying, anyway? Why not bring his suspension out into the open right now, since, whatever he said, it would soon be general knowledge.

66

'Pint of your usual?' the landlord asked.

Woodend nodded automatically, but his mind was already being distracted by the man who had just emerged from the toilets and taken the free seat at Terry Taylor's table. What made him worthy of scrutiny was that he was a very unlikely drinking companion indeed for the builder. Whereas Taylor's suit had a muted elegance about it, the other man was wearing a loud check jacket which might possibly have been expensive, but certainly had no style about it. And there were other contrasts, too. Taylor had a corpulent figure and face which bore witness to long business lunches followed by several expensive French brandies. His guest, on the other hand, had a hard, wiry body and tight, pinched features.

'So are you makin' any progress in this murder up at the farm, Charlie?' the landlord asked.

'You know I can't tell you anythin' about the nature of police inquiries,' Woodend said. Then he realized he was just avoiding the issue again. 'The fact is,' he continued, 'I don't *know* anythin'. My boss has decided I'm a bit too direct for his likin', an' I've been suspended. It's only temporary, of course – until the misunderstandin's been cleared up – but still, it means I haven't got much to do with the investigation.'

'Oh . . . I see,' the landlord said. 'Well, if you'll excuse me, Charlie, there's other customers to serve.'

And by taking two or three quick side-steps, he removed himself to the other end of the bar.

So this was what it was like to be a leper, Woodend thought grimly. This was how bent bank managers must feel when their respectable neighbours realize that they've come under investigation. Except that there was a difference, he told himself, a *big* difference – because bent bank managers knew that they'd done something wrong, and he was convinced that he hadn't.

He drained his pint. 'Another one when you're ready, Arthur,' he called across the bar.

The landlord jumped slightly, then turned to his barmaid and said, 'Can you serve Mr Woodend, Elaine?'

The barmaid nodded. 'Pint of best, Charlie?'

'That's right,' Woodend answered, thinking: No sudden change in *your* attitude to me, is there, Elaine? But then you don't know what Arthur knows about me. Yet!

Elaine slid his pint across to him, and Woodend, for want of anything better to do, turned his attention back to Terry Taylor and his companion. They really did look an incongruous pair, he thought, but he'd been a policeman long enough to know that incongruous pairings were nothing out of the normal.

There could be any number of reasons why Taylor had chosen to spend his time with the man in the flashy jacket. He might be one of Taylor's sub-contractors, negotiating a deal for supplying windows for Moorland Village. On the other hand, he could be Taylor's customer – one of those spivs who had made so much money just after the war, and now wanted to spend some of it on a lavish, garish house with Greek columns everywhere and a swimming pool in the basement filled with champagne. If that *was* the case, then maybe the tasteless Merc outside belonged to him.

Other possibilities presented themselves to his fertile imagination. The man could be a private detective who Taylor had hired to watch his wife. Or – and Woodend felt a grin coming to his lips as the thought occurred to him – he could be a private detective who *Mrs* Taylor had hired to watch her husband, and who Taylor was now attempting to buy off.

The conversation at the table had been fairly amiable up to that point, but now it was obviously becoming heated. Taylor's jaw had set as hard as his double chins allowed, and the man in the flashy jacket had started to wag his finger like a pedantic schoolmaster.

Woodend found himself putting words in their mouths and playing out their imaginary conversation in his mind.

'The pictures are very explicit, Mr Taylor. I couldn't even have imagined half the things you did with that blonde lady friend of yours.'

'Surely everybody's entitled to a little fun now and again?'

'Of course they are, Mr Taylor. But you're old enough to know that fun has to be paid for.'

If that really was what they were talking about, then the conversation was verging on blackmail. But blackmail very rarely became a police matter, because most of the victims, while not exactly *willing* to stump up the money demanded, usually preferred that to the alternative.

Fun *did* have to be paid for, Woodend thought, suddenly sombre again. *Everything* in life had to be paid for. And he himself was now paying the bill for being the sort of policeman who did his job the way he'd decided it *should* be done, rather than sticking to the rules laid down by some stuffed shirt who hadn't come into contact with a real criminal for years.

Terry Taylor stood up, so violently that he knocked his stool flying over behind him.

'Don't you *dare* threaten me!' he said loudly – and then, realizing that his words must be carrying across the whole pub, he made his voice drop again to a harsh whisper.

The man in the check jacket did not appear to be the least intimidated by Taylor's outburst of temper. As he looked up at the flabby builder, the expression on his face was one of mild – though cold – amusement.

Taylor wheeled round, and headed towards to the bar. It was when he was about halfway there that he caught sight of Woodend. For a second it looked as if he would stop dead in his tracks, then he forced a friendly smile of recognition to his face and kept on walking.

'Didn't see you there, Chief Inspector,' he said jovially.

'No, I didn't think you did,' Woodend replied. 'Are you havin' any trouble, Mr Taylor?'

'Trouble?'

'Only it seemed to me that you didn't exactly enjoy whatever it was you were hearin' over there.'

The smile drained away from Taylor's face. 'I don't like people watching me when I'm having private conversations.'

'Then maybe you shouldn't have them in public places,' Woodend suggested.

'And as for troubles,' Taylor continued, walking towards the door but determined not to leave without delivering a parting shot, 'if the rumours I've been hearing about you are true, then I'd say you've got too many troubles of your own to go worrying about anybody else's.'

Nine

There had been no fresh fall of snow that morning, but there was no sign of a thaw, either, and as Woodend negotiated the slippery path from Crown Rise to the duck pond in Corporation Park, he was starting to feel hemmed in by the banks of complacent, glistening crystals.

He had spent a bad night, haunted by dreams of disgrace and even, at one point – God help him! – of execution. Some time during the night – he had not bothered to check the clock to see when it was exactly – he had climbed out of his clammy bed and, uncharacteristically, had poured himself one large whisky after another. Now, several hours later, he still suffering from the hangover, and the excessive light which nature had laid on was beginning to seem like a personal insult.

He stopped, and looked around him. Several stumps of Sunday-snowmen grinned at him through their crumbling pebble-mouths. A large dog ran happily towards the park gates, kicking up a trail of snow behind it and ignoring its owner's loud appeals for it to come back that minute. A couple of old-age pensioners tottered cautiously forward, using their walking sticks to test the ground ahead of them for icy booby-traps. Of any stern-faced men with open police notebooks, there appeared to be no sign.

'Paranoid,' Woodend told himself. 'You're gettin' paranoid, Charlie Woodend.'

But, as the old joke went, it was hard *not* to be paranoid when everybody was against you.

71

He had reached the duck pond. Most of it was frozen over, but someone – probably a council workman – had broken the ice around one edge, and the ducks, impervious to the cold, had taken to the water. The municipal cafe lay just ahead. In the summer months – if you were prepared to accept that Whitebridge *had* a summer – the cafe did a thriving trade, but now the green metal shutters were bolted down all around the bar.

There was a bench just beyond the cafe, and on it was a blonde-haired woman who seemed to be using her open paper more as a disguise than a source of information.

Woodend sat down beside her. 'Got any good news for me today, Monika?' he asked.

'*Good* news?' Paniatowski repeated, still hiding behind her newspaper. 'You've got to be joking!'

'Then you'd better tell me the *bad* news, hadn't you?'

'DCI Evans isn't working alone. He's brought a whole team in with him, and they've all been asking questions about you.'

'What kind of questions?'

Paniatowski shrugged, and her paper rustled. 'They're all pretty much on the same lines as the ones that Evans asked me yesterday. How much did you pay for your house? Where did you go on your holidays? Do you have any expensive hobbies? That kind of thing.'

'They're not still tryin' to prove that I'm bent, surely to God?' Woodend asked.

'You're a pretty good detective, sir,' Paniatowski replied. 'What do *you* think?'

'*I* thought they'd have given that up as a non-starter by yesterday afternoon at the latest.'

'Then you thought wrong.'

Was there a hint of doubt creeping into her voice? Woodend wondered. Was even Monika starting to believe that where there was smoke there must be at least a *small* fire?

72

'How's the case developin'?' he asked.

'Are you sure that you still want to bother your head with that after what I've just—'

'Has anythin' new broken since the last time we spoke about it?' Woodend snapped.

'We've got no more answers than we had yesterday,' Monika Paniatowski said resignedly, 'but we certainly seem to have come up with one hell of a lot more questions.'

'Well, at least that shows the investigation's goin' somewhere,' Woodend said. He paused, to give Paniatowski space to speak, and when it became obvious that she wasn't going to take the opportunity, he forced himself to press on. 'Do you want to tell me what these questions of yours are about?' he asked.

'They're about Wilfred Dugdale, mainly,' Paniatowski said, sounding reluctant.

'*What* about Dugdale?'

'His family has been farming the same piece of land for the last three generations, but Dugdale himself has never been much of what you might call a son of the soil.'

'Meanin'?'

'He never showed much enthusiasm for farming when he was growing up – at least, according to some of his older neighbours – and shortly after his twenty-first birthday he jacked it in all together and moved away from the area.'

'When did he come back?'

'Not until after his father had died, which was around seventeen years ago. He'd have been in his early fifties himself, by that time.'

'An' what was he doin' durin' the missin' years?'

'Nobody we talked to seemed to have the slightest idea – or the slightest interest, for that matter.'

'Do you know why he came back at all? Was it because he realized *somebody* had to run the farm?'

'That may have been his original plan, but if it was, he

didn't stick to it for long. He made a half-hearted attempt at farming the land for a year, then he sold all his equipment – ploughs, tractor, animals, the whole caboodle – and he hasn't planted a crop or milked a cow since.'

Woodend thought about the farmhouse, with all its expensive furniture. 'So what's been his main source of income since he gave up farmin'? Have you checked to see if he's been drawing the dole?'

'It was one of the first things we did. The Ministry of Labour has never heard of him. And I'll tell you something else that's very strange – he's of pensionable age now – he has been for more than two years – but he's never bothered to draw his entitlement.'

'So where does his money come from?'

'Nobody knows. The favourite theory back at the station is whatever he did while he was away, he made himself a fortune from it, and has been living on the interest ever since.'

But why would a man who was independently wealthy – or at least very comfortably off – ever decide to return to the draughty stone farmhouse of his childhood? Woodend wondered. 'Anythin' else?' he asked.

'You remember I told you that we'd found lots of sets of fingerprints in the farm?'

'Yes.'

'From what we now know, it would have been surprising if we *hadn't* found them.'

'An' why's that?'

'The neighbours say that he had a great many visitors – especially late at night.'

'The nearest neighbours must be a mile away from Dugdale's Farm,' Woodend said. 'How could they possibly know how many . . . ?' He paused again. 'They'd have noticed the headlights, wouldn't they?'

'That's right,' Paniatowski agreed. 'On the moors you can see a set of headlights for miles.'

'Speakin' of the fingerprints, what's been happenin' with them?'

'Scotland Yard has done us really proud. The technical lads down there must have spent all night checking the prints out, because they phoned through the results just before I set out to meet you.'

'Go on.'

'And if you're hoping for a break from that direction, you're in for a disappointment. The Yard came up with the same results as our fingerprint people did. None of Dugdale's visitors appears to have had a criminal record.'

'I don't like that,' Woodend said thoughtfully.

'I don't like it either,' Paniatowski agreed. 'It would have been much easier for us if the Yard had come up with positive identification. But it didn't, and that's the end of it.'

'You're missin' the point.'

'And what point would that be?'

'If you collected twenty sets of prints in a real villains' pub like the Burnin' Bush in Whitebridge town centre, you'd expect to find a match for a fair number of them in our records, wouldn't you?'

'Naturally.'

'Now say you took the same number of prints in somewhere highly respectable – like, for example, the Women's Institute. You'd be very surprised if you found even one set that matched any we'd got on file. Agreed?'

'Agreed. But what's all this—?'

'Those are the two extreme cases. But what would happen if we took a random sample from people in the shoppin' precinct an' didn't get a single match there? Wouldn't you find it strange that not one of the people printed had committed even a minor crime like drunk drivin' or petty theft?'

'I suppose so.'

'Twenty sets of prints from Dugdale's Farm an' no match. Statistically, that's very unlikely.'

'Very unlikely, but not completely impossible – as the results from the Yard clearly show,' Paniatowski countered. 'Anyway, I think you already explained the lack of matches away.'

'Did I?'

'Of course you did.' Paniatowski grinned, just as she might have done in what she was now coming to think of as 'the old days'. 'Wilfred Dugdale's guests *were*, in fact, all members of the Women's Institute – possibly the Witches Coven Section.'

Woodend returned her grin. 'Now there's a thought. After all, we did find a dead virgin (human sacrifice for use of said coven) up at the farmhouse.'

The moment the words were out of his mouth, he felt terribly ashamed of himself.

What was happening to him? he wondered. How could he make jokes about the poor bloody girl who had lost her life in Dugdale's Farm? Could it be that the longer he was kept away from the investigation, the less he saw the victim through the eyes of a caring bobby – and the more he saw her through the eyes of a salacious reader of the sensational press?

'We've got to find this murderer,' he said passionately.

'We're doing all we can,' Paniatowski replied.

And it was clear to him that once again they were talking about entirely different sets of 'we's'.

'I want to be useful,' he said – and although he was not a man to plead for anything, it sounded to him very much as if he were pleading now.

'You *are* useful, sir,' Paniatowski said awkwardly. 'We're bouncing ideas off each other just like we always did.'

'I want to do more.'

'Like what?'

Woodend gestured helplessly with his big hands. 'I don't know. Anythin' at all. Give me somethin' to look into that

76

you haven't got the time, or the inclination, to look into yourself.'

Paniatowski shook her head regretfully. 'I have detective constables to do that for me, sir. Besides – for the moment at least – you don't have any official standing.'

For the moment at least!

'You're right,' Woodend agreed. 'I don't have any official standin'. But you'll still keep me in touch with developments, won't you?'

'I'll . . . I'll do my best,' Paniatowski promised. She glanced down at her watch, though Woodend was sure she knew exactly what time it was. 'I have to be getting back.'

'Of course you do, lass.'

Paniatowski stood up, folded her newspaper, and dropped it into the bin. Woodend watched her as she walked up the slippery path towards the park gates. There was only so far he could push her, he thought. She was already running a big enough risk just by meeting him and keeping him abreast of the investigation – to ask for more could make her shut down on him entirely. She owed him – and they both knew it – but she would not sacrifice her own career in a desperate attempt to save his. And who could blame her?

He lit up and watched as the smoke from his cigarette drifted through the chill air. He was waiting – like a starving dog – for Monika to throw him a few scraps from the investigation to chew on. And she might just do that, whatever she had said about him having no official status. But he was not certain that he could stand the wait – was half-convinced that before he got the scraps, the hunger which was gnawing away inside him would drive him mad.

So what was he to do? As far as he could see, he had only one option. If he could not investigate the murder as the police officer in charge of the case, then he would just have to investigate it as a private citizen.

Ten

Turner's was the fourth moorland farm Woodend had visited that afternoon. It was closer to the main road than the one which belonged to the missing man, but other than that, with its thick stone walls and heavy slate roof, it was almost the twin of Wilfred Dugdale's property.

Woodend parked in front of the main building, and climbed out of his car. The chill wind which was blowing, unhindered, off the moor, enveloped him immediately in its icy fingers. He stuck his hands firmly in his overcoat pockets, and shivered.

The oak door of the farmhouse swung open, and a man stepped out into the yard. He was short and broad. His face was as wrinkled and weather-beaten as a gnarled oak tree, which probably meant he was the same age as Wilfred Dugdale, if not a little older. He was in his shirtsleeves, and if the cold scything in from the moors was bothering him, he certainly didn't show it.

'Mr Turner?' Woodend asked.

'That's me. How can I help yer?'

'I'm a reporter,' Woodend lied. 'I'm writing a story on the murders up at Dugdale's Farm.'

The old man's eyes narrowed. 'Work for the *Whitebridge Evenin' Telegraph*, do you?' he demanded.

Woodend forced a laugh. 'Nothin' as grand as that, Mr Turner. I'm what they call a freelance.'

'A free-what?'

'I write the story first, then I try to sell it to whichever paper shows an interest.'

'A man your age should have a proper job,' the old farmer told him disdainfully. 'A job where you can make good use of them strong arms an' broad shoulders of yours.'

'Blame it on me old dad,' Woodend told him. 'It was always his ambition to see me end up wearin' a collar an' tie to work.'

The old farmer nodded sagely. 'Well, maybe your dad was right, at that,' he conceded. 'There's so much of the work done by machines these days that there's little room left for a bit of honest hard labour.' He paused for a second. 'So you're writin' a story, you say?'

'That's right.'

'Well, I don't see what use we can be to you. We're too far away from Dugdale's to have heard anythin' here.'

'I appreciate that you can't tell me anythin' about the murders, but I was wonderin' if you could give me any background information on Mr Dugdale himself,' Woodend said.

The old farmer's eyes hardened. 'I haven't spoken to Wilf Dugdale for over forty years,' he said.

'I see.'

'An' if we both live for *another* forty years I won't be speakin' to him in that time either. So if you're lookin' for background information, as you call it, then you'd better take yourself off somewhere else.'

A white-haired woman appeared in the porch behind Turner. 'We weren't expectin' company,' she said.

'He's not company,' her husband told her. 'He's one of them reporters, writing a story on Wilf Dugdale. I told him we didn't know nowt.'

The old woman ran her eyes quickly up and down Woodend. 'So you're a reporter, are you?' she asked.

'That's right,' Woodend agreed.

79

The old woman nodded, though it was plain to him that she didn't believe a word of it. 'You'd better come inside then, hadn't you?' she said.

'We can't help him, so what's the point of that?' her husband asked. 'He'd just be wastin' his time as well as ours.'

'You're probably right,' Mrs Turner agreed. 'But while he's wastin' it, he can get a good, strong, hot cup of tea down him – an' by the look of him I'd say he could use one.'

The old man shrugged. 'I hadn't thought of that,' he admitted.

'That's the trouble with you, Jed Turner,' his wife said good-naturedly. 'You never *do* think of things like that.' She turned back to Woodend. 'Come inside, lad, an' get some of that chill thawed out of you.'

She went back into the house, and the two men followed her. The living room lay immediately beyond the porch. It had a flag floor, broken up occasionally by pieces of carpet which looked as if they were nothing more than mill off-cuts. There was a battered oak table under the window, and a number of mismatched armchairs arranged around a blazing log fire. The air near the doorway was almost as cold as it was on the outside, but nearer the easy chairs the fire threw out a semicircle of heat which was far more welcoming than anything a central heating system could have possibly produced.

This was how Dugdale's Farm should have looked, Woodend thought. This was *exactly* how it should have looked.

'Sit yourself down, then,' Mrs Turner said.

Woodend lowered himself into a creaking leather armchair with bits of horsehair sticking out of the arms. Mr Turner simply stood where he was – his backside to the fire – as if he were uncertain what to do next.

'You might as well take the weight of your feet, an' all, Jed,' Mrs Turner said. She smiled at Woodend. 'I won't be a minute makin' the tea. The kettle's always kept just off the boil in this house.'

Jed Turner, after some hesitation, sat down on a chair at the extreme edge of the semicircle. He did not offer to resume the conversation they had begun outside, and since Woodend did not wish to push him for any more information until his wife returned, they sat together in an awkward silence for the two or three minutes it took the old woman to make the tea.

Mrs Turner re-entered the room with three steaming mugs of tea on a battered tin tray. Woodend took a sip of his. It tasted heavily of tannin, and was strong enough to make bricks out of – which was just the way he liked it.

'You said you hadn't spoken to Mr Dugdale for over forty years, Mr Turner,' he said, when he'd taken a couple more sips of tea. 'Is there any particular reason for that?'

'Aye, there's plenty of reasons for it,' the old farmer replied. 'But none that I want to go readin' about in a newspaper.'

'He was away from Whitebridge for a good few years, wasn't he?' Woodend said, trying another tack. 'Do you have any idea where he went?'

'None at all – an' I don't care, neither. He should have stayed away for ever, if you want my opinion.'

Woodend turned his attention to Mrs Turner. 'Do you have any idea—' he began.

'No, she does not,' Jed Turner interrupted him – but not before Woodend had had time to read the flicker in the old woman's eyes.

'So there's really not much you can tell me about him, is there?' Woodend asked.

'I can tell you that he's a real bad bugger – allus was – an' that if it turns out he was responsible for them killin's up at that so-called farm of his, I wouldn't be the least surprised.'

81

'A real bad bugger?' Woodend repeated. 'What exactly do you mean when you—?'

'I've said all I'm *goin'* to say on that particular matter,' Turner snapped. He stood up, and placed his half-finished mug of tea on the stone mantelpiece with an air of finality. 'So now, if you wouldn't mind . . .' he continued, gesturing towards the door.

'Let the lad finish his drink before you turn him out into the cold again,' Mrs Turner said. 'An' while he's doin' that, you could make yourself useful an' go an' fetch some more logs for the fire.'

Turner glanced down at the pile which already stood by the fireplace. 'We've plenty of—'

'I know you of old, Jed Turner,' his wife said with mock severity. 'There might be plenty of wood for now, but later on – when we're runnin' low – you'll be moanin' that it's too dark an' miserable to go an' fetch some more. So you're better doin' it now.'

Turner gave Woodend an uncharacteristically friendly look – a look which said that even if Woodend didn't have a real job, they were both still men and so both understood that when you were dealing with women it was easier just to do what they wanted, however unreasonable that might seem. Then he rose to his feet and headed for the door.

Mrs Turner waited until her husband had closed the door behind him before saying, 'We haven't got long, so you'd best save time by bein' straight with me right from the start.'

'Straight with you?' Woodend repeated.

'You're not really a reporter at all, are you?'

Woodend looked into the woman's faded, but still intelligent, eyes and decided there was no point in pretending any longer.

He grinned. 'Was I that obvious?'

'Well, you weren't very good at it, if that's what you

mean. But even if you'd been able to carry it off better, it still wouldn't have worked. As far as my Jed's concerned, the world revolves around this farm – but I read the papers.'

'An' you've seen my picture in them?'

'More than once. An' my niece once pointed you out to me. She works in the police canteen in Whitebridge, an' always speaks very highly of you. Says you're not stuck up like some of the buggers in plain clothes she has to serve.'

Woodend grinned, then grew serious again and said, 'So if you knew I wasn't who I said I was, why didn't you tell your husband right away?'

The old woman smiled. 'Partly because of what my niece said about you, and partly because I was curious. You may not believe this, but we don't get many bobbies pretendin' to be reporters round these parts. Do you want to tell me what it's all about?'

'I can't investigate the murder in the way I normally would because I've been suspended from duty,' Woodend confessed.

'Suspended from duty,' the old woman repeated. 'Did you do somethin' wrong?'

Woodend shook his head. 'I don't think so.'

'So if it's really nothin' to do with you any more, why are you still workin' the case?'

'Because I think that I have a better chance of solvin' it than anybody else does,' Woodend said. 'An' because I don't think it's right that a kid should be robbed of her life before she's had the chance to even start livin' it fully.'

The old woman nodded slowly, as if she were prepared to take his explanation at face value. 'Have you got any children of your own, Mr Woodend?'

'One. A girl. She's trainin' to be a nurse in Manchester.'

'I've had six. Of course, they're all grown up now, an' have their own families.' The old woman paused. 'My youngest granddaughter's about the same age as the poor kiddie who was killed up at Dugdale's Farm. Do you think it was Wilf Dugdale that killed her?'

'Do you?'

'Not a chance. Wilf has been a bit of a bugger in his time – my Jed's quite right about that – but he's no murderer.'

'You've got somethin' you want to tell me, haven't you, Mrs Turner?' Woodend guessed.

The old woman looked down at her lap. 'Maybe,' she said hesitantly. 'I'm not sure.'

'Whatever you have to say won't go beyond these four walls,' Woodend coaxed. 'If Mr Dugdale's innocent, then what you tell me won't hurt him. An' if he's guilty, don't you want to see him behind bars?'

'When Wilf had that big row with his dad an' moved away, he went to Rochdale,' Mrs Turner said quickly, as if she wanted to get the words out before she changed her mind. 'The first street he lived in was called Derby Avenue. He lodged at Number Forty-six. I don't know how long he stayed there, or where he went after that.'

'How do you know all about this, when your husband doesn't?'

Mrs Turner gave him a sad smile. 'You've already guessed that, haven't you, lad?'

'Perhaps I have,' Woodend agreed.

'Wilf Dugdale was a good lookin', well-set-up, young feller forty-odd years ago,' Mrs Turner said. 'An' I was no drudge myself.'

'I'm sure you weren't,' Woodend agreed.

'The difference between us – an' it was a big difference in them days – was that I was married – an' he wasn't.'

'Is that what he had the blazin' row with his father about, just before he left home?'

'Old Clem Dugdale had very strict morals. He wasn't goin' to harbour a sinner under *his* roof.' There was a hint of a smile on the old woman's face again. 'Especially a sinner who wasn't a very good farmer.'

'Did your husband ever find out what had been goin' on?'

'Let's just say that he had his suspicions.'

'When Wilf Dugdale moved down to Rochdale, you went to visit him, didn't you?'

'A few times.'

'What made you stop goin'?'

'I got pregnant with our Harold.'

'An' whose baby was he?'

'My husband's,' Mrs Turner said with sudden, unexpected ferocity. 'Well, he *had* to be, didn't he? Because even if I could have got a divorce, Wilf would never have married me.'

'So you didn't see him again?'

'Not until he came back to the farm after his father died. An' then it was only from a distance.' A tear trickled down her wrinkled cheek. 'It was too late for me by then, you see. I was too *old* to start again.'

The front door swung open and Mr Turner entered the room, laden down by logs.

'Are you still here?' he asked his unwelcome guest.

Woodend rose to his feet. 'I was just leavin',' he said. He turned back to the old woman. 'Thank you for the cup of tea.'

'You're welcome,' Mrs Turner said. 'I hope you find what you're lookin' for.'

'Me, too,' Woodend agreed.

Old farmers like Jed Turner did not shake hands unless they were buying or selling cattle, so Woodend merely nodded to him and stepped through the front door and out into the cold winter air.

He was getting somewhere at last! he thought as he lit up a cigarette. He had discovered something that all the efforts and all the resources of the Central Lancs police force had failed to come up with.

He gazed out on to the snow-covered moors – where Wilf Dugdale might, at that very moment, be lying frozen stiff – and wondered what he should do with his discovery. All his training dictated that he should immediately communicate his findings to his superior, DCC Ainsworth – but his instincts told him that would be a big mistake, both for the investigation and for his own teetering career.

He took a deep drag on his cigarette, and wondered which was the quickest way to Rochdale.

Eleven

The housing estate was on the outskirts of Rochdale, just off the road leading to Todmorton. It consisted of row upon row of neat, semi-detached dwellings with red-tiled roofs, large bow windows and small, but well-tended, front gardens. The streets had names like Willow Close and Cedar Drive, and if such places had existed when they were both growing up, Woodend would have been willing to bet that Mickey Lee would have ended up in just the kind of home he now owned.

Woodend walked up a path flanked by garden gnomes and a flower bed which looked forlorn in the dead of winter but would, no doubt, be a blaze of colour once the spring came around again. He came to a stop at the recently painted front door and rang the bell. From the hallway he heard a tinkling musical chime announcing his arrival.

The man who answered the summons had grey, clipped hair and a perpetually worried, sulky expression etched into his face. Though they had sat next to each other all the way through Sudbury Street Elementary School, the other man could have been the senior by at least ten years, Woodend thought – and then he wondered if that was what *all* middle-aged men told themselves when suddenly faced with a contemporary.

'Hello, Mickey,' he said.

'Hello, sir,' the grey-haired man replied, without much enthusiasm.

Sir! That was a bad sign!

'I wasn't "sir" to you the last time you an' I met,' Woodend said, with a conviviality that he didn't really feel. 'It was at the federation dance, as far as I can recall.'

'It was.'

'An' if I remember rightly, you called me "Charlie, you miserable old bugger".'

'That was a social occasion,' Lee said, not willing to give an inch. 'This isn't.'

'So you know why I'm here, do you?'

'I know that there's been a double murder up on the moors near Whitebridge. An' I know you'd probably be leadin' the inquiry yourself, if you hadn't been suspended.'

Bad news travelled very fast, Woodend thought – but then, what had he expected?

'I need your help, Mickey,' he admitted. 'To be honest, I need it pretty badly.'

'I'm not sure that, under the circumstances, that would be appropriate,' Lee said, stony faced.

'We've been pals since we were kids,' Woodend cajoled. 'I even went out with your sister Joyce for a while.'

'That was a long time ago – before I'd settled for bein' a humble desk sergeant close to home, an' you'd gone down to London to become a hot-shot chief inspector.'

'I've pulled you out of a few nasty scrapes in your time,' Woodend reminded him.

'An' now you've come to collect your debts?'

Woodend shrugged awkwardly. 'It's not somethin' I like doin', but I don't seem to have any choice.'

Lee sighed theatrically. 'Well, now you're here, I suppose you'd better come inside.'

He led Woodend down a neat hallway into a carpeted lounge which had three plaster ducks flying on the wall.

'Joyce not around?' Woodend asked.

'She's doin' shift work up at the hospital.'

'Our Annie's trainin' to be a nurse,' Woodend said. 'She started in September.'

'Joyce *has* to work, you see,' Lee said, as if Woodend had never spoken. 'We can't get by on just a sergeant's pay.'

Then why don't you do something about it? Woodend thought. Why didn't you put in for promotion while you had the chance? But Mickey Lee had never been one to show much initiative.

'Would you like a beer?' Lee asked. 'I think there's a couple of bottles in the fridge.'

It was tempting, but Lee was just the sort of man to regard one beer as enough to square off all accounts.

'As you've already pointed out to me, Mickey, this isn't a social visit,' Woodend said.

Lee nodded. 'So why *are* you here?'

'We're lookin' for an old farmer, a feller called Wilfred Dugdale—' Woodend began.

'What's all this "we" business?' Lee interrupted him. 'I know the *Whitebridge police* are lookin' for him – I read that in the papers – but since you've been suspended, I can't see what it has to do with you.'

'I'm conductin' my own investigation.'

'You're *what*?'

'You heard me the first time.'

Lee shook his head. 'The whole of the Central Lancs police can't find this feller, an' yet you think you can do it on your own? Grow up, Charlie.'

It wasn't going to be easy, Woodend thought, but at least Lee was calling him 'Charlie' again.

'I know somethin' they don't know,' he said. 'Dugdale used to live at Forty-six Derby Road, Rochdale.'

'Then it's your duty to make whoever's in charge of the case aware of that as soon as possible.'

Woodend sighed. 'I'm out on a limb,' he admitted. 'If I

can come up with somethin' which will help to solve these
murders, I might just be able to stop my career from goin'
down the drain. But knowin' that the feller used to live in
Rochdale isn't nearly enough.'

'You want me to find out what I can about this Dugdale
feller, do you?'

'That's about the long an' short of it.'

Lee shook his head again. 'I'm five years away from
drawin' my pension. I've got an unblemished record, you
know . . .'

'I'm sure you have.'

'. . . an' I'd like to keep it that way.'

'I'm not askin' you to do much,' Woodend said. 'All I
want is for you to come up with a bit of background on
him. What he did for a livin'. Who he associated with. That
kind of thing.'

'In case you've forgotten, the man's right at the centre
of an investigation into a serious crime.'

'I know he is, Mickey. I wouldn't be interested in him if
he wasn't, now would I?'

'If the bosses back in Whitebridge find out I've been
askin' questions about somethin' which is no concern of
mine . . .'

'They won't.'

'But if they do . . .'

'Then you could turn it to your own advantage – say
you were only tryin' to do your bit to help the investigation.'

'An' just *how* would I go about justifyin' that?'

'Jesus, it shouldn't be too difficult,' Woodend said exasperatedly. 'Use your initiative.'

But as he'd reminded himself earlier, even at school
Mickey Lee hadn't had much initiative.

'Spell it out for me,' Lee said.

'All right,' Woodend said wearily. 'You can tell them that

when you read about Dugdale in the papers, you remembered seein' his name in some report or other an'—'

'What if they ask me to produce the report in question?'

'Show them a report on another Dugdale. Or on a Duggins or Dugson. Tell them that you made a genuine mistake. Bloody hell, man, they're not goin' to come down on you like a ton of bricks for showin' a little enthusiasm for your job, even if it doesn't lead anywhere.'

'I'm not so sure of that.'

'Anyway, like I said, that won't happen. The brass in Whitebridge might have bloody big ears, but even theirs aren't large enough to hear a few casual conversations goin' on in a station twenty miles away from their offices.'

For a moment it looked as if Lee would agree, then he said, 'I know I owe you a few favours, sir – but this is *too* big a risk.'

He should have known, Woodend thought. He should have recognized from the start that if there were a world championship for Jobsworth of the Year, Mickey Lee would win it hands down.

'I'd have done it for you, you know,' he said, making one last effort.

'*You'd* have done for it for somebody you hardly even knew,' Lee replied, a little sadly. 'But, you see, you're not me.'

'No, I'm not,' Woodend agreed. 'You'd best get on with whatever you were doin' when I turned up like a bad penny. I'll see myself out.'

'One thing before you go,' Mickey Lee said.

'An' what might that be?'

'If you tell anybody you've been here, I'll deny I even let you through the door.'

'You amaze me,' Woodend told him.

Twelve

Not too many cars went down the dirt track which ran alongside the Woodends' cottage, but there were enough of them during the week for Charlie Woodend not to find himself wondering who it was every time he heard a vehicle carefully negotiating its way down the rutted road. So he did no more than register the rumble of a car as he was preparing his bedtime cocoa at the end of the long day which included his visit to Rochdale. And even when he heard the car's engine die, the driver's door slam, and the sound of footsteps coming towards his front door, he was no more than mildly curious.

He glanced up at the grandfather clock. It was well after midnight. Chances were his visitor was some poor, hapless motorist who had taken a wrong turning and found himself wandering the labyrinth of country lanes with no idea of which turn to take next.

It came as something of a surprise, when he answered the urgent knocking at the door, to find Monika Paniatowski standing there. And it was even more surprising – possibly even shocking – to see the state the sergeant was in.

Paniatowski's eyes were red. The silky blonde hair drooped in rat's tails over her shoulders. And the shoulders themselves had developed an uncharacteristic droop since the last time he'd seen her.

'I promised myself an early night for once,' Paniatowski said tiredly. 'I thought I'd fall asleep the minute my head hit the pillow. But I didn't. I couldn't go to sleep however hard I tried.'

'I know *that* feelin' well enough myself,' Woodend said sympathetically.

'So in the end, I gave up. I got dressed again, and for the last couple of hours, I've just been driving around. I didn't mean to come here – at least, I don't think that I did. It wasn't until I realized what that bloody lane of yours was doing to my suspension that it even registered that I was anywhere near your house. Then I saw your downstairs light was still on, and it seemed like a good idea to stop. Would you mind if I came in for a few minutes?'

'Of course not, lass,' Woodend said. 'Step inside an' make yourself comfortable.'

Paniatowski flopped down heavily on the sofa. 'God, life's an awful bloody thing, isn't it?' she said. 'You don't happen to have any vodka in the house, do you, sir?'

'You emptied the bottle the last time you were here. But there's some twelve-year-old single-malt whisky sittin' in the cupboard, if you'd like to try that instead.'

'That'll do,' Paniatowski said dismissively, as if he had offered her methylated spirits.

Woodend poured his sergeant a large shot, then watched her as she knocked it back with scant regard to its delicate flavour.

'What's on your mind, lass?' he asked gently.

Paniatowski gave a half-hearted shrug. 'You? The investigation at Dugdale's farm? The clutch on the MGA? I don't know any more. My judgement's so shot that I can't work out what's important and what isn't.'

'Do you want to talk about the case?'

'If you like – not that that'll take us long. We're getting nowhere fast. DI Harris is happy enough, because he's having   much fun playing Big Chief that he hasn't even oticed how low the team's morale is. And as for

93

Mr Ainsworth – well, Dick the Prick seems much more interested in nailing you to the wall than he is in finding out who blew that poor bloody girl's face away.'

Should he tell her about Dugdale? Woodend asked himself. Should he give away the one card he still had in his hand?

'I've found somethin' out that might help the investigation, an' since it doesn't look like it's goin' to be much use to me any more, you might as well take the credit for it yourself,' he said.

Paniatowski's tired eyes were suddenly alive and intelligent again. 'What is it?' she asked.

'It's about Dugdale. For at least some of his missin' years, he was livin' in Rochdale. I don't really know if that bit of information will lead you anywhere positive – but it's all I've got to give you.'

'It might help,' Paniatowski said. 'But if there's any credit to be extracted from it, I'll make damn sure it goes to you.'

Woodend shook his head. 'That'd be a waste of time, lass,' he said regretfully. 'From what you've told me about what's been happenin' in the last couple of days, my stock's so low that if I turned up at the station tomorrow with the murderer in tow, an' his confession in my hand, Ainsworth would still probably arrest me as an accomplice.'

The phone rang shrilly, making Paniatowski jump. 'Are you expecting a call?' she asked, sounding panicked.

'At this time of night? No, I'm not.'

The same thought was running through both their minds, Woodend realized – that the caller was DCC Ainsworth, demanding to know what Paniatowski was doing at the cottage of a man currently under investigation.

It was a ludicrous idea, of course. It would never have crossed Ainsworth's mind that one officer would go out on a limb for another officer. And even if it had done, Paniatowski – despite her present state – could not

94

have failed to notice if she'd been followed down the country lane.

So it was insane to think – even for a moment – that it was Ainsworth on the other end of the line. But the fact they *had* both thought it showed just how screwed up their minds were.

Woodend picked up the receiver. 'Yes?'

'Is that DCI Charlie Woodend?' asked a familiar voice.

'Mickey? Mickey Lee?'

'No names,' the caller said hastily. 'No names, an' no follow-ups. This is a once-only call. Understood?'

'Understood.'

'An' after it, our account's squared?'

'Absolutely.'

There was a pause as if, even at this stage, Lee was contemplating hanging up, then he said accusingly, 'You never mentioned the fact that Wilfred Dugdale's got a criminal record!'

'I didn't know he had.'

'Are you playin' straight with me?'

'Yes,' Woodend said.

'You're sure?'

'I swear I am.'

'You always did play straight,' Mickey Lee said grudgingly. 'All right, here's what I've got for you. Dugdale *did* live in Rochdale for a fair number of years before the war. He worked as a builder's labourer, on an' off, but most of the time he was drawin' the dole. In other words, he was a typical scrounger, livin' off the fat of the land while me an' my missus have to work our balls off to meet the mortgage payments every month.'

But Dugdale hadn't shown any signs of being a scrounger since he'd got back to Whitebridge, Woodend thought. Far from it – he was fully entitled to an old age pension, but he'd never bothered to register for it.

'Go on,' he said encouragingly.

'Dugdale was suspected of any number of minor crimes durin' his time in Rochdale.'

'What kind of minor crimes?'

'Breakin' an' enterin'. Fencin' stolen goods. That kind of toe-rag stuff. He was pulled in for questionin' a couple of dozen times, but the bobbies in charge of the cases could never make anythin' stick.'

'If they couldn't make anythin' stick, why does Dugdale have a criminal record?'

'I'm comin' to that. One night back in 1938 he got into a fight in a pub called the Dun Horse.'

'A serious fight?'

'Serious enough. He went for the other feller with a broken bottle an' cut him up pretty badly, too, by all accounts. Anyway, to make a long story short, he was charged with GBH, an' drew an eight stretch.'

Woodend felt his pulse start to race. He was on to something, he thought – at last, he was on to something.

'You're absolutely sure of all this, are you?' he asked.

'Certain. If you want more details, I can give them to you.'

'All right.'

'He served his time in Strangeways, an' his cellmate for most of his sentence was a nasty young tearaway who went by the name of Philip Swales. Both Dugdale an' Swales were released at the same time – June 1946.'

Right around the time Clem Dugdale, Wilfred's father, had finally popped his clogs. And Wilfred, finally free to go wherever he wanted to after eight long years in prison, had heard about his old man's death and come back to Whitebridge to claim his inheritance.

'Did he—?' Woodend began.

'That's it,' said the voice on the other end of the line. 'That's all I've got – and that's all you're gettin'. *Ever.*'

The line went dead. Woodend replaced the receiver on its cradle, and turned back to Paniatowski.

'Accordin' to the man I've just spoken to, Dugdale did time in Strangeways for GBH,' he said, with the new hope he felt evident in his voice. 'He attacked another feller in a pub in Rochdale. An' it must have been a pretty nasty attack, because he served eight years.'

Paniatowski frowned worriedly. 'Don't go getting carried away, sir,' she cautioned him.

'What do you mean by that?'

'Just what I say: however desperate we are, there's no point in trying to twist the facts so that they'll fit into a convenient theory.'

'Is that what I was doin'?'

Paniatowski nodded. 'I'm afraid I think that it was. So Dugdale's got a record for violence. What does that really prove? Getting into a heated pub brawl – even a particularly nasty one – is an entirely different matter to shooting two people, one of them a girl, in cold blood.'

'You think I'm tryin' to pin the murders on Dugdale?'

'Aren't you?'

'No, I'm not. This isn't about Dugdale at all.'

'Then what is it about?'

'The Central Lancs police force.'

Paniatowski's frown deepened. 'You've lost me.'

'Think about it,' Woodend urged.

Paniatowski did. 'If Dugdale has a criminal record, then his fingerprints should be on file,' she said finally.

'Go on.'

'And it's almost inconceivable that none of the prints that Battersby lifted from the farmhouse belonged to the owner of the place.'

'Agreed. So we should have got a match – and we didn't. Now why do you think that is?'

'There are two possible explanations,' Paniatowski said,

speaking slowly and carefully. 'The first one is that DC Battersby made a lousy job of doing the comparisons.'

'It wouldn't be the only time there's been a slip-up of that nature,' Woodend said, playing Devil's Advocate.

'But Battersby didn't just do the comparisons only once – he did them a second time.'

'That's right, he did.'

'And after that, they were sent down to Scotland Yard. So if a mistake was made, it had to be made *three* times, by *two* different sets of people. And I simply can't see that happening.'

'Which leaves us with the other possibility, doesn't it?' Woodend said. 'An' that is . . . ?'

'That the reason there was no match was because Dugdale's prints were never submitted for examination.'

'Or, at least, they were never submitted to *Scotland Yard.*'

'Or at least they were never submitted to Scotland Yard,' Paniatowski echoed.

'That information I gave you on Dugdale earlier . . . about where he was durin' the missin' years . . .'

'Yes?'

'Forget what I said about sharin' it with the rest of your team. I think you should keep it to yourself for a while longer.'

'Do you really?' Paniatowski asked.

'Do you think I'm wrong about that?'

'In a way. But it's more a question of degree than anything else.' Paniatowski gave him a tired – perhaps even vaguely optimistic – smile. 'You don't *think* we should share the information about Dugdale with the rest of the team yet – whereas I'm bloody *sure* that we shouldn't.'

Thirteen

The pale blue Ford Anglia, which Woodend had borrowed from one of his neighbours, blended in well with the other cars parked on the early-morning streets of Birkdale, a housing estate located on the south side of Whitebridge.

The estate was a fairly new development. It was considered by many people in Whitebridge to be a highly desirable place in which to live, and its residents – drawn from the ranks of primary school teachers, clerks, driving instructors and factory foremen – were quietly complacent about having had the foresight to move into it. Yet despite their complacency, even they would be prepared to admit that Birkdale could not compare with the Castlewood Estate, a recent project of T. A. Taylor and Associates, on the north side of town. All the houses in Castlewood were detached, and were occupied by solicitors, factory managers and doctors. Such places were well beyond the reach of people like them – and of low-ranking police officers like DC Clive Battersby.

Woodend glanced through the windscreen of the Anglia at Battersby's house and those on either side of it. The one to the left had an elaborate nameplate on the front wall, announcing that it was called 'Camelot'. The one to the right had a brass carriage lamp over its door. Battersby's house had neither a nameplate nor a carriage lamp. Even from a distance, the Chief Inspector could see that the front windows could have done with a good cleaning and that the paint on the front door was starting to flake.

'Are you sure that Clive's the one we should be looking at?' Paniatowski asked, from the passenger seat of the Anglia.

'He's not the *only* one,' Woodend replied. 'He isn't even one of the main players. But he's certainly involved in some way in the whole bloody mess – because the prints from Dugdale's Farm could never have gone missing without his co-operation.'

DC Battersby's front door swung open, and the detective constable himself stepped out. He was wearing a shabby camelhair coat which was open wide enough to reveal a chain-store blue suit, a badly ironed white shirt and a dark, carelessly knotted tie.

'How long is it now since his wife ran off with the coal man?' Woodend asked.

'A year? Eighteen months?'

'He's not standin' up particularly well to the difficulties of copin' on his own, is he?'

'Not well at all.'

'On the other hand, he doesn't really look rough enough to have called in sick – especially in the middle of an important murder inquiry.'

Battersby walked down his path, and came to a halt in front of a battered old Morris Minor.

'Is that his own car?' Woodend asked.

'It's certainly what he's been driving lately – but he used to have a Ford Cortina.'

'It's not a swop I'd have made,' Woodend said.

Battersby took his keys out of his overcoat pocket, selected one by feel, and tried to slide it into the lock in the driver's door. When the key refused to go in, he looked first down at his hand, then glared up at the sky – as if he suspected God of playing a malicious trick on him.

As he was selecting another key, the ring slipped out of his hand and clattered on to the pavement.

'He's nervous,' Woodend said.

'Very,' Paniatowski agreed.

Battersby retrieved the keys, opened the door successfully this time, and climbed into the car. He had some difficulty getting the vehicle started – probably because he was being too impatient – but eventually the engine coughed into some kind of life, and the Morris pulled away from the curb.

Woodend waited for a few seconds, then followed in the Anglia.

'Aren't you afraid he'll spot us?' Paniatowski asked, noticing the absence of other traffic.

'The state he's in at the moment, he wouldn't spot us if we were Bertram Mills' Circus on his tail,' Woodend replied.

At the edge of the Birkdale estate the Morris Minor turned right, on to the main road.

'He's going into the centre of Whitebridge,' Paniatowski said. 'Isn't that a bit of a risk, when he's supposed to be at home sick?'

'Maybe he's goin' to see his doctor,' Woodend said.

But neither of them really believed that that was where Constable Battersby was heading.

They passed the sign which welcomed careful drivers to Whitebridge, and reached a road junction. The new shopping centre lay to the left, the police headquarters to the right. Battersby made a left turn.

Woodend pulled up at the curb. 'This is as far as you go,' he told Paniatowski.

'Why?'

'Because the way things are at the moment, it wouldn't be very clever of us to be seen in the same car.'

'To hell with that,' Paniatowski said fiercely.

'I appreciate your loyalty,' Woodend told her. 'But stayin'

with me now would be crossin' the line between support an' stupidity.'

'Sir—'

'Out!'

Paniatowski opened the passenger door, stepped out on to the icy pavement, and slammed the door again with rather more force than was strictly necessary. Woodend waited until she was clear of the car, then pulled out into the stream of traffic again.

Battersby parked at one end of the car park on top of the shopping centre, Woodend – playing it carefully – parked at the other. By the time the Chief Inspector was getting out of the Anglia, the fingerprint expert had already reached the stairs.

Woodend sprinted across the asphalt, then took the stairs two at a time. As he reached the shopping level he caught sight of Battersby heading towards the central piazza.

The detective constable walked hurriedly passed a Curry's electrical store, William Hill's bookmakers, a dry cleaner's and a butcher's. When he drew level with T. A. Taylor's Turf Accountants, he dived through the door as if he had spotted an oasis in the middle of a desert.

If he was in such a hurry to place a bet, why hadn't he gone into William Hill's? Woodend wondered.

But he already knew the answer – a gambler will only willingly pass the nearest betting shop when his line of credit there has completely dried up.

Woodend waited for a minute, then pushed the door of the betting shop open and stepped inside. There were already a few gamblers gathered, some studying the racing form and others filling out their slips. Battersby was standing at the counter, arguing with the young clerk who was unfortunate enough to have been on duty when he arrived.

'I've told you twice already, I simply can't authorize a

bet of that size, except on a strictly cash basis,' the clerk was saying.

'An' I'm tellin' you that Mr Taylor himself has extended my credit by another hundred quid,' Battersby protested.

The clerk ran his eyes up and down Battersby's shabby overcoat.

'Mr Taylor himself has extended your line of credit, has he?' he asked contemptuously. 'Do I look like I was born yesterday?'

A door at the back of the shop opened, and a second clerk – a man in his mid-forties – emerged.

'Are you havin' some kind of trouble with the customer, Jack?' he asked his colleague.

'The gentleman wants to place a big bet, Mr Bairstow,' the younger clerk said disdainfully. 'The problem is, he's got no cash on him, so he wants to put it on the slate.'

'I see,' Bairstow said thoughtfully. 'An' might I enquire what your name is, sir?'

'Battersby. Clive Battersby.'

'*Detective Constable* Battersby?'

'Yes, that's right,' Battersby said, sighing like an addict who thinks that it's just possible that he might get his fix after all.

'How much was it you were plannin' to bet?'

'Only twenty quid.'

Bairstow smiled. 'Well, if we can't trust the police to honour their debts, who can we trust? Accept the bet, Jack.'

The junior clerk shrugged, as if to say it was none of his business if his boss wanted to go playing silly buggers. The senior clerk, having cleared up the problem, retreated to the back room again. With hands that were visibly shaking, Battersby reached for a betting slip. And Woodend – having heard enough – made his way quietly out of the shop.

A few minutes later, the betting shop door swung open

again, and Constable Battersby – the collar of his overcoat turned up despite the fact that the shopping centre was well heated – stepped out. Once more he looked neither left nor right, but instead headed straight towards the Weaver's Arms, a modern precinct pub which fondly imagined that it could hide its newness by the strategic placement of a few artefacts from a hand-loom weaver's cottage.

Battersby pushed the swing doors open and walked up to the bar. 'Whisky,' he said.

'What brand?' the barman asked. 'Bell's? Johnny Walker's? Black an' White?'

'Anythin' will do. Just make it quick. An' you'd better make it a double, an' all.'

The barman measured out the drink from the optic. He placed the glass in front of his customer, and Battersby slid a five-pound note across the counter. Then, without waiting to be given his change, the constable knocked the whisky straight back.

'Give me another one of them,' he told the barman, placing the empty glass on the bar.

Woodend walked up behind him, and tapped him lightly on the shoulder. The effect was even more dramatic than he might have expected. First Battersby jumped as if he'd been electrocuted, then he swung round to face Woodend as though he feared he was under attack.

'Hello, Clive,' Woodend said. 'I think it's time we had a little talk. Don't you agree?'

'I . . . I . . .' Battersby gasped.

Woodend took the other man by the arm, and half led, half dragged him over to a table in the corner.

'Sit down,' the Chief Inspector said.

'I don't . . . you can't make me . . .'

'Sit down before I knock you down,' Woodend growled.

Slowly and sullenly, the detective constable sank down on to one of the rustic stools.

Woodend took a seat opposite him. 'How long have you had this gamblin' problem, Clive?' he demanded.

'It's not a problem,' Constable Battersby protested. 'I've got it well under control.'

'You're talkin' like one of those winos you see dossin' down on the Boulevard.'

'I am? How d'you mean?'

'They've got things under control, too. Accordin' to them, the only reason they get pissed out of their heads an' then fall asleep in their own vomit is because they like it.' Woodend shook his head mournfully. 'Come on, Clive. You know me better than to think I'm goin' to walk away from this just because you tell me everythin's all right.'

'It . . . it all started when Vera left me for that big flashy bastard who used to deliver the coal,' Battersby said. 'I felt so *alone* after she'd run off, if you know what I mean.'

'Yes, I know what you mean.'

'Goin' down to the bettin' shop now an' again seemed to make things a bit more bearable for me. I'd ask the other punters what horse they thought I should put my money on, then we'd all stand there together an' watch the race. It was almost like bein' part of a family.'

'Then the bug really started to bite, did it?'

'I'd only put ten bob on at first, but before I knew what was happenin' I was bettin' a quid. An' then two.'

'I just heard you bet nearly two weeks' wages on a single horse,' Woodend pointed out.

Battersby's left eye started to twitch. 'That was different. I got a hot tip on that one. The nag can't lose.'

'I also heard you say that Terry Taylor himself had personally guaranteed you an extended line of credit of up to a hundred pounds.'

'I . . . he . . .' Battersby stuttered.

'Has he, or hasn't he?' Woodend barked.

'Well . . . yes . . . he has.'

105

'Now why should he have done that?'

'Because he knows I'm good for it.'

'Well, that leads us on to another interestin' question,' Woodend said. 'You tell me he knows you're good for it, but what I'd like to find out is how he knows you *at all*.'

'What do you mean?'

'With all the other pies Terry Taylor's got his fat fingers in, I don't suppose he finds he's got much time to spend in his bettin' shop. So it's unlikely you met him there. An' I'm really not sure where else you could have met him. I don't imagine you move in the same social circles, do you?'

'I met him at the races,' Battersby said unconvincingly.

'What races?'

'Er . . . Doncaster. Yes, that's right – it was Doncaster. He heard me talkin' to somebody else, an' he must have recognized my accent because he asked me if I was a Whitebridge man. Well, I said that I was, an' then we got chattin' – as you do at the races.'

'An' on the strength of that he's prepared to subsidize your gamblin' addiction?'

'Like I said earlier, he knows I'm good for it.'

'How much do you owe him already?'

Battersby shrugged awkwardly. 'A hundred an' fifty quid.'

'You're lyin' to me!'

'Or maybe a bit more.'

'I'm guessin' it's *a hell of a lot* more.'

'An' what if it is?' Battersby demanded, suddenly showing some spirit. 'What's it got to do with you? You're not even my boss any more. You've been suspended.'

'So I have,' Woodend agreed. 'But it's *you* we're talkin' about at the moment, isn't it? I remember what it's like tryin' to get by on a detective constable's wages. It's tough enough just meetin' your regular payments, so where are you goin' to find the money from to pay off your big gamblin' debts?'

'I'll work them off somehow.'

'Oh, I'm sure you will,' Woodend agreed. 'In fact, I think you've already started.'

'What are you insinuatin'?'

'Why did Terry Taylor want you to switch the fingerprints you got from Dugdale's Farm?' Woodend demanded.

'I don't know what you're talkin' about!'

'Yes, you do. Wilfred Dugdale's prints never went down to London, or Scotland Yard would have matched them up with those on his record straight away. So somebody else's prints were sent instead – somebody *without* a record. You're the only one who could have made that substitution. I already know why you did it – for the money. What I'm interested in now is why Terry Taylor should ever have *wanted* it done.'

'I don't have to talk to you,' Battersby whined.

'No, you don't,' Woodend agreed. 'But you'd be a fool not to take the chance when it's offered to you. I always look after my team – you know that – an' I'll do the best I can for you. Let me help you, because no bugger else will. No bugger else gives a *damn* about what happens to you.'

There was a flicker of hope in Battersby's eyes. 'Could you save my career, sir?'

Woodend shook his head. 'I could lie to you about that – an' the state you're in, you'd probably believe me. But I'm goin' to be honest with you, instead. All right?'

'All right.'

'This whole business has gone much too far for there to be a hope of savin' your career. But if you co-operate fully with me, I might just be able to keep you out of prison.'

Battersby made a superhuman effort, and struggled to his feet. 'I've got to think it over,' he said. 'I've . . . I've got to . . . to . . . go somewhere on my own . . . where I can think about it.'

He put his hand over his mouth, and rushed away. He only just made it through the door into the shopping centre before he doubled up and was violently sick.

Fourteen

With Woodend in the passenger seat, Monika Paniatowski pulled off the main road and drove on to
the Birkdale estate. There was even less traffic this time
than there had been earlier. The men – and many of the
women – were now all at work, and these were not the
kinds of households which could afford to run second cars
for non-working wives.

Their arrival had been noted, Woodend thought. House-
wives vacuuming their front rooms, and mothers walking
their well-wrapped-up babies, turned their heads in frank
curiosity at the sight of an unfamiliar car on their familiar
territory. They probably wouldn't have paid half as much
attention to the borrowed Anglia he'd been using earlier.
But it didn't matter a damn that they'd been spotted. The
time for caution was over. There was no need to play your
cards close to your chest when you had a winning hand –
and a winning hand was exactly what Clive Battersby had
dealt them in the Weaver's Arms.

'This had better work, sir,' Paniatowski said, the hint of
uncertainty in her voice showing that she did not quite share
her boss's optimism. 'We only get one shot at it, so it had
better work.'

'There's no way it can fail,' Woodend assured her.

'Battersby's probably scared half to death and—'

'Of course he is, but that can only work to our advantage.
Look, he was on the verge of tellin' me everythin' I needed

to know in the shoppin' precinct. Since then, he's had a couple of hours to realize he hasn't got any option but to co-operate. An' seein' the two of us standin' there on his doorstep will be the final straw. He'll give us Terry Taylor – and Terry Taylor will give us both the motive for the murders an' the name of the murderer.'

And in a few hours at the most, I'll be back in my own office, as if the nightmare I've been livin' through had never happened, he added silently.

'What if he's so frightened that he's done a runner?' Paniatowski asked worriedly.

'That'll delay matters – but not for long,' Woodend argued. 'He won't get far, an' once he's taken into custody he'll probably be more willin' than ever to spill his guts. In fact, lookin' at it from that angle, it might even speed things up if he decides to cut an' run.'

But though his words sounded confident – though he told himself that he really believed them – he still breathed a sigh of relief when he saw the battered Morris Minor parked in front of Battersby's house.

Woodend and Paniatowski got out of the car and walked up the path which led to the detective constable's front door. Coming from inside the house, they could hear the sound of loud music. Woodend recognized it. 'Winter', the last movement of Vivaldi's *Four Seasons*. He would not have thought that Battersby was a man for the classics.

The music really *was* very loud. 'It's a wonder the neighbours don't complain about the noise,' Paniatowski said.

Woodend grinned. 'There aren't many perks to bein' a bobby,' he said, 'but one of the few we do get is that neighbours will always think twice before they complain about us.'

They reached the front door. Woodend raised his arm to ring the bell, only to find Paniatowski's hand restraining it.

'Better not, sir,' the sergeant said.

'Why?'

'Since I'm the only one who's still got official standing, I'd like to be the one who handles things from here on. If you don't mind, that is.'

'I don't mind,' Woodend said.

Why should he? This impotence was only temporary. In a few hours he would back firmly in the driving seat.

Paniatowski rang the bell. They waited. They should have been able to see a distorted image of Battersby entering the hallway through the frosted glass in the front door, but they didn't.

'He probably can't hear us ringing over all that bloody noise inside,' Paniatowski said.

She pressed the bell again – and this time she kept her finger on it.

Woodend took a step to the side. The curtains in the bay window were half open, and he could see through the gap into Battersby's living room.

It was the sofa he saw first – a rather threadbare one with a floral pattern. And then he noticed the pair of legs which were sticking out from beyond it!

'Get out of the way!' he told Paniatowski.

'What's the matter, sir?'

'Don't ask questions, Monika – just get out of the bloody way!'

Paniatowski moved clear of the door. Woodend braced himself, then lashed out with his right leg. His boot made contact with the lock. The door juddered, but held firm. He swung again, and this time the lock groaned and gave, and the door swung, complaining, open.

Woodend rushed into the hallway, and from there into the lounge. But he already knew that he was far too late. He had seen the legs through the window – now all that was left to do was to see the *rest* of what was left of Battersby.

The detective constable was lying on his back. He had a

shoe and sock on his left foot, but his right foot was naked. The big toe of the right foot was jammed up against the trigger of a shotgun, the barrel of which was in his mouth. Much of the upper part of his head was missing. Bits of brain, and what looked like an ocean of blood, had been spattered on the wall and skirting board.

'Oh my God!' Paniatowski said.

Then she walked quickly over to the radiogram, and pressed the eject button. The mechanical arm swung off the record, and the room was suddenly – eerily – quiet.

Woodend looked again at the bloodied pulp which had been the head of the man he'd been talking to only that morning.

'Jesus!' he exclaimed, to no one in particular.

'Get out of here, sir!' Paniatowski said urgently.

'What?'

'Get the hell out of here!'

'But I can't just leave Battersby—'

'There's nothing that you or anybody else can do for the poor bastard now, and if it comes out that you were with me when I found the body, we'll both take a fall.'

She was right, Woodend thought – there *was* nothing anybody could do for Detective Constable Clive Battersby now.

As he stepped out of the front door, he could hear that Paniatowski was already talking into her radio. He walked quickly down the path and out on to the street. The snow was falling again – quite heavily – but his mind was in such a state of turmoil that he didn't even notice it.

His chances of being quickly reinstated had died with Battersby, he told himself. And, even worse, without the information the constable could have given him, he was no nearer to finding the man who killed the poor bloody kid up at Dugdale's Farm.

He kept on walking, more out of instinct than from a desire to reach anywhere specific. He had covered perhaps half a mile when the ambulance – warning lights flashing and siren blaring – screamed past him.

Fifteen

When night fell on most days of the year, all that could be seen through the front window of the Woodends' cottage was the black impenetrability of the moors. But there were a few winter evenings – and this was one of them – when the layer of snow which was covering the inhospitable ground sucked what little light was available into itself, and the moors shimmered with an eerie glow.

Woodend had no idea how long he had been sitting there in front of the window, a glass of malt whisky clutched in his big hand. He did not even know how many times he had got up from his chair to refill the whisky glass. Though his body had not left the cottage since it had got back from the Birkdale Estate, his mind had been ranging far and wide.

Battersby's death had not just been a defeat for him – it had also been a far-too-convenient escape for someone else. The detective constable had been the weak link near the very end of the chain. And now he was gone. Was that mere coincidence? Woodend didn't think so.

He pictured how things must have happened. Battersby would have been sitting in his kitchen – finally coming to accept that he had no choice but to turn to his old boss for help – when he heard the doorbell ring.

Had he looked through the window to see who it was? Or had he just assumed it was a neighbour come round to borrow a cup of sugar, or a door-to-door salesman trying to sell him the latest miracle cleaning fluid?

It didn't really matter *what* he'd thought, because when he had opened the door he'd found himself facing neither the neighbour with her cup, nor a salesman with a suitcase and an ingratiating smile, but some hard-lookin' fellers with grim expressions on their faces.

How many of them would there have been, Woodend wondered. Two? Three?

It would have taken at least three, he decided.

The hard-lookin' fellers would have backed him into his lounge, deaf to all his protests that their secret was safe with him. While two of them stood in the doorway, blocking any chance of escape, the third would have put the record on the record player, turning up the volume very loud to cover the sound of the explosion which was to follow.

Battersby must have worked out what was about to happen by then, and had probably begun to plead with them to let him live. But it had done him no good! Two of the men had grabbed him and held him on the floor, while the third had bent over him and forced the shotgun barrel into his mouth.

How he must have struggled, knowing that he was fighting for his very life. And how pointless he must have known that struggle would be, even from the very beginning.

The barrel would have hurt his teeth and the roof of his mouth. He would have found breathing difficult, and there was probably the taste of oil on his tongue. He would have heard the click of the trigger being pulled back, and for one brief instant have known he was as close to death as anyone ever gets. And then . . . and then, nothing.

His killers would have taken off his right shoe and sock, wiped the gun clean of their own prints, and placed it where they wanted it to be found. Then they would have left and walked calmly down the street.

Terry Taylor – or whoever it was who was behind Terry Taylor – must now be thinking he was in the clear. But he

115

was wrong! Battersby's death may have closed the most obvious route to a solution, but over the last few hours Woodend had come to realize that it had opened several new ones.

There would be bruises from the struggle on Battersby's arms and legs. There might be scrapings of his killers' skin under his fingernails. No one – not even that bloody fool DI Harris – would be able to pretend it was anything but murder. A full-scale inquiry would have to be launched. Hundreds of people would be interviewed. Someone on the estate would be bound to have seen the killers or their vehicle, and be able to provide a description. And then it would just be a case of the police following a piece of string until they got to the end. The descriptions would lead them to the murderers, the murderers would lead them to Taylor.

The builder had made a big mistake when he'd decided that the best way to escape being implicated in the first two deaths was to sanction a third.

The telephone rang, and Woodend dashed across the living room to pick it up.

'Monika?' he asked, almost breathlessly.

'No, it's me, sir,' said a male voice.

Bob Rutter!

'How are things goin' down in Hendon?' Woodend asked, injecting his voice with a lightness he did not feel. 'I hope you're learnin' somethin' – even if it's only which bums to suck up to.'

'I'm not calling to talk about me – I'm calling because of what's been happening to you,' Rutter said.

'Oh! So you've heard, have you?'

'Paniatowski rang me up.'

'That was nice of her,' Woodend said, thinking that if Paniatowski and Rutter were speaking to each other voluntarily then he must be in an even worse mess than he'd thought he was.

'I was wondering if there was anything that I could do to help you,' Rutter said.

'Your best plan might be to pretend you've never heard of me,' Woodend told him, bitterly.

'I'm not just making polite conversation, here – I mean it,' Rutter replied, his tone falling somewhere between stern and earnest.

'I know you do,' Woodend said, chastened. 'But even if you were up here in Whitebridge, I doubt you could do much. Stuck in London, you're about as much use as . . .'

He paused.

'Has something occurred to you?' Rutter asked.

'Aye, it has,' Woodend agreed. 'You know Terry Taylor?'

'The builder?'

'That's the man.'

'Is he a suspect?'

'I think so – but I doubt DI Harris would agree with me.'

'I'd be worried if he did. DI Harris is an idiot. But you still haven't told me how I can help.'

'I've just remembered readin' an article about Taylor in the *Evenin' Telegraph* a few months back. It was one of them back-slappin' pieces which is more an advertisement than information. But one fact's stuck in my mind. He said that before he came to Whitebridge, he had a very modest jobbin' builder's business in Southwark, South London.'

'And you want me to go down to Southwark and see what I can sniff out about him?'

'If you can find the time.'

'I'll *make* the time.'

'You're a good lad,' Woodend said sincerely.

'You're a good boss,' Rutter replied.

Woodend put down the phone, and walked back to the window. Suddenly, now that he'd remembered that article, it was all starting to make sense.

He'd been wondering where Taylor had managed to find men who would commit murder for him – men willing to hold a struggling police constable down while a shotgun was forced into his mouth – and now he thought he knew. They'd be old pals of Taylor's, men he'd drunk with when he'd been a jobbing builder in London's gangland.

If only Bob could make that connection – if only he could prove that a bunch of criminals with a reputation for violence had travelled from London to Whitebridge shortly before Battersby met his death . . .

The phone rang again. It *had* to be Paniatowski this time, he thought – and it was.

'Have you got the preliminary results of the autopsy yet?' Woodend asked.

'Yes, I have,' Paniatowski replied, in a flat – almost dead – voice.

'Well, come on, lass! What does it say?'

'That the injuries sustained were entirely consistent with a successful suicide attempt,' Paniatowski said, as if she were quoting.

'That can't be right!' Woodend protested. 'There must have been bruisin' which couldn't have been self-inflicted. Get Doc Pierson to check the ankles an' upper arms again.'

'It wouldn't do any good.'

'How do you know?'

'Because I was there for the entire autopsy. If there'd been any bruising, I'd have seen it myself. Besides, there's other evidence which points to suicide.'

'What other evidence?'

'It was Battersby's own gun, for a start.'

'I don't believe that.'

'I've seen the licence.'

'Whoever's behind all this has got enough influence to be able to tamper with the fingerprint evidence. Compared

to that, slippin' a false firearm licence into the files would
have been a doddle.'

'It was Battersby's own gun,' Paniatowski repeated
firmly. 'Hardcastle and Duxbury have been out shooting
with him on the moors a few times. They've positively
identified it.'

It couldn't be suicide, Woodend told himself. It just
couldn't be.

Because if it was, they had lost their best lead without
gaining anything to replace it.

Because if it was, he knew he'd soon be asking himself
exactly what it was that had caused the constable to take his
own life.

'So it was Battersby's gun,' he conceded. 'That doesn't
have to mean that Battersby was the one who pulled the
trigger, does it?'

'And then there's the note he left,' Paniatowski said.

'Are you sure it's genuine?'

'The experts have been over it. There's no doubt that
Battersby wrote it himself.'

'An' what did he have to say in this note of his?'

'The usual stuff that suicides always write,' Paniatowski
replied – just a little too quickly.

'Be more specific, Sergeant.'

'Oh, you know the sort of thing,' Paniatowski continued
uneasily. 'That he'd made a real mess of his life. That he
was sorry for all the trouble he'd caused. Like I said, the
usual stuff.'

If that was all it was, why did she seem so unhappy?

'There's still more, isn't there?' Woodend demanded.

Paniatowski said nothing.

'I said there's more, isn't there?'

Another pause.

'Yes, there's more,' Paniatowski finally admitted.

'So tell me what else he said.'

119

'He said he hoped that you'd forgive him.'

'Me? He hoped *I'd* forgive him?'

'That's right, sir.'

'Oh, Sweet Jesus!' Woodend groaned.

'Don't take it personally.'

'How else can I take it? If I hadn't backed him into a corner in the Weaver's Arms an' put the pressure on him to come clean, he'd still be alive.'

'He didn't kill himself because of what you said to him. He killed himself because he'd done wrong and couldn't face the consequences. You were the one who found out about it, but it could have been me or anyone else on the team who came up with the goods.'

But it wasn't you or anyone else on the team, Woodend thought. It was *me*. I didn't pull the trigger – but I might as well have done.

'Are you all right, sir?' Paniatowski asked.

'I'm fine,' Woodend lied. 'Listen, I need time to do some thinkin' about where we go from here, so I'm goin' to hang up now.'

'You wouldn't like me to come round, would you?'

'I didn't realize you were unconscious in the first place,' Woodend said, making an attempt at humour.

'You know what I mean,' Paniatowski persisted. 'Don't you want some company?'

'You get your beauty sleep, lass,' Woodend said. 'Ring me first thing in the mornin', an' I'll tell you the brilliant new idea which I'm bound to have come up with by then.'

He replaced the receiver on its cradle and took another sip of his malt whisky. Walking back to the window, he looked out at the moors and felt as if his energy – his will to go on fighting against the odds – was being sucked from him as surely and steadily as the snow was sucking in the light.

He needed to find a new direction for his investigation to take. He needed to come up with some blinding insight which would act as the opener for a can of worms he had yet to locate.

He was not sure that he was up to the task, because he knew that at the same time as one part of his mind was working on the intricacies of the case, there would be another part of it – perhaps a larger part – which was wrestling with his feelings of guilt over Battersby's death.

It was going to be a long, long, night which was stretching ahead of him – and probably a fruitless one.

Sixteen

They came for him just before dawn broke.

Woodend had been expecting them for several minutes, ever since he'd first heard the sirens screaming and – looking out of an upstairs window of the cottage – had seen the lights on their roofs flashing dementedly as they made their way down the country lanes.

There had been no need to send three cars to bring him in. One would have served the purpose perfectly well. There'd been no need for the flashing lights and sirens, either – unless, of course, they'd hoped to spook him into making a break for it. But they knew him better than that – knew he'd never run. No, the lights and sirens had been used only to create a spectacle, as part of the stage craft in the play which he was already coming to think of as *The Lamentable Fall of Charlie Woodend.*

Even the arrival of the convoy had been carefully timed – so that his neighbours would be woken from their beds and forced to watch the spectacle through sleep-filled eyes.

Standing in his living room, still dressed in last night's clothes, Woodend watched the cars pull up outside his cottage, and understood it all. DCC Ainsworth was not out merely to harm him, he wanted to destroy him completely – and so far, he was forced to admit, the bastard hadn't missed a trick.

Two young constables got out of the lead car and walked up the steps to the front door. Even sending them to do the

122

job had been a deliberate choice, Woodend thought, a ploy designed to deny him the dignity of being dealt with by his equals. Besides, young bobbies were more impressionable than their older colleagues – if anybody could be guaranteed to spread the news of what had happened, it would be them.

Woodend opened his front door. 'What can I do for you, lads?' he asked – going through the motions, playing his assigned part in the script that someone else had written.

'We've come to take you down to the station, sir,' said one of the constables, a kid who would have been playing conkers at the time when Woodend was counting the corpses in the death camp at Belsen.

'Am I under arrest?' the Chief Inspector asked.

'No, sir. Not yet.'

'So if I refuse to come . . . ?'

The constable looked down at his boots in obvious embarrassment. 'You know the procedure better than I do, sir,' he mumbled. 'It'd be much easier all round if you co-operated with us.'

Much easier, Woodend agreed. And, after all, why should he go out of his way to make things difficult for these kids who were only doing what they'd been told to do?

'I'll just get my coat,' he said.

The constable coughed. 'If I was you, sir, I'd pack an overnight bag, as well,' he advised.

'I see. So things have already gone *that* far, have they?'

'Don't know anythin' about that, sir. Just know that Mr Evans said it would be better if you brought a few things with you.'

Woodend threw a change of underwear, a clean shirt, a pair of socks, his shaving stuff and a well-thumbed copy of Dickens's *The Mystery of Edwin Drood* into a bag.

'Do you need to cuff me?' he asked the fresh-faced constable.

123

The young man seemed to blush, even at the thought of it. 'No, sir. We've been told that isn't necessary.'

Well, at least he'd been spared one indignity. But then that had probably been part of the plan too – a part aimed at allowing him to hold on to just a tiny flickering flame of hope, so that when that flame was finally snuffed out, he would be all the more devastated.

So, the handcuffs might be absent now, but they would be brought out at some stage or other, he was sure of that. And even as he stood there on his own doorstep, he could almost hear the metallic click as they were clamped around his wrists.

Woodend had spent more time in this interview room than he cared to remember. But he had never sat at this side of the table, with his eyes looking directly at the door which led to freedom – a door which, like so many other men before him, he knew he would be passing through only under police escort.

He turned his attention to the two policemen who were sitting opposite him. It was almost comical to see the look of troubled concern on Ainsworth's drink-mottled face, as the DCC tried – with very little success – to slip into the role of the sympathetic member of the interrogation team. The bullet-headed Chief Inspector Evans was experiencing no such difficulties in finding his role. His face was even more pinched than usual, and his eyes burned with a blood lust. If there were such a thing as reincarnation, he would almost certainly come back as a slavering Dobermann, like the four which guarded Terry Taylor's building site.

'I will ask you again, Mr Woodend, do you want to see a solicitor?' Evans said.

Woodend shook his head.

'Would you please answer the question verbally, so it can be noted down, Chief Inspector?'

How easy it was to forget the procedures, Woodend thought. How easy to stop thinking like the methodical bobby he had been all these years, and to slip straight into the criminal's skin.

'No, I do not wish to see a solicitor,' he said for the benefit of the WPC who was recording the interview on her shorthand pad.

Ainsworth sighed wearily, pretending that he was not enjoying any of this at all.

'Are you going to tell us what we want to know straight away, Charlie?' he asked. 'Or are we going to have to drag it out of you?'

'That depends,' Woodend told him. 'What exactly *is* it that you'd like to know?'

'Who's this man Tideswell?' DCI Evans barked. 'Is that his real name, or just an alias?'

'Tideswell? I used to know a feller called *Fred* Tideswell when I was just a little kid,' Woodend said reflectively. 'He was a tackler up at the old British Empire Mill. But he was gettin' on in years then, so he must be dead an' buried by now. An' as far as I can remember, he had no family to speak of.'

'We're not talking about him – and you know it! What about the *other* Tideswell? W. M. Tideswell?'

'I've never heard of him.'

'Yet this same man, who you claim never to have heard of, deposited five hundred pounds in your account at the Royal Lancaster Bank on Whitebridge High Street?'

'I know nothin' about that.'

'Nobody gives five hundred pounds to a complete stranger,' Evans pointed out.

'They do if they're tryin' to fit him up. An' that's what's happenin' here. I'm bein' fitted up.'

DCI Evans laughed, dryly and humourlessly. 'How many times have you sat on this side of the table and heard some toe-rag who's as guilty as sin make just that same claim?'

'Often enough,' Woodend admitted. 'But that doesn't mean that now an' again somebody who says it might not actually be tellin' the truth.'

Ainsworth, still grappling with playing the part of benign uncle, shook his head regretfully.

'Tell us the rest, Charlie,' he urged. 'Then at least we can say in mitigation that you co-operated with us.'

Woodend picked up his packet of Capstan Full Strengths and lit one up without offering them around. 'There is no *rest* to tell.'

'Are you claiming this is the only bribe you've ever taken?' DCI Evans demanded.

'That's a bit like the "When did you last beat your wife?" question, isn't it? I haven't taken any bribes at all.'

'Then how did the money get there?'

'The bankin' system's specifically designed to stop other people from takin' money out of your account – not to prevent them puttin' it in.'

'So you still maintain that this Tideswell man was prepared to say goodbye to five hundred pounds of his money just to fit you up?'

'Who said it was his own money?' Woodend asked.

'If it wasn't his, then whose was it?'

Taylor's, Woodend thought. Bloody Terry Taylor's!

'I don't know,' he said aloud.

'Will you please give me the details of all other bank accounts, apart from the one in the Royal Lancaster, which are held in your name?'

'There are no others.'

'So it would come as a complete surprise to you to learn that the Amalgamated Cotton-Industrial Bank of Skelton has just such an account on its books?'

'No.'

'No? But you've just told us, on the record, that you don't have any other accounts.'

'Nor do I,' Woodend agreed. 'But whoever's out to get me is doin' a thorough job of it, so I'm not surprised a second account exists. When was it opened, by the way? Yesterday?'

'According to the bank's records, you opened that account eleven months ago.'

Woodend took a deep drag on his cigarette. 'Eleven months, eh? Well, I'm willin' to bet that if you look at those records closely, you'll find the ink isn't even dry yet.'

'Tideswell has been paying five hundred pound a month into that account,' Evans said, as if Woodend had never spoken. 'In other words, it now contains five and a half thousand pounds. It would have taken you over four years to earn that much money legitimately. I can see how it must have been a big temptation to you.'

'Do you really think any jury is goin' to believe that I'd be stupid enough to open bank accounts in my own name, an' then have bribes from this Tideswell feller paid straight into them?'

'You wouldn't be the first bent bobby to act in that way,' Evans said. He clasped his hands in front of him, as if he were a lay preacher about to deliver a sermon. 'That's the trouble with officers who go bad, like you have, Mr Woodend – you're all so cocksure you're completely fireproof that you don't bother to take even the most elementary precautions.'

'So accordin' to you, Mr Evans, I'm not only greedy, but I'm also *thick*,' Woodend said.

'As I told you just a moment ago, you wouldn't be the first to be so blatant about it – not by a long chalk.'

'It's getting rather smoky in here, don't you think, Chief Inspector?' Ainsworth said to Evans.

'I beg your pardon, sir?'

'I said, it's getting rather smoky in this room. It must be difficult for a non-smoker like you to tolerate. Why don't you go outside, and get a few breaths of fresh air?'

'I'm all right for the moment,' Evans said.

'But you'd be even *better* for a short break,' Ainsworth insisted. He turned to the WPC. 'You can take a break, too, Constable.'

They would have to have had the sensitivity of concrete not to take such a heavy hint. DCI Evans and the woman constable stood up and stepped out of the room.

Ainsworth waited until the sound of their footsteps had receded down the corridor, then turned his attention back to Woodend. 'Well, this is a *real* mess you've found yourself in, isn't it, Charlie?' he said.

'For once, I agree with you,' Woodend replied.

'And I still want to help all I can,' Ainsworth continued. 'If you'll stop screaming about being fitted up, and just take your punishment like a man, I'll make sure the prosecution asks the judge to impose a minimum sentence.'

'For a while, I thought Evans might be in on all this,' Woodend said. 'But he isn't, is he?'

'I don't know what you're talking about.'

'Evans is just a dupe – but a very useful one. People may not like him very much, but they know he's fundamentally straight an' honest. So if he believes that I'm guilty, then I must be.'

'We *all* believe you're guilty, Charlie.'

Woodend shook his head. 'No, you don't. For a scam like this to have a chance of workin', it needs two things goin' for it.'

'It's pointless to still try and pretend that—'

'The first is a hell of a lot of money to splash around. Well, that's really no problem for a rich feller like Terry Taylor, is it? But the second thing it needs is the co-operation of somebody inside the force – somebody quite high up.'

'And that's me?' Ainsworth asked.

'An' that's you,' Woodend agreed. 'I've been sittin' here wonderin' what's makin' you do it. I've never liked you – you were never my kind of bobby – but I've always thought you got more pleasure out of makin' the people around you jump through hoops than you did from worldly goods. An' I still think I'm right about that. So if it's not the money you're after, what *is* in it for you? Has Taylor got friends who can help you make Chief Constable? Or do you have political ambitions? Has he offered to see to it that, in the course of time, you become the Honourable Member for Whitebridge?'

'You're losing your marbles,' Ainsworth said dismissively.

'Am I?' Woodend asked. 'Or have I finally started to see things as they really are? You told me to take my punishment like a man. That's funny.'

'Is it?'

'*Very* funny, coming from a feller like you – a feller who isn't enough of a man to stop play-actin' even when there are only two of us here.'

Ainsworth's already red face flushed with anger. 'You want me to stop play-acting?' he hissed. 'You want me to be straight with you? All right, I will be. There's only one person to blame for the situation you find yourself in now – and that's Charlie Woodend.'

'Me?'

'You! If you'd just been willing to lie low for a while, you'd have waltzed your way through the Disciplinary Board hearing and come out at the other end smelling of roses. But you couldn't do that, could you, Charlie? You just had to keep sticking your nose into things that were none of your business.'

'Murder *is* my business.'

'And you simply can't see beyond it, can you? You just go barging in without any thought of the consequences –

without even considering the innocent lives you might be destroying in the process.'

'What innocent lives?'

'Battersby's, for a start.'

'He was scarcely innocent.'

'Maybe not – but he didn't deserve to die either, did he?'

'No,' Woodend admitted, feeling a fresh pang of his recurring guilt. 'He didn't deserve to die.'

'And he's only a marginal case, at best. You could have wrecked dozens of lives! Dozens!'

'An' what's that supposed to mean, exactly?'

Ainsworth, who had been riding on a crest of anger, seemed suddenly to recall where he was, and what he was saying. 'Nothing,' he told Woodend. 'It means absolutely nothing.'

The two men fell silent for perhaps half a minute, then Woodend said, 'Shall we get the formal chargin' over with now?'

'Yes,' Ainsworth said. 'As soon as DCI Evans returns, we'll get the formal charging over with.'

'I'm sorry about this, sir,' the sergeant said as he rolled the new detainee's fingers over the inkpad.

'It's all right,' Woodend told him.

As had been the case with the interview room, the holding cell area took on an entirely new aspect when viewed from the other side of the fence. It had seemed so neutral and antiseptic when he'd visited it in the past. Now it felt full of menace. And the cells! He was well aware that they were perfectly adequate – not much smaller than the spare bedroom back at the cottage, as a matter of fact – yet they *appeared* so cramped and confined.

'Photograph next, sir,' the sergeant said, leading him through to a second small room where the camera was permanently mounted.

'I've not had my picture taken since I was dressed up as Henry VIII at the fancy dress ball,' Woodend said.

'Just sit on the stool, sir,' the sergeant said, his voice as bland as the expression on his face.

Woodend sat.

'Look straight at the camera, sir.'

A flash.

'Now turn your head to the side, please.'

A second flash.

'Should you wish to consult a lawyer—' the sergeant began.

'I know my rights,' Woodend interrupted him.

'I'm sure you do, sir,' the sergeant said levelly, 'but I am still obliged by police procedure to remind you of them.'

Woodend nodded. 'Of course you are. Sorry, Sergeant.'

'Should you wish to consult a lawyer or telephone one friend or relative, then you are entitled to do so.'

But who would he call? There was no point in worrying Joan – far better to wait until he was out on bail and could explain the situation to her face-to-face. And he couldn't ring Monika Paniatowski, because a record of the call would be kept – and people might start asking why he'd *needed* to call her.

'Sir?' the sergeant said.

'There's nobody I want to speak to. We've completed all the paperwork, haven't we?'

'Yes, sir.'

'Then if you wouldn't mind showin' me to my cell . . .'

'Of course, sir.'

'I got a parkin' ticket once,' Woodend said, as the sergeant led him down the corridor.

'Beg pardon, sir?'

'I said I got a parkin' ticket once. In Accrington, it was. Left the car too close to a zebra crossin'. An' up until today, that's the only illegal thing I've ever been charged with.'

131

'We all get parkin' tickets at one time or another, sir,' the custody sergeant replied.

'But most of us don't get charged with corruption – is that what you're sayin'?'

'No sir, I'm not. I'm just sayin' that most of us have had parkin' tickets at one time or another.'

They both fell silent, and the only noise to fill the air was the sound of their feet on the tiled floor. They reached the cells and the sergeant opened one of the doors.

'We don't know each other very well, but we do *know* each other,' Woodend said. 'Do you really think I'm guilty of corruption, sergeant?'

'It's not for me to say, sir,' the other man replied. 'My job's to see that you get fed properly and that your rights aren't violated. I wouldn't like to go much further than that.'

'Quite right,' Woodend agreed, chastened. 'I'm sorry to have put you on the spot like that.'

He stepped over the threshold of the cell, and heard the door click closed behind him. He looked around. A bed, a wash basin, and a toilet alcove which was not visible from the door.

He placed his bag on the floor, and sat down on the bed. You are in deep, deep trouble, Charlie, he told himself.

DCC Ainsworth probably wouldn't oppose his bail in court the following morning, but even once he was out on the street again, he was not sure that he could do himself any good. He needed the police records and a dozen trained men at his disposal. As it was, he wasn't even sure that Monika Paniatowski would dare to help him any further.

He had to find a way to get something on Terry Taylor, he told himself. Once he'd done that, everything else would fall into place like iron filings around a magnet. But where the hell could he begin?

He looked around at the walls and the metal door. If

things went the way Ainsworth had planned they should, a prison cell would become as familiar to him as his own home. More familiar – because work so often kept him away from the cottage, but once in jail, the cell would become the centre of his world.

How long a sentence would he get?

Five years?

More?

It would probably depend on just how thick the Crown Prosecutor chose to lay it on – corrupt officer, callously abusing his position of trust, etc – and which judge he had the luck to draw.

However long or short the sentence he was given, it wouldn't be an easy stretch to serve – ex-bobbies were not exactly the most popular inmates in prisons, and the other prisoners would be sure to find a thousand ways to make his life a living hell.

He tried to read, but simply could not focus his attention on *The Mystery of Edwin Drood*. The day dragged on, and gradually turned into night. Woodend lay on his narrow bed, and gazed up at the cell ceiling. Occasionally there was some noise to distract him – a bellicose drunk being processed, a muted conversation as one officer went off duty and another took his place, the sergeant's footsteps as he made his slow, steady rounds – but mostly there was nothing to keep his mind occupied but his own dark thoughts.

He must have eventually fallen asleep without noticing it, because suddenly he was very cold, and when he looked up at the window he saw that dawn was starting to break.

Seventeen

It was early afternoon when the custody sergeant appeared at the door of Woodend's cell with two uniformed constables.

'We're here to escort you to the magistrates' court, sir,' one of the officers said, in a flat featureless voice.

'Both of you?'

'Both of us.'

'Do you really think that's necessary?'

'I couldn't say, sir. We're just obeying orders.'

'An' whose orders might they be? DCC Ainsworth's?'

'No, sir. The sergeant's.'

But the order would have *originated* from Ainsworth, Woodend thought as he walked down the corridor, flanked by his escort.

The timing of his appearance before the magistrates had been another of Ainsworth's masterstrokes, Woodend admitted grudgingly. The DCC could have used his influence to arrange a special closed session of the court if he'd wished to, but that wouldn't have suited his purposes at all. Better – far better – to have Woodend arraigned in open court under the critical gaze of a general public whose view of humanity had already been distorted by having sat through dozens of cases of drunk and disorderliness, shoplifting and child neglect.

It wasn't even a case of kicking a man when he was down – always an Ainsworth speciality – it was kicking him when he was down *and* out.

*   *   *

The magistrates' court was an impressively oak-panelled room which often seemed far too grand a setting for the display of pathetic human weaknesses which were pronounced on within its walls, but for the grave matter of indicting a fallen angel, it was just right.

Woodend was not surprised to discover that he knew all three of the magistrates socially. In a town the size of Whitebridge, everyone of a certain standing knew everyone else of that same standing – and even his lack of dress sense and quirky nature were not *quite* enough to debar him from being at the edges of the elite.

Two of the magistrates were men already well into middle age – local head teachers who, from the vantage point of the bench, could follow the progress of the more recalcitrant pupils who had passed through their hands. They had fixed, neutral expressions on their faces as they looked at him, but their eyes were full of the censure they reserved especially for those who had held positions of responsibility and had let the side down.

The third magistrate was younger – and a woman. Polly Johnson was a rising star of the town's social services department. The last time Woodend had seen her had been a garden party she'd thrown as a wake for the half of that garden she was about to lose under a compulsory purchase order.

'I love those trees,' she told Woodend, when she'd had perhaps a little too much to drink. 'I've looked after them as well as if they were my children. Now they're going to be cut down. And why? Because I don't have the *right kind* of influence. If I'd been a Mason, this would *never* have happened.'

Now, as she looked down at Woodend in the dock, there was none of the condemnation in her eyes he had found in the eyes of her fellow magistrates. Rather, there was open puzzlement – as if she couldn't quite understand what he was doing there at all.

Not that it made much difference one way or the other what any of the magistrates thought of him, Woodend realized. This was a purely formal hearing in which the charges were read out, he pleaded not guilty, and the bench ruled that the case would be tried, at an appropriate time, by a higher court.

Bail was not opposed by the police – why should it have been, when he didn't have a card left in his hand which was worth playing? – and less than two minutes after entering the dock, Woodend found himself standing outside in the lobby again.

'You can leave through the back door if you like, sir,' said one of his uniformed escorts.

'An' why would I want to do that?'

'Most people in your situation usually prefer to avoid the press if they possibly can.'

'So the press is here, is it?' Woodend said – thinking, even as he spoke: Of course it's here! What else did I expect? Bent bobby brought up before the beaks! I'm a big juicy story.

'Thing is, it's not just the local boys,' the constable said. 'There's a television crew from BBC Manchester as well.'

It was tempting to just slip quietly out of the back door, Woodend thought. It would certainly save Joan, still at her sister's house, from the humiliation of seeing him on the evening news. But it would also look suspiciously like he was running away – that he had something to hide.

'I think I'll go out through the front,' he said.

'Please yourself,' the constable replied indifferently.

Woodend opened the main door and stepped out. Yes, the press was there all right – notebooks and cameras at the ready. He recognized many of the faces, but there was one he had expected to see, and didn't – Elizabeth Driver, the crime reporter from the *Daily Globe*, the woman who had made it her personal mission to blacken his name ever since the Westbury Hall case. It was not like Liz Driver to miss an opportunity like this, and Woodend wondered what could possibly have happened to her.

The air was chilly, and he could see patches of ice on the steps which led down to the street. If he went arse over tip now, it would seem almost symbolic of his fall from grace, he thought.

He grasped the rail for support, and the moment his hand wrapped around it, he realized he had made a mistake – understood that he must look like a man so shaken by his experience in the courtroom that he was forced to clutch the rail for support. But there was no help for it now – to release his grip would merely be another confession of uncertainty.

He made his way carefully down the steps, while the reporters moved in like a pack of ravening wolves who have sensed their prey's weakness.

It was the BBC man – the true aristocrat among the waiting hacks – who stepped the furthest forward, thrusting his microphone aggressively right into Woodend's face.

'Were you surprised to be released on bail, Chief Inspector Woodend?' he demanded.

'Of course I wasn't surprised,' Woodend replied. 'There can't be a single person in this whole town who doubts for a second that I'll turn up for my day in court.'

'You sound as if you're actually looking forward to it.'

'I am. I want this travesty ended as quickly as possible.'

'So you're saying the charges which have been laid against you are completely unfounded?'

'I pleaded not guilty, didn't I?'

The reporter smirked. 'That's what they tell me,' he said. 'But come on, Chief Inspector, the police must have been very sure of their ground before they moved against one of their own.'

'What do you intend to do now, Mr Woodend?' one of the other reporters – a mere print journalist – called out.

'I have no further comment to make.'

'Don't you have any plans to try and clear your name?' the reporter persisted.

But his tone suggested that whatever Woodend might try to do, it would be a wasted effort – because black was black, and it wouldn't change colour just because some bent bobby wanted it to.

A breathless-looking young woman with black hair suddenly appeared from around the side of the courthouse. So that was where Elizabeth Driver had been – waiting in ambush for him at the back door.

Had that been her own idea? Woodend wondered. Or had she been put up to it? Was this just one more example of Ainsworth directing the drama which, as far as the DCC was concerned, could only be allowed to have one ending?

Woodend glanced up the street; at the cars covered with a thin layer of freshly fallen snow; at the early-afternoon shoppers who had stopped their shopping to watch the spectacle being played out in front of the courthouse; at the two uniformed policemen who knew him well, but now were pretending not to notice him at all.

And suddenly, it all felt just too much. Felt as if the street was beginning to close in on him – and would continue to close in until it fitted him like a straitjacket, denying him the possibility of even the slightest movement.

'I said, do you have any plans to try and clear your name?' the reporter asked for a second time.

'Didn't you hear what I said, you stupid bastard?' Woodend demanded angrily. 'I told you I had no further comment to make – an' I bloody meant it.'

Eighteen

'I'm sorry I wasn't there for you in court,' Monika Paniatowski said.

'I know you are, lass,' Woodend replied.

But as he looked at her standing there on the doorstep of his cottage, dressed in a sheepskin jacket which seemed almost to engulf her, he was thinking: She looks so small and vulnerable. Why have I never noticed that before?

'I wanted to be there – but I just wasn't brave enough,' Paniatowski mumbled.

'There's a big difference between bein' brave an' bein' foolhardy,' Woodend told her. 'An' if you'd turned up, foolhardy is what it would have been. It wouldn't have done me an ounce of good – an' it would have been professional suicide for you.'

Paniatowski nodded gratefully. 'Can I come in?'

'Are you sure you want to?'

'Yes.'

'Even if I told you that DCC Ainsworth's behind this attempt to fit me up? That he'll do whatever he has to – an' I mean *whatever* – to see me behind bars? An' if that includes crushin' a detective sergeant along the way, he won't hesitate for a second?'

'You're not telling me anything I didn't know already. Ainsworth has to be behind it – because the thing wouldn't work without him. And I'd *still* like to come inside.'

'You're a good lass,' Woodend said.

Paniatowski smiled. 'Good? I'm one of the best.'

'Aye, you certainly are that,' Woodend agreed. 'Let's get out of the cold, shall we?'

Paniatowski followed Woodend into the living room. A fire was blazing away in the grate, and the sergeant warmed her hands before shucking off her sheepskin jacket.

'Any progress?' Woodend asked, without much evidence of hope in his voice.

'Not so as you'd notice. We still haven't found Wilfred Dugdale, and we've no more idea now who the victims are than we had when we found the bodies on Sunday.'

'Nobody's phoned in to report a friend or a member of the family has gone missin'?'

'*Lots* of people have phoned up. They always do on cases like this one. Even once we'd eliminated the nutters, we were still left with a fair number of callers who did seem genuinely concerned. But it didn't get us anywhere. All the girls who the genuine callers were worried about were either too old or too young, too tall or too short – or simply turned up at home again.'

'An' the man?'

'We've had less calls about him – as you'd expect – and they all led to dead ends, too.' Paniatowski lit up a cigarette. 'How bad was it in court?'

'It was bloody awful,' Woodend admitted. 'Even worse than I'd expected it to be. But frettin' over that won't get us anywhere. Let's stick to the case. You really haven't got any leads at all?'

'I didn't say that.'

'Didn't you?'

'No. I said the investigation led by *DI Harris* hasn't got any leads. But then he's not looking at it from the same angle as you and I are, is he?'

'The angle bein' Terry Taylor?'

'That's right.'

'An' you think you might be on to somethin'?'

'I think that in investigating Taylor, we might be wading into deep water – *very* deep water which is not only mined, but is probably full of sharks as well,' Paniatowski said ominously.

'You want to be a bit more specific?'

'For the last couple of days I've been spending as much time as I could get away with looking into the history of Terry Taylor's business dealings. And I've discovered that the bigger his company has grown, the more local authority contracts he's won.'

'I'm all for diggin' up dirt on the bastard, but I don't see where you're goin' with this,' Woodend said. 'The larger a company is, the more contracts it's *bound* to win.'

'True,' Paniatowski agreed. 'But he's not the only big builder in the Whitebridge area, is he?'

'No. There must be three or four more, at least.'

'Yet last year, T. A. Taylor and Associates managed to secure over fifty per cent of the available council contracts.'

Woodend whistled softly. 'That does seem high,' he admitted.

'There's more. In the cases where sealed bids had to be submitted, Taylor's were always the lowest. Not usually! Always! And he didn't significantly undercut the next lowest bidder – he carefully calculated it so that it was *just* low enough to win the contract.'

'You're sayin' that he knew what the other bids were goin' to be in advance?'

'Either that, or he's had the devil's own luck. Then there's the case of Moorland Village.'

'What about it?'

'Over the last few years, several other developers have come up with similar schemes, but they've all been turned down on the grounds that they'd be spoiling an area of great

141

natural beauty. So why did Taylor's request get such an easy passage through the planning committee?'

'You think he's got the council in his pocket?'

'He doesn't need to have them all,' Paniatowski said cautiously. 'It doesn't have to be even the majority. But he *has* to have enough of the councillors on his side to give him the edge when it comes to a vote.'

'You think he's spreadin' his money around?'

'It certainly looks that way.'

'But even if that's the case, what the bloody hell has it got to do with the murders up at Dugdale's Farm?' Woodend asked. 'An' what has it got to do with *me*? He's spent a small fortune to make sure I'm in the position I'm in now, an' I still don't know why. I can see him tryin' to nobble me if I was investigatin' municipal corruption, but I'm not.'

'I know,' Paniatowski said heavily. 'It just doesn't make sense, does it?'

'It's time for the local news,' Woodend said, walking over to the television and switching the set on.

'You're sure you *want* to watch it?'

Woodend nodded. 'Best to see just what I'm up against.'

The set warmed up, and the local newscaster appeared, sitting authoritatively behind his desk.

'. . . *weathermen confidently predict that a thaw will begin in the next day or so* . . .' he was saying.

'Maybe then, we'll find Wilfred Dugdale,' Paniatowski said.

'If he's out there to find.'

'If he's not, then where the hell is he?'

'I don't know,' Woodend admitted. 'I've just got the feelin' that the moors is not the right place to be lookin' for him.'

'*And now to return to our main story of the day,*' the newscaster said. '*The Central Lancashire police continue to come under heavy fire from all sides. Not only are there apparently no new leads in the double murder at Dugdale's Farm, but today one of Whitebridge's senior policemen, Detective Chief Inspector Woodend, appeared in the magistrates' court charged with corruption. Here's Tom Eccles report on the case.'*

Eccles appeared, standing in front of the magistrate's court. There was no sign of the smirk which had been on his face when he'd questioned Woodend earlier. Instead, the expression he displayed for the camera was one of earnest concern, as befits a dedicated reporter whose only interest is in uncovering the truth.

'*Chief Inspector Woodend was pale, but steady, as he stood before the magistrates this morning to be told that there was sufficient evidence for the case of bribery against him to go ahead,*' Eccles said. '*Later, out on bail, he had this to say to me . . .*'

A new image filled the flickering black-and-white screen – a middle-aged man with a haunted expression on his face.

'*Didn't you hear what I said, you stupid bastard?*' the on-screen Woodend demanded angrily. '*I told you I had no further comment to make – an' I bloody meant it.*'

'You should never have said that,' Paniatowski said.

'Aye, it wasn't too clever of me,' Woodend agreed.

But then there was very little he'd done over the previous few days that he didn't regret.

Eccles was back on the screen. '*Mr Woodend faces two charges of corruption at this present moment, but unofficial police sources have hinted that more may follow,*' he said.

'Have you got that?' Paniatowski asked angrily. 'Do you understand what it means? They not only want you buried, they want to make sure the grave's so deep there's no chance you'll ever claw your way out of it.'

'*Deputy Chief Constable Richard Ainsworth had this to say . . .*'

Ainsworth's head filled the screen. '*Without wishing to prejudge Chief Inspector Woodend's case, I am prepared to promise you here and now that if there are any rotten apples in the police barrel, we will seek them out and destroy them,*' he said.

'*You obviously believe that Mr Woodend is guilty as charged,*' the reporter persisted.

'*That is up to a judge and jury to decide.*'

'*But you would never have brought the case if you had not already decided there are good grounds for such a verdict.*'

There was a pause – just long enough to be called 'significant' – then Ainsworth said, '*Obviously there is a case to answer, or Chief Inspector Woodend would not have made his court appearance this morning. Yet as his commanding officer, it is obviously my hope that Mr Woodend will, in the fullness of time, be cleared.*'

Woodend twisted the knob viciously, and turned off the set. 'He's not leavin' much to chance, is he?'

'He can't afford to,' Paniatowski said. 'The way things stand now, he's either got to pull you right down – or take a fall himself. So he's no choice but to put as black an interpretation on your actions as he can.'

But he didn't have to enjoy it so much! thought Woodend, who could see right through the mask of solemnity to the glee which lurked just below the surface.

I should have left by the back door of the magistrates' court, like that constable suggested, he told himself.

But he hadn't. Instead, he'd exposed himself to the press and given that bastard Ainsworth even more ammunition to fire at him.

'We're not dead yet,' Paniatowski said, putting a brave face on it. 'There's always Taylor.'

Yes, there was always Taylor. In the face of all the evidence, Woodend was forced to accept that Taylor had not used his South London criminal connections to help him eliminate Clive Battersby; but he might have used them in *other* ways, and if Bob Rutter could find just one link, there might be a way to get the investigation back on track again.

As if it could read his mind, the phone chose that moment to ring, and it was Rutter on the line.

'What have you got for me, Bob?' Woodend asked eagerly.

'Nothing!' Rutter said despondently.

'Nothin'!'

'Absolutely bugger all!'

'Are you tellin' me that Taylor was a model citizen when he lived in Southwark?'

'No. I'm not telling you that. I'm telling you that he didn't live in Southwark *at all*.'

'You're absolutely sure of that?'

'I must have talked to a couple of dozen people since you called me. All kinds of people. Other builders, council officers, officials at the rates office – you name it and I've spoken to them. Nobody called Taylor was ever a jobbing builder in Southwark – nobody even matching his description was involved in the building trade.'

It was just another blow at the end of a few days which seemed to have consisted of nothing but blows. But this one fell the hardest of all. Even if Terry Taylor *was* bent, they had no way of proving it now. And without Taylor, they had no leads at all.

Woodend thanked Rutter for his efforts and hung up.

'There must be another way to get at him,' said Monika Paniatowski, who had picked up enough of the conversation from Woodend's end of it to understand what was happening.

'How *can* you get at a man who's built a wall round himself in the present and seems to have no past at all?' Woodend asked gloomily. 'Terry Taylor arrived in Whitebridge

with nothin', an' now he's one of the richest men in town.
Where did he come from? We don't know. How did he get
to be so successful so fast? We don't know. We don't know
anythin', Monika.'

Paniatowski glanced down at her watch. 'I'd better go
before I'm missed back at the station,' she said. 'Don't
worry, sir. Taylor's got a weak spot – everybody has – and
we'll find it in the end.'

'Maybe you're right,' Woodend agreed half-heartedly.

The phone rang again.

'That's probably the press,' Paniatowski said.

Woodend shook his head. 'This number's unlisted. It'll be
somebody I know.' He paused, an anguished look coming to
his face. 'It'll be Joan.'

'I'll see myself out,' Paniatowski told him.

Woodend nodded and picked up the phone. 'Hello? . . .
I thought it would be you, love . . . Yes, I've seen the
news myself. I looked a right bloody, idiot, didn't I? . . .
What? . . . I didn't tell you because I didn't want you to
worry . . . No, of course there's nothin' to worry *about*.
If I didn't believe in British justice winnin' through in the
end, I wouldn't be in the job I am in . . .'

Paniatowski closed the front door quietly behind her,
shutting herself off from the warmth inside and feeling
the outside cold immediately wrap around her. She owed
Charlie Woodend, she told herself – she owed him more than
she could ever hope to repay. And she desperately wanted to
help him out of the mess he was in. But despite her earlier
assurances to him, she had no idea what to do next.

She reviewed the case quickly in her mind. They could
not find the farmer in whose home the murders had been
committed. They had no idea who the victims were, or
why they had been killed. Both Terry Taylor and DCC
Ainsworth were deeply involved in the case in some twisted,
hidden way, but she'd didn't know why – couldn't even

begin to imagine what possible interest a successful local businessman and a high-ranking police officer could have in the deaths of a badly dressed middle-aged man and an expensively dressed young girl who appeared to have no reason for being in an isolated country farmhouse so early on a Sunday morning in the middle of winter.

She lit up a cigarette and gazed out at the moors again. Was Dugdale somewhere out there, buried under the snow? And if he wasn't, where the hell *had* he disappeared to?

'Come out, come out, wherever you are,' she said softly to the missing farmer.

Nineteen

The sun had only just started to rise on the day after Woodend's appearance before the magistrates' court, but the stocky, red-faced woman who was walking across the farmyard with a large zinc bucket in each hand looked as if she had been up and about for hours.

Monika Paniatowski parked her MGA, and walked over to the woman.

'I wonder if you could help me,' she said.

'You're not from the police, are you?'

'That's right.'

The woman shook her head, wonderingly. 'We've had the bobbies round here twice since the murders. I don't know what I can tell you now that I haven't told you already.'

Neither do I, Paniatowski thought.

But there seemed to be nothing else left to do but to go over old ground in the hope that she could glean something she'd missed before.

'I was just wondering if you'd noticed anything unusual last Sunday,' she said.

The red-faced woman sighed. 'We're four miles from Dugdale's Farm, an' half a mile from the main road. If the Martians had landed between here an' Dugdale's, we probably wouldn't have noticed it.'

The farmhouse door opened, and an old man, heavily wrapped up and carrying a walking stick, stepped into the yard.

Death of an Innocent

'You're never goin' to go out in this weather, are you, Dad?' the woman asked.

'I won't be long,' the old man replied defensively. 'Just want to get a breath of fresh air in me lungs.'

'You'd be much better off stayin' inside, where it's warm.'

'I won't be long,' the old man repeated, turning to make a slow, shaky break for freedom.

'He won't listen to me,' the red-faced woman resignedly said to Paniatowski. 'He never would. He's been in bed all week with a bad chest. But will he learn? Will he heck as like. I told him when he went out last Sunday that he was askin' for trouble, but he would still insist—'

'Did you say last Sunday?' Paniatowski interrupted.

'That's right. That's when he caught the cold.'

'The day of the murders?'

'I suppose it was, now I think about it.'

'And what time did he take this walk of his last Sunday?'

'Round about the same time as now.'

'Thanks for your help,' Paniatowski said, turning away and setting off after the old man.

She caught up with him just as he reached the track that led to the main road. 'Can I talk to you for a minute?' she asked.

'Talk as long as you like,' the old man said. 'I've got plenty of time on me hands.'

'Your daughter was just telling me that you went for a walk last Sunday morning.'

'And so I did. What's that got to do with the price of fish?'

'I was wondering if, while you were out on your walk, you happened to see anything unusual.'

'Anythin' to do with them murders, you mean?'

'Yes.'

149

The old man shook his head. 'Much as I'd like to, I'm afraid I can't help you there, lass.'

They had continued walking slowly onwards as they talked. The farm track was on a slight incline, and when they reached the top of it, they could see the Moorland Village spread out before them.

'They should never have allowed that soddin' abomination to be built,' the old man grumbled. 'It's not natural, is it?'

Paniatowski smiled. 'That's just what my boss says.'

'Then he must be a very wise man. An' he must like this bloody awful weather as much as I do – because at least it seems to be holdin' the destructive buggers up for a bit.'

'Yes, they can't have been doing much for the last fortnight,' Paniatowski agreed.

'Now, you're wrong there.'

'Am I?'

'Aye, you certainly are. They were workin' on the bloody place last Sunday mornin'.'

Woodend was surprised to see Paniatowski again so soon, and even more surprised that she seemed to be so much more animated than she'd been the last time they'd spoken.

'I've been talking to an old farmer by the name of Obediah Metcalfe,' she said, as she warmed her hands in front of the fire. 'He's retired now, but he lives with his daughter and her husband at Pickup Farm, and he likes to go for walks early in the morning.'

'So what?' Woodend said. 'Pickup Farm must be at least four miles away from Dugdale's.'

'It is,' Paniatowski agreed, 'but it's less than *half* a mile from the Moorland Village, and when he was out on his walk last Sunday, he heard the sound of heavy plant being moved behind the fence. What do you think of that?'

I think you're clutchin' at even wispier straws than I've been grabbin' for, Woodend thought.

But aloud he said, 'So they were workin' on Sunday morning. What does that prove? Maybe they're behind schedule, an' they were puttin' in a bit of overtime to try to catch up.'

Paniatowski shook her head firmly. 'They weren't putting in any overtime. I talked to the site foreman myself, not more than half an hour ago, and according to him, none of his workers have been up at the site since the bad weather brought work to a halt.'

'Nobody at all? Not even his night watchman?'

Paniatowski grinned. 'Think back to when we met out there. Did you notice anything in particular?'

'Dogs!' Woodend exclaimed. 'Four bloody big, slaverin' Dobermanns with teeth like razors.'

'Exactly! You don't need a night watchman when you've got beasts like those on the loose.'

'I still don't see where you're goin' with any of this,' Woodend confessed.

'That's because you haven't heard the rest yet. Before the machinery started up, our Mr Metcalfe saw what he considered to be quite an unusual amount of traffic for a Sunday morning—'

'Well, he would have done, wouldn't he?' Woodend interrupted. 'There'd been a double murder just up the road.'

'But what struck him particularly was that there were three cars which didn't just go by, but actually drove on to the building site itself. The first one he saw was a Jag—'

'That'd be Terry Taylor.'

'Exactly!'

'Well, when all's said an' done, it *is* his site, an' he's got the right to do what he wants on it.'

'Terry Taylor doesn't normally drive heavy machinery.

151

He's too important for that. He pays other people to do his dirty work.'

'Maybe his parents never gave him a toy bulldozer when he was a kid, an' now – when there's nobody else around – him an' his mates like to play with the real thing,' Woodend suggested.

Paniatowski looked worried. 'What, in God's name, is the matter with you, sir?' she asked.

'Nothin' – as far as I know. Why do you ask?'

'Because you're not acting like yourself at all!'

'Aren't I?' Woodend challenged.

'No, you're bloody not.'

'An' in what particular way do you think that I've suddenly stepped out of character?'

'Normally, when I bring you something new during the course of an investigation, you're over the moon about it. This time, all you seem to want to do is pick holes in everything I tell you.'

'Isn't it my job to see if I can pick holes in your argument?'

'Yes, but only when I've finished outlining it. You're usually such a good listener – but today I feel as if you're fighting me every step of the way.'

Was it possible she was right, and that was *just* what he was doing? Woodend wondered.

Could it be that he was deliberately setting out to crush any hope of escaping from the dark tunnel in which he found himself trapped, simply because he couldn't bear the disappointment of having his hopes dashed again?

If that were the case – if he really *were* thinking like that – then Dick the Prick need not bother to fight him any more, because the bastard had already won.

'Let's hear the rest of it, Monika – an' this time I'll try to be a bit more positive,' he promised.

'Taylor's Jag had come from Whitebridge, but the second

car came from the other direction. And it wasn't a big fancy job like you'd be expecting one of Taylor's mates to be driving – it was a yellow Austin A40.'

'*The* yellow A40!'

'It has to be, doesn't it?'

'Did this Metcalfe feller happen to see who was in the car?'

'He was too far away to get a good look – and, anyway, I suspect his eyes are not what they were – but he's sure there were two people in the car, and that the passenger was white-haired.'

'Dugdale has white hair!'

'So do thousands of other men in this neck of the woods,' Paniatowski cautioned.

'Aye, you're right,' Woodend agreed. 'Go on, lass.'

'The A40 turned on to the site, and then, a few minutes later, the third car arrived. It came from the same direction as the A40 had, but it was a much more impressive vehicle altogether.'

'You're gettin' as bad as Bob Rutter when it comes to paddin' a story out,' Woodend said, regaining some of his old spirit. 'What exactly do you mean by sayin' it was a more impressive car altogether?'

'I mean that it was a Volvo.'

'A Volvo! Ainsworth's?'

'How many Volvos are there in Lancashire?'

'Not a lot.'

'And what are the chances that two of the few that *are* around would have been travelling down the same stretch of country road at the same time on a Sunday morning?'

'Virtually nil.'

'Then I think we can assume that DCC Ainsworth was the driver.'

'So let's see if I've got this straight,' Woodend said. 'A short time after the murder, Taylor arrives at the buildin' site. A few minutes later, an old A40 turns up, an' the passenger is a white-haired man who may – or may not – have been Dugdale. We're not sure of the exact timin', but it must have been roughly when that reporter, Bennett, was discoverin' the bodies.'

'You're sure of that?'

'Yes I am, because otherwise, Bennett wouldn't have passed the A40 on the road to the farm.'

'You're right, of course,' Paniatowski said.

'Then the third car arrives,' Woodend continued. 'A Volvo driven, presumably, by our beloved Deputy Chief Constable, who hasn't gone home, as he told me he was intendin' to do, but has driven straight to Moorland Village.'

'Correct.'

'An' it's right after Dick the Prick arrives on the scene that the machinery starts up.'

'That's about it,' Paniatowski agreed.

'Why didn't Metcalfe report all this earlier?'

'He's been in bed ever since then with a nasty cold. He didn't even know we were looking for the A40 until I told him.'

Woodend looked into the fire. He had poked it a few minutes earlier, and now it was blazing brightly. He began to think that his own hopes might just be starting to be rekindled, too.

'You've done a brilliant job, Monika,' he said.

'I may have opened a new line of inquiry, but we're still a long way from getting a result,' Paniatowski said, a touch despondently.

'What's happened to you, Sergeant?' Woodend asked. 'Five minutes ago you were as bubbly as a shaken-up bottle of lemonade. Now you look as if you're expectin' the roof to drop in on you.'

'Five minutes ago, I believed we'd got a really good lead,' Paniatowski confessed.

'You were right. It *is* a really good lead.'

'Maybe, but now I've thought about it for a while, I don't see how we can use it.'

'Don't you?' Woodend asked, sounding more cheerful than he had in a long time. 'Then it's a bloody good job that at least one of us has still got a brain-box that hasn't been left out in the rain, isn't it?'

What had Cloggin'-it Charlie seen which had so obviously passed her by? Paniatowski wondered.

'You've got a plan, haven't you? she asked.

'I wouldn't go quite that far, but I may just have what could be the beginnin's of an idea.'

'And do you want to tell me what it is?'

Woodend looked slowly around his living room, a slight smile playing in the corners of his mouth.

'I'm very fond of this old cottage of mine,' he said. 'It reminds me of where I used to live when I was a kid. But, do you know, Monika, there are times when I think that it's not quite the sort of place that other people would expect a feller with the rank of Detective Chief Inspector to live in.'

He was going weird again, Paniatowski thought. Charlie Woodend was not the kind of man to give a bugger what other people thought. And even if he *had* suddenly started to care about the opinions of others, why the hell was he talking about it now, of all times?

His career was hanging by the slenderest of threads. Unless a miracle came to pass, the chances were that he wouldn't have a rank at all in a few months' time, only a number. And as for choosing where to live, that choice would be made for him by the judicial system – and wherever it was, he'd be seeing the world through a set of bars.

'Aye, I think it's about time I started raisin' my sights a bit,' Woodend continued. 'I really should give some serious consideration to movin' into a residence which is more in keepin' with my position in society.'

He'd gone cheerfully mad, Paniatowski thought. That was the only possible explanation. The strain he'd been under for the last few days had finally pushed him over the edge.

'If we could just get back to the case for a minute, sir . . .' she said, as tactfully as she could.

'Yes, it's time for a change,' Woodend said, ignoring her. 'An' since I've got a bit of unexpected free time on my hands, now seems the ideal opportunity to go house huntin'.'

A slow smile spread across Paniatowski's lips. 'Oh, now I get it,' she said.

Twenty

T he estate agent who worked for T. A. Taylor and Associates (Properties) said his name was George Fletcher. He drove an aggressively red Vauxhall Velox, and it was plain from the way he talked on the journey out to the Moorland Village that he had either not heard of Woodend's problems or would have been prepared to be pleasant to Judas Iscariot himself if it could have assured him of a sale.

'The whole concept of the development is that it will be a *real* village,' he said, as they drove across the moors.

'A real village,' Woodend repeated.

'That's right,' Fletcher said, as if he were inordinately pleased that his potential customer had grasped a particularly difficult point. 'There'll be a pub – with a genuine thatched roof. There'll be shops and a community hall for the use of boy scouts, amateur dramatic societies, et cetera, et cetera. The village will have its own general works department, too. It's going to be a model for what can be done if only we dare to transform our dreams into reality.'

'As long as the "we" that you're talkin' about happen to be filthy rich,' Woodend said dourly.

Fletcher wrinkled his nose up, as he would have done if he'd detected a particularly bad smell coming from under the dashboard.

'Not rich, Mr Woodend,' he said. 'You only have to be moderately prosperous to share in Moorland Village – to become a part of the golden rural future.'

Woodend looked around him. The thaw had arrived in earnest. Slush lay piled up by the sides of the road, and though the moors still had snow on them, there were now islands of green floating in the sea of dirty white.

The 'dream which was soon to become a reality' loomed up ahead – surrounded by its high wire fence. Early on Sunday morning, four men had met behind that fence. One of them was probably the richest man in Whitebridge; the second, one of the county's most senior police officers and the third an old farmer who had not actually farmed his land for over fifteen years. Who was the fourth man? And where were he and Dugdale now?

The main entrance to Moorland Village had big double gates, and though one of them was firmly closed, the other was half open. Fletcher drove his Vauxhall Velox carefully through the gap. Immediately ahead of them were two rows of neo-Georgian detached houses, separated by a morass of slush, which would eventually be turned into a street.

'There's going to be a village green,' the estate agent enthused. 'With a duck pond.'

And floating on it would be mechanical ducks that were radio-controlled from the general works department, no doubt, Woodend thought dryly.

Fletcher pulled up on a stretch of asphalt which had been designated a temporary car park. Along the edge of the asphalt stood several lorries and some earth-moving equipment.

'They've been standing there idle for over two weeks now,' the estate agent said. 'Bloody shame! Bloody weather!'

But it wasn't true. At least *some* of the vehicles had been on the move the previous Sunday, because a retired farmer called Obediah Metcalfe had heard them when he was out on his walk.

'Shall we go and take a look at the show house, Mr Woodend?' Fletcher suggested.

'Aye, we might as well.'

As he opened the passenger door and stepped out, Woodend heard the sound of furious barking. He turned towards the source of the noise. Just to the left of the main gate was a rectangular prefab with the words 'Site Office' written over the door. Two cars were parked by the side of it, and chained to sturdy posts beyond them were four large Dobermanns, straining against their leashes.

'Are those dogs always chained up?' Woodend asked – though he knew from his previous visit that they weren't.

The estate agent laughed. 'Always chained up?' he repeated. 'They wouldn't be much use as guard dogs if they were, now would they?'

'So why are they chained up now?'

'They usually are when there's somebody working in the site office. You see, they've been trained to attack anybody and everybody – with the exception, of course, of Mr Taylor and a couple of his security people.'

Woodend and Fletcher walked towards the show house, their Wellington-booted feet squelching in the slush.

'Now's the time to buy, while the property market's still relatively low,' the estate agent said, 'because – mark my words, Mr Woodend – it'll soon be on the rise again.'

They had reached the front door of the show house, and Fletcher pulled a key out of his pocket.

'Look at that finish,' he said, pointing at the door. 'That's none of your pine veneer rubbish that you get in most new houses these days – it's genuine hardwood, all the way from South America.'

'Nice,' Woodend said.

'And that's real brass around the lock. I tell you, Mr Woodend, you're lucky to find quality like this any more.'

Fletcher guided Woodend through the hall, the kitchen

159

and the lounge with its big picture windows. They went upstairs and the estate agent showed the policeman the four bedrooms – all of them, as he did not fail to point out, large enough to take a full-sized double bed.

'Are you impressed with the place?' Fletcher asked, when the tour was finally over.

'Very,' Woodend lied.

'And you think you might like to buy?'

'It's certainly a possibility.'

'People are very cautious when it comes to purchasing a house,' Fletcher said. 'And I can understand that myself. It's a very big commitment, as I'm always at pains to point out. But I've been in the business for a long time and, believe me, Mr Woodend, your first instinct is almost always the right one. If you don't act on it, you could find yourself regretting it forever. So if you like the place, why don't we go back to the office and start the paperwork?'

'If it's all the same to you, I'd like to take a few minutes to walk around the site,' Woodend said.

'But there's nothing to see as yet – except, of course, for a couple of acres of slush. Now back at the office, I've got proper artist's impressions of what it will look like when—'

'I want to get a feel of the place,' Woodend said firmly. 'Besides, I think better when I'm walkin' around.'

'Building sites can be very rough places, you know, Mr Woodend,' Fletcher warned him.

'What did you do in the war?'

'I was in the Pay Corps – in Aldershot. Why?'

'I was part of the D-Day Invasion of France, myself,' Woodend said. 'The beaches we had to land on were mined an' fortified, but we didn't worry too much about that, because we were more interested in all the stuff the Germans were firin' at us from the tops of the cliffs.'

'I'm afraid I don't quite see—'

'If I came through that all right, I think I can just about manage a stroll round a buildin' site without doin' myself much harm. Don't you?'

The estate agent shrugged. 'I suppose so. If you think a stroll will help you to make up your mind, Mr Woodend . . .'

'I'm sure it will.'

'. . . then I'll be in the site office when you want me.'

Woodend walked to the end of the row of mock-Georgian houses, then stopped and looked around him. Half the building site had already fallen victim to the developers' bulldozers and excavators, but the rest of it was relatively untouched and – as with the moors on the other side of the fence – patches of green grass were beginning to appear through the melting snow.

The question was not whether there had been activity on the site the previous Sunday, Woodend thought. He was sure that there had been. What mattered was *where* that activity had taken place. And *why*?

He started to cross the strip of undeveloped land that separated him from the chain-link fence. It was unlikely that Taylor and Ainsworth had used the heavy equipment to do anything to the part of the site which had *already* been dug up, he argued, yet why should they have bothered to—?

He came to an abrupt halt. Just ahead of him enough snow had melted to reveal a patch of bare earth about the size of a bath towel. Excavations? But why there, rather than closer to the finished buildings?

Dragging his Wellingtoned right foot along the ground, he cleared a trail through the sludge from the exposed patch of earth to the point at which the excavation finished and the grass began again. That done, he returned to his starting point, and made a fresh trail in the opposite direction. When he hit grass a second time, he stopped and examined the line in the slush.

161

'Just about two yards wide,' he said to himself. 'Now let's see how *long* it is.'

He repeated the process, working at right angles to his original line. It took him a couple of minutes to discover that the excavation had been about four yards long, and another five minutes to scrape the slush back into its original position – masking the fact that he had ever been there.

He was on the point of heading back to the site office when the sun, suddenly emerging from behind a cloud, cast its rays on a small patch of brightness in the nearby grass. Woodend moved closer and saw that the object was a fleck of yellow paint. He put his hand in his overcoat pocket, took out one of the small plastic bags he always carried with him, and dropped the fleck into it. He wasn't *certain* he knew what he'd found – but he thought he had a pretty good idea.

There was a third car parked next to the site office now – an E-type Jaguar. Its owner, a man in a yellow safety helmet and an expensive blue suit, was standing in front of the office. He was not alone. Mr Fletcher, the estate agent who would sell his houses to anyone – even a bent bobby – was with him. Fletcher was hanging his head, and Taylor was waving his hands agitatedly. It was clear to Woodend that the agent was on the receiving end of a tremendous rocket.

The two men noticed Woodend's approach simultaneously. Taylor let his hands drop to his sides, and Fletcher hastily stepped forward to speak to his prospective buyer.

'Mr . . . Mr Taylor was just telling me that I should never have allowed you to wander around the site on your own,' the estate agent said nervously. 'It's a question of the insurance, you see. The company would have been liable if there'd been an accident.'

'But there wasn't, was there?' Woodend asked. 'So you've got nothin' to worry about.'

Terry Taylor took a few steps forward, so that he was

standing next to Fletcher. He smiled. His teeth were very white and regular, but even all the expensive remedial dentistry they had obviously undergone did not quite hide the evidence of earlier neglect.

'Chief Inspector Woodend! What a pleasant surprise!' Taylor said in a voice full of flat Northern vowels, but with a hint of Southern springiness lurking just below the surface. 'My man Fletcher, here, tells me that you're interested in buying into Moorland Village. Is that right?'

Woodend shook his head. 'Not really. I got used to livin' in the town when I was down in London, an' I've got used to livin' in the country now I'm back in Lancashire – but this place is neither the one thing nor the other.'

'You'd be surprised how quickly people can adapt,' Fletcher said earnestly, attempting to compensate for his earlier gaffe by clinching a sale now. 'Why, we had this customer in one of our earlier developments who'd lived in a flat all his life, but I saw him the other week and he said that buying one of our houses was the best move he'd ever—'

'Don't you have some work you should be getting on with, Fletcher?' Terry Taylor interrupted.

'I beg your pardon, Mr Taylor?'

'Work!' the builder repeated. 'In the office!'

A sudden look of comprehension crossed Fletcher's face. 'Oh . . . er . . . yes, I suppose I do,' he said weakly.

'Then you'd better go and do it, hadn't you?'

'Right away, Mr Taylor.'

Taylor watched Fletcher until he had disappeared through the site office door, then turned back to Woodend, and smiled again. It was a smile totally devoid of warmth, Woodend thought – almost an *inhuman* smile.

'Imagine that fool Fletcher trying to sell you a house on this pricy estate when the government will soon be providing you with somewhere to live for absolutely nothing,' he said.

Woodend shivered – though not with the cold.

'I have to be goin',' he told the builder.

'But before you consider extreme outcomes like going to jail, it's always best to look around for alternative solutions,' Taylor continued, as if he hadn't spoken. The builder glanced down at his expensive wristwatch. 'Do you happen to know a pub called the Last Chance Inn, Mr Woodend?'

'Out on the moors? Near Hoddlesworth?'

'That's right.'

'I think I've been past it a few times, but I can't say I've stopped an' gone inside.'

'It's got a little restaurant attached to it. The chef is French. He does a very decent lunch.'

'Thanks for the tip,' Woodend said. 'I'll remember it the next time I'm in the area.'

Taylor smiled again. 'I mustn't be making myself clear. What I'm trying to say to you is that, as it's almost my lunchtime, I thought I'd pop over there. And if you'd care to join me . . .'

'I wouldn't.'

'Don't be so hasty,' Taylor urged. 'When two people have business to discuss, it's always better to do it over lunch.'

'But we *don't* have any business to discuss. I've told you already, I'm not interested in buyin' one of your houses.'

'And given your current, somewhat precarious, situation, I wouldn't dream of selling you one of them, even if you *were* interested. But that's not the kind of business I'm talking about – and we both know that, don't we?'

'Aye,' Woodend conceded. 'I suppose we do.'

'So will you join me?'

'As long as we each pay for our own grub.'

'Why don't you let me treat you?' Taylor suggested. 'I'm a rich man. I can afford it.'

'I've no doubt you can,' Woodend replied. 'I'll bet you

spend more on little luxuries than I earn altogether. But that's not the point, is it?'

'Then what is the point?'

'I wouldn't want to put myself in a position where I could be accused of bein' beholden to you.'

Taylor chuckled. 'Given the position you're *already* in, I would think it's rather late in the day for you to be worrying about minor matters like a free meal,' he said.

Twenty-One

Terry Taylor was an excellent – if aggressive – driver, sitting behind the wheel of an excellent – if aggressive – car, and though some of the lanes were narrow and the slush was slippery, they were making excellent time.

They were mid-way between two remote moorland villages when Taylor turned to Woodend – the humourless smile firmly back in place again – and said, 'Don't you think you're taking something of a chance by accepting my invitation, Mr Woodend?'

'Why should I?'

'Because, given that you apparently seem to think I'm some sort of law-breaker—'

'"Criminal's" the word you're graspin' for, Mr Taylor,' Woodend interrupted. 'An' I don't *think* anythin'. I *know*. You're as big a villain as I've come across in a long, long time.'

'So, as I was saying, given your poor opinion of me, isn't it rather foolish of you to agree to come out here, to the middle of the moors – where anything could happen?'

Woodend ran his eyes slowly up and down the other man's frame.

'You're a big feller, Mr Taylor,' he said finally. 'An' I reckon you must have been quite a hard man in your time. But you've been livin' the good life for quite a while, an' now I could take you with one hand tied behind my back and the other one pickin' my nose.'

Taylor laughed. 'But suppose I'd not planned to hurt you myself,' he said. 'Suppose I'd arranged to have some of the brutes I employ on my building sites – men who'd break their own mothers' bones for a couple of pounds – waiting in ambush further up the road?'

'Then I'd be in big trouble,' Woodend admitted. 'But you haven't arranged that, have you?'

'How can you be so sure?'

'Because if you ever did decide to have the crap knocked out of me, you'd arrange for it to happen at a time when you were havin' afternoon tea with the Mayor an' all his council.'

Taylor threw back his head and laughed even louder this time. 'I wasn't *really* threatening you, you know,' he said.

'Yes, you were,' Woodend contradicted him. 'I know you'd no intention of actually carryin' the threat out – for the moment, anyway – but you were interested in findin' out just how frightened you could make me if you really tried. Well, now you know, don't you?'

'Are you really as calm as you seem?'

'What do you think?'

'I think you're far too intelligent not to appreciate the dire situation you're in, and that it will only take a little pressure from me to make that brave front you're putting on crumble away into a hundred tiny pieces.'

'Maybe you're right,' Woodend said. 'We'll soon see, won't we?'

'Yes,' Terry Taylor agreed. 'We'll soon see.'

The Last Chance Inn was situated in a small village at the very edge of the moor. From the outside it looked a simple, honest structure, built from huge blocks of dressed stone and topped by a heavy slate roof. The inside, by way of contrast, was all false smoothness. Fake polished beams had been put up to hide the genuine rough beams that ran across the ceiling. The flag floor had been covered with a thick swirling carpet. Horse brasses, which had once adorned working horses on show days, now decorated the lounge. The whole place was a designer's dream of what an eighteenth-century pub would have looked like – if, that was, the people living back in the eighteenth century had shared his rather effete tastes.

It was still early for lunch, so Woodend and Taylor had the restaurant to themselves. Taylor gave the menu a cursory glance, then said to the waitress, 'I'll have the sirloin steak. I like it well done.'

Woodend took more time to study his menu. 'Does the mixed grill include black puddin'?' he asked finally.

'Yes, sir.'

'Then that's what I'll have.'

Taylor waited until the waitress had retreated into the kitchen, then leaned across the table and said, 'That was a very nice touch, Mr Woodend.'

'What was?'

'Oh, you know what I'm talking about. Pretending to be interested in the food. Insisting on black pudding, as if you really wanted it. When all the time, your stomach's so knotted up with fear that even the *thought* of something solid is enough to make you feel sick.'

'I did a bit of amateur boxin' in the Army,' Woodend said. 'My lads enjoyed seein' me fight – it was good for their morale to know that *their* sergeant could knock down pretty much anybody he came up against. But I never really cared much for it as a sport myself. It wasn't the gettin' hit that bothered me, you understand. I just got bored with all that dancin' round the ring an' tryin' to look dangerous. It seemed to me that if you were goin' to have a fight, the best thing you could do was stop poncin' about an' just get on with it.'

'In other words, you're saying I should stop poncing around myself and get to the point.'

'Aye, that's what I'm sayin'.'

'All right. But before we begin in earnest, I suppose I'd better just check that I'm working from the right assumptions. I haven't got things wrong, have I? You *are* investigating me?'

'You haven't got things wrong,' Woodend confirmed.

'And your visit to Moorland Village this morning was part of that investigation?'

'That's right.'

'What, exactly, were you looking for?'

Woodend shrugged. 'Anythin' at all that might add to the picture I've been buildin' up.'

'And *was* there anything?'

Woodend suppressed an almost overpowering urge to look across at the coat rack, where his overcoat – the pocket of which contained the fleck of yellow paint – was hanging.

'Until the jigsaw puzzle's complete, you never know how vital any particular piece of it is goin' to be,' he said.

'You didn't answer my question,' Taylor pointed out.

'I know I didn't,' Woodend countered.

Taylor sighed. 'I told Dick Ainsworth . . . You do know about Dick Ainsworth's involvement in all this, too, I take it?'

'I'd have to be pretty thick not to, now wouldn't I?'

'Yes – and you're certainly not that. As I was saying, I told Dick Ainsworth it was the wrong move to go after a man like you with a big stick. But he simply wouldn't listen.'

'So what alternative are you proposin'?'

'The carrot, of course. As things stand, you could go to prison for a long time.'

'You're not tellin' me anythin' that I don't already know.'

'Perhaps not, but that outcome – a long prison sentence – is still by no means inevitable. If you were to consider—'

The waitress returned with the bottle of wine Taylor had ordered. The builder went through the ritual of sniffing the wine before taking an exploratory sip. Watching him, Woodend gained the distinct impression that this particular activity – like so much else of the man's behaviour – had been meticulously learned in later life, rather than naturally acquired when he was growing up.

'Excellent,' Taylor pronounced, smacking his lips. 'I think you'll rather enjoy this particular little wine, Mr Woodend,' he continued, gesturing, with a nod of his head, that the waitress should fill the Chief Inspector's glass.

Woodend raised his arm and put his right palm across the top of the glass. 'Bring me a pint of your best bitter with my mixed grill, would you, love?' he said to the waitress.

Taylor shot him a hostile look, and when the waitress had left again he said, 'Are you deliberately trying to annoy me, Chief Inspector?'

'Aye, I certainly am,' Woodend agreed. 'An' if I say so myself as shouldn't, I think I'm makin' a pretty good job of it. But let's get back to what you were sayin' before we were interrupted.'

'If you were to stop trying to nail me, I wouldn't have to keep on trying to nail you,' Taylor told him.

'It's a bit late for that kind of speech, isn't it? Aren't I well an' truly nailed already?'

'Not necessarily.'

The waitress returned with their plates – and Woodend's pint.

Taylor attacked his steak with gusto. 'Most things in this life can be reversed if you know the right way to go about it,' he said, after he had chewed and swallowed the first chunk. 'The evidence against you at the moment looks as solid and substantial as the police station where you spend most of your underpaid working life. Yet if it's handled in the right way, it could all collapse as suddenly as a house of cards.'

'The law doesn't work that way,' Woodend told him, pushing his various pieces of meat unenthusiastically around his plate.

'There's no reason why the law shouldn't work in any way *we* wanted it to. Say, for example, that Dick Ainsworth was to uncover fresh evidence that showed conclusively that you'd been fitted up.'

'For that to be at all convincin', somebody else would have to go to jail instead of me.'

'But of course.'

'Who? You?'

Taylor chuckled. 'You really can have a delightful sense of humour on occasion, Mr Woodend. No, I would not be the one to do time.'

'Then who would?'

Taylor speared another piece of steak. 'The exact details are really of secondary importance,' he said. 'But, believe me, finding a replacement for you is absolutely no problem for me at all. There are any number of men I'm acquainted with who regard prison as their second home – and would see it as a bonus if they were actually *paid* for going inside.'

'So you get some poor toe-rag to give evidence in court that he tried to fit me up . . . ?'

'Exactly.'

'An' that he was doin' it on the instructions of some mysterious Mr Big – who the police will look for, but never actually find?'

'It would be regrettable, but the big fish often do slip out of the net that catches all the minnows.'

'An' what happens to me?'

Taylor sliced off another piece of steak, and Woodend

found himself wondering if the builder always enjoyed his food so much.

'What happens to you?' Taylor asked. 'You'll be a hero. You'll return to your duties in the Central Lancs Police with a totally unblemished record. Or, if you would prefer it, you could come and work for me.'

'For you?'

'I have extensive business interests, Mr Woodend, and I need – or could decide I needed – a new head of security. It would be an interesting, fulfilling job – and I could certainly afford to pay you a lot more than you're earning as a chief inspector. So what do you say to my offer?'

'I say that you can take your offer an' stuff it up your backside, you crooked bastard!'

Taylor did not seem to take any offence. Instead, he looked down at Woodend's plate.

'I thought, for all your talk about black pudding and boxing, you wouldn't be able to manage to eat much,' he said, 'but even so, I'd imagined you'd have made a more valiant stab at it than you have.'

'The Frenchies never could cook,' Woodend said defensively. 'They can bugger up anythin' – even decent English grub.'

'You're like a bad poker player who knows he should act as if he's got a good hand, but just can't seem to make the effort. You know you'll hate yourself if you accept my offer, but you also know – deep inside yourself – that that's exactly what you *are* going to do.'

'I'd rather go to jail for the rest of my life than make a deal with you,' Woodend said.

But he didn't sound convincing – even to himself.

'Have you ever actually been to jail?' Taylor asked. 'I don't mean as a visitor – I mean as an inmate.'

'No, I haven't. Have you?' Woodend replied, showing just a little of his old spirit.

172

'You'll never come out again, you know,' Taylor said, ignoring his question. 'Not an ex-policeman like you. However short your sentence is, you'll never live to see the end of it.'

'Shut up!' Woodend said weakly.

'But you won't mind the thought of dying – at least, you won't towards the end,' Taylor continued relentlessly. 'In fact, it will seem like a blessed release after all you've endured.'

Woodend stood up, and clamped his hand over his mouth. 'I have to go to the bog,' he muttered through his fingers.

'Yes, that does seem like a good idea,' Taylor agreed. 'And while you're there – bent double over the toilet bowl and puking up all your fear – you should give some serious thought to what we've just been discussing.'

Woodend lurched towards the exit, but before he finally left the room, he glanced quickly over his shoulder. Taylor was no longer eating. Instead, he had laid his knife and fork down, and was gazing intently at the wall.

Woodend made his way into the corridor. The waitress who had served them their meal was leaning against the door, seizing the opportunity for a quick, illicit smoke. When she saw a customer approaching, she cupped her hand to hide the cigarette.

'Where's the phone?' Woodend demanded.

'Beg pardon, sir?'

'The phone. The bloody public phone.'

'It's over there. In the bar.'

Woodend pushed the bar door open, and stepped inside. There were a number of customers spread around the room, but the phone – thank God – was unoccupied. He reached in his pocket for change, lifted the receiver, and dialled a Whitebridge number.

'Police headquarters,' said a starchy female voice on the other end of the line.

'Put me through to Sergeant Paniatowski.'

'Who shall I say is calling?'

'Mr Blenkinsop.'

'And what is the nature of your call, Mr Blenkinsop?'

'Sergeant Paniatowski knows all about it. She's been expectin' to hear from me.'

'If you could just give me a few details—'

'I've got some information that could crack this Dugdale's Farm murder case wide open for you, but if I'm not talkin' directly to Sergeant Paniatowski herself in the next half minute, I'm goin' to hang up. An' who'll get the blame for that? You bloody will!'

'Just hold on for a moment, sir,' the woman said hastily, and a few seconds later a new voice said, 'Paniatowski.'

'It's me. Can you talk?'

'If I keep my voice down. What's this about?'

'I'm at the Last Chance Inn in Hoddlesworth. I've been havin' lunch with Terry Taylor.'

'You've what!'

'You heard. Half an hour ago, on the way over, he threatened me with violence. He didn't mean it at the time, but now that his other plans aren't goin' to work out as he expected them to, it might have started to look like a very attractive prospect. So I need somebody to get me out of here in a hurry.'

'I'll come right away,' Paniatowski said. 'Where will I find you? In the pub?'

'No, not there. Just drive slowly through the village, an' stop when I wave you down. An' one more thing . . .'

'Yes.'

'Before you leave the station, call the Last Chance. Say you're from Taylor's office, an' you need to speak to him urgently.'

'And then?'

'When he comes to the phone, hang up.'

'Do you want to tell me what this is all about?'

'Later,' Woodend promised. 'I'll give you the whole story later. For the moment, just do what I ask.'

He replaced the phone, and made his way back to the dining room. On the threshold, he paused, took out his handkerchief, and made a great show of wiping his mouth.

'*Have* you been sick, Mr Woodend?' Taylor asked, as the Chief Inspector resumed his seat.

'It's none of your bloody business whether I have or I haven't,' Woodend told him.

'Then let's get back to what *is* my business,' Taylor suggested. 'Have you thought over my offer?'

Woodend looked down at the table. 'I don't want to go to prison,' he mumbled.

Taylor smiled. 'Of course you don't, Mr Woodend. What man in his right mind would?'

'But before I agree to do what you want, I'll need some pretty solid guarantees.'

'Tell me what they are, and I'll see if it's possible for me to accommodate them.'

The waitress re-entered the room. 'Is one of you gentlemen a Mr Taylor?' she asked.

Taylor nodded. 'That's me.'

'Well, your office wants you on the phone. They say it's urgent.'

Woodend read the conflicting thoughts crossing the builder's face. On the one hand, Taylor was loath to leave the pond when his fish was hooked and almost ready to land. On the other, he didn't want to make a deal when the rules of the game might have just changed.

He stood up. 'I won't be a minute, and when I come back we can iron out the final details,' he said. He turned to the waitress. 'Where's the phone?'

'In the public bar, sir.'

Taylor made his way to the bar. When he picked up the

phone the line was still active, but the moment he said, 'Terry Taylor here,' it went dead.

He slammed down the receiver and went back to the restaurant. Some new diners had arrived in his absence, but there was no sign of Woodend. He examined the table for a clue to the other man's disappearance. Woodend's food – largely untouched – was next to the empty pint pot under which Woodend had left two pound notes. Taylor's own meal and wine glass were still in place. But something was missing.

Taylor closed his eyes and tried to visualize the table as it had been before he left the room to answer the non-existent phone call. And suddenly he knew what was wrong. Woodend had refused wine, but a glass had been provided for it anyway – and now that glass was gone.

Twenty-Two

S canning the distance for any sign of Paniatowski's MGA, Woodend found his mind drifting back to January 1945.

It had been one of those occasions when he had thought his personal war was almost over – and then suddenly discovered that it wasn't. The Germans, who had been retreating since D-Day, had unexpectedly launched the counterattack that would become known as the Battle of the Bulge.

It had been a messy, piecemeal battle – the forest so thick that only limited use could be made of heavy artillery, the weather conditions so poor that for much of the time air support had been impossible.

And it had been a desperate battle – the last major stand of an almost-defeated, under-equipped remnant of the once mighty German Army.

During the course of the fighting, Woodend had been cut off from the rest of his unit, and found himself alone in the forest. But was he really alone? he'd wondered nervously, as he'd stood there listening to the sound of distant gunfire. Or was he, even at that moment, in the gun sights of a German soldier who felt as isolated and confused as he did?

He felt those nerves return to him now, as he stood in the centre of a copse of trees only a few hundred yards from the Last Chance Inn.

What was his new enemy – Terry Taylor – doing at that moment? he asked himself.

Had Taylor assumed that the man he'd tried to bribe had dashed off on to the moors in a blue funk? Did he no longer think of Woodend as a danger? Or had he, immediately he'd seen the empty chair at the table where the Chief Inspector had been sitting, put a call through to the hard men he had threatened to use earlier? And were those same hard men even now making their way to the village?

The roar of a small sports car made Woodend break cover, and seconds later he was standing in the centre of the road, waving his arms furiously. Paniatowski expertly brought her car to a halt just beside him, and Woodend quickly crammed himself into the passenger seat.

'Where to?' the sergeant asked.

'A pub,' Woodend gasped.

'Which pub?'

'Any pub – as long as it's not one where we're likely to run into some of Terry Taylor's lads.'

Woodend took a long, grateful swig of the pint that Paniatowski had just brought him from the bar.

'If I do say so myself, I handled Terry Taylor like a master,' he said, with an uncharacteristic complacency, which had replaced the nerve-jangling tension he'd felt earlier. 'I'm particularly proud of the show I made of insistin' there should be black puddin' with my mixed grill, then hardly touchin' the food when it arrived. He really thought that showed that while I might be actin' confidently enough on the outside, I was actually scared to death just under the surface.'

'And weren't you?' Paniatowski asked.

'Wasn't I what?'

'Were you scared?'

Woodend grinned ruefully. 'I was bloody terrified,' he admitted. 'I still am, as a matter of fact. But then, so is he.'

'From what you've said so far, it doesn't seem that way to me at all,' Paniatowski replied sceptically. 'Would you like my assessment?'

'Aye, go on.'

'I'd say he thinks he's holding the winning cards, and all you're sitting there with is a bust hand.'

Woodend shook his head vehemently. 'You're wrong about that. He knows that there are some very important cards he *should* have in his hand which are missin' – but he's tryin' his best to prevent me from realizin' that, too.'

'Is that what your gut instinct's telling you?' Paniatowski asked dubiously.

'Yes, but it's more than just instinct,' Woodend said, noticing for the first time that his sergeant was not riding the same wave of optimism as he was himself. 'An' it's not blind hope born out of desperation, either – in case that's what you're thinkin'.'

'I never—'

'I'm no rat caught in a trap, desperately believin' there has to be a way out, even when there isn't one.'

'I didn't mean to suggest you were.'

'No, you'd never have put it so bluntly – but that's what was on your mind, wasn't it?'

'Maybe,' Paniatowski confessed.

'Listen, Monika, if he felt as secure as he's pretendin' to be, he'd never have come out in the open the way he did, an' made me an offer. The fact that the offer *was* made tells me that he's worried I'll find somethin' that will damage him – or maybe that I already have.'

'Or perhaps you're just a loose end that he wants to tie up for the sake of tidiness.'

'No!' Woodend said empathetically. 'That's what he wants me to think, but it's not true. He seems so much in control that he makes the pope look insecure – but it's all an act. His whole bloody life is an act. Taylor isn't anybody but the person he invented for himself when he first appeared in Whitebridge.'

'Maybe—' Paniatowski said.

'Maybe nothin',' Woodend cut in. 'While I was lookin' at him across the table, he was all self-assurance an' mockin' eyes. But when he thought I *wasn't* lookin' at him any more – when he thought I was on the way to the bog to spew up my ring – his face changed. I turned around suddenly at the door, an' what I saw was a very worried man.'

'What exactly is it that you think he's worried about?' Paniatowski asked, still unconvinced.

Woodend reached into his pocket and took out the plastic bag. 'He's worried that I might come up with somethin' like this.'

'A fleck of paint?'

'Aye, the paint itself – an', probably even more importantly, *where* I found it.'

'Where *did* you find it?'

'While I was walkin' round the site, I came across signs of recent excavations. Somebody had dug an oblong hole about four yards by two, an' then filled it in again. I found the fleck of paint nearby.'

'I'm still not on your wavelength,' Paniatowski confessed.

'One of the first things I asked you to do when we got to the farm last Sunday was to see to it that roadblocks were set up. Remember?'

'Of course I remember.'

'An' those roadblocks were in place for most of the rest of the day, weren't they?'

'Yes?'

'But with no result. *Now* do you see what I'm gettin' at?'

'The Austin A40!' Paniatowski exclaimed.

'The *yellow* Austin A40 that Obediah Metcalfe spotted

enterin' Moorland Village when he was out for his Sunday
mornin' walk – an' which hasn't been seen since. Put
that together with the fact that the old man heard the
machinery bein' started up, an' you're led to the inevitable
conclusion that—'

'That they buried the A40!'

'Exactly.'

'But why, in God's name, should they want to do that?'

Woodend scratched his head. 'I don't know. But it has
to be important, because I think it was the fact that I was
nosin' around the site – more than anythin' else I've done
durin' the course of this investigation – which made Terry
Taylor nervous.'

Paniatowski took a sip of her drink. 'Perhaps there's
something *in* the car,' she suggested. 'Something they didn't
want us to find.'

'Like what?'

'Stolen goods?'

'Like televisions and washin' machines?' Woodend asked,
relieved to find that his sense of humour was returning.

Paniatowski, taking the remark at face value, shook her
head. 'No, something much smaller than that,' she said.
'Something that has quite a high value for its size. Antiques,
perhaps. Or whisky and cigarettes.' A new idea occurred to
her. 'Couldn't that have been how Taylor got his start? We
know he built up T. A. Taylor and Associates from virtually
nothing, but he had to have got a little initial capital from
somewhere, didn't he? Couldn't his legitimate businesses
have been founded on the money he made from crime? And
if that were the case,' she continued, growing more and more
enthusiastic, 'wouldn't a remote place like Dugdale's Farm
have been the ideal place to hide all the contraband?'

'It's certainly a theory. But just how do the two murder
victims come into the picture?'

'The murdered man may have been in the same sort of

business himself,' Paniatowski suggested. 'He could even have been in partnership with Taylor and Dugdale. Then he had an argument with them over how to divide up the spoils, and he got himself killed.'

'An' the girl? Just how does she fit in?'

'Perhaps she was the dead man's bit of stuff. He took her with him because—' Paniatowski came to a sudden halt, and frowned exasperatedly. 'No, that wouldn't work, would it?'

'Why not?'

'Quite apart from her age making it unlikely that she was his mistress, we know from the post-mortem examination that she died a virgin. So . . . so maybe she was the other victim's *daughter*.'

'It would be very convenient for our investigation if she was,' Woodend agreed, 'but how do you explain away the clothes?'

'You mean, the fact that the girl's clothes were expensive, whereas the man's were cheap?'

'An' not only cheap, but shabby as well. Is it really likely that any feller would spend quite so much on his daughter, an' then dress himself in little more than rags?'

'Some men do dote on their daughters,' Paniatowski said. 'I'm looking at one of them right now.'

But even as she spoke, she was thinking how unconvincing her argument sounded. Woodend was right. Even the most doting father would not have dressed his daughter so much better than he dressed himself. And not even the most selfish of daughters would have allowed him to.

'So you think that there's nothing at all to connect the two victims, sir?' she asked.

'If there *is* a connection – apart from them bein' in the same place at the same time, when somethin' went seriously wrong – then I can't see it,' Woodend admitted. 'But let's get back to the car. We're almost certain that it was buried, an' we're certain that there's somethin' incriminatin' inside it. So sooner or later – probably sooner, after my visit to Moorland Village today – Terry Taylor's goin' to realize it's too dangerous where it is, an' decide to move it. That's why I want him watched.'

Paniatowski looked dubious again. 'If Mr Ainsworth is as involved with Taylor as you seem to think he is—'

'Taylor virtually admitted to me that he was when were havin' our cosy little lunch together in the Last Chance.'

'– then the last thing he's going to do is to sanction using my team to watch his mate.'

'I know that,' Woodend agreed. 'That's why you'll only be able to use lads who are off-duty.'

'Let me get this straight,' Paniatowski said slowly. 'You want me to ask the lads to put their careers on the line to save your skin.'

'No. I'm askin' them to do it because, if they don't, there's every chance that whoever killed that poor little kiddie will get away with it.' An awkward grin came to his face. 'Of course, there's always the possibility that by catchin' the murderer, my skin *might* be saved.'

'It's asking a lot,' Paniatowski told him.

'Yes, it is. That's why you shouldn't pressure anybody into it – why we'll only use volunteers. An' I can think of a few probables off the top of my head. There's Hardcastle, for a start. You saw how upset he was out at the farm. He wants to catch this bastard as much as I do.'

Paniatowski nodded gravely. 'For the sake of everybody's daughter everywhere,' she said.

'Then there's Duxbury. He should have been a sergeant by now, but thanks to Dick the Prick, he isn't. Drop a hint to him that what you're doin' might help to shaft the DCC, an' he'll be willin' enough to help.'

'Got it all worked out, haven't you, sir?' Monika Paniatowski asked admiringly.

'I'm glad I give you that impression, because that's what a leader should do – but, in point of fact, I'm makin' it up as I go along.'

'That's comforting to know,' Paniatowski said, with a slight smile. 'I assume, since you're expecting me to organize this surveillance operation, you're also expecting me to be one of the volunteers working on it.'

'An' won't you be?'

'Well, of course I bloody will!'

Woodend suppressed a sigh of relief. 'There's one more thing we need to talk through,' he said. 'The fingerprints.'

'What about them?'

'The check on the dead man's prints didn't lead us anywhere, but that check was carried out by DC Battersby, who we now know was in Terry Taylor's pocket all along.'

'So you want them checked again?'

'That shouldn't be a problem, should it?'

'Technically, no. His body's still on ice in the morgue, waiting for someone to come and claim it. But if Ainsworth and Harris find out I've been doing it behind their backs—'

'You're sunk,' Woodend supplied. 'But if they find out about *any* of the things you've been doing behind their backs the last few days, you're probably finished anyway.'

'So I might as well be hung for a sheep as a lamb?'

'It's your choice,' Woodend said. 'It's always been your choice, right from the beginnin'.'

'I suppose it has,' Paniatowski agreed. She sighed. 'All right, I'll take the prints and send them down to the Yard.'

'We can minimize the chances of discovery if we don't go through the official channels,' Woodend said. 'I've still got a few mates at the Yard who'll do a foreigner for me. I'll give you their names. An' one more thing.' He reached into the pocket of his sports coat and placed a wine glass on the table. 'Get the prints on this glass checked, too, while you're about it.'

'Whose are they?'

'Terry Taylor's. It's the wine glass he used at lunch.'

'Have you lost your mind, sir?' Paniatowski demanded. 'I know we'll have to take some bloody big chances if we're ever to crack the case – but this is ridiculous!'

'Listen, Monika—'

'Taylor would have to be a complete fool not to have noticed that his glass had gone missing. He's probably on the phone to Ainsworth right now, telling him all about it. And you want to hand that same poisoned chalice to me!'

'If Taylor noticed anythin', it was that there was no glass where I'd been sittin',' Woodend said calmly.

'You swapped them over?'

'Aye. An' I poured what was left of his wine into my glass.'

'I sometimes forget just how smart you are,' Paniatowski said.

'Oh, I'm all there with my cough drops,' Woodend agreed. 'Well, when you're hangin' on by your fingertips, you bloody well have to be, don't you?'

'Shall I take you back home now?' Paniatowski asked.

'Aye. But not to my home – to yours.'

'Come again!'

'Apart from everythin' else he's dirtied his hands with over the years, Terry Taylor's up to his neck in two murders now. He's not goin' to think twice about makin' it three.'

'You think he'd have you killed?'

'I don't know. But for some strange reason, I don't feel like takin' the chance.'

Paniatowski thought for a moment. 'What if Ainsworth suspects you're staying with me?' she asked.

'Even Dick the Prick would never think you'd be quite so bloody stupid as to hide me.'

'And if any of my nosy neighbours find out I've got a man staying with me?'

185

'They'll probably just think I'm your bit of rough trade.'

'That wouldn't do much for my reputation, would it?' Paniatowski asked.

'No, it wouldn't,' Woodend agreed, grinning. 'But it would certainly do a hell of a lot for mine.'

Twenty-Three

He'd been a self-imposed prisoner in Paniatowski's flat near the top of Whitebridge's only tower block for less than forty-eight hours, yet the boredom was so crippling that Woodend felt as if he'd already served a long sentence with no time off for good behaviour.

He'd glanced through Paniatowski's slim library, but there was nothing there to interest him. Her record collection included none of the traditional jazz he liked to listen to. He'd tried watching television, and had found his mind wandering back to a case he could only control – completely unsatisfactorily – from a distance. And though Monika had been thoughtful enough to see the fridge was well stocked with bottles of beer, it just wasn't the same as a pint drawn straight from the wood.

Woodend walked over to the lounge window, drew back the flowery curtains, and looked down on the town spread out before him. He stood in silence as the dark clouds began to lose their blood-red edge, and the streets beneath them slowly sank into the darkness of a winter early night.

He had grown up in this town, he reminded himself. No, that wasn't strictly accurate. Better to say he'd been brought up in the same space as this town now occupied. Because the Whitebridge of his boyhood was no more. Many of the streets he'd played in had gone forever – victims of the bulldozer and the demolition ball. The old covered market, where his grandmother had taken him every Friday as regular

187

as clockwork, had been replaced by a concrete monstrosity which was some bright spark's idea of the future. Even the buildings which had survived the relentless march of progress now seemed so oddly out of place that they could almost have been mistaken for intruders.

The abandoned mills stood forlornly against the skyline – as if harbouring the faint hope that they would eventually hear the sound of clogs again on the cobbled streets which led to them. The railway station, a confident, bustling place in the eyes of the young Charlie Woodend, had somehow acquired the same quaintness as the little old lady in whose reign it had been built.

Woodend turned around and faced the thoroughly modern room he found himself in. G-Plan furniture. The latest radiogram – which hardly looked used at all. Light wood and soft furnishings everywhere. If his granny were still alive to see this, she'd have thought she'd landed on a different planet.

He heard the key turn in the lock, and swung round expectantly – though not without a little dread.

Paniatowski entered the lounge, a thick brown envelope under her arm. 'You're absolutely sure that the prints on that glass you gave me were Taylor's, are you?' she asked brusquely.

What did that mean? Woodend wondered.

That his mates at the Yard hadn't been able to find a match?

'Well?' Paniatowski demanded.

'Taylor was drinkin' out of it,' Woodend said. 'There may be other prints on it, but some of them *had to* be his.'

'In that case, it's just remotely possible that we may still be able to pull you out of the shit,' Paniatowski told him.

Woodend felt his heart start to beat a little faster. 'What have you come up with?'

Paniatowski sat down on the sofa, then stood up again

almost immediately, as if she were too tense to remain still for long.

'The Yard has identified the prints on the prints on the wine glass as belonging to Thomas Arthur Tasker.'

T. A .T. – as in T. A. Taylor and Bloody-Associates!

'What kind of form has Mr Tasker got?' Woodend asked.

'He was born and brought up in Hove. He was a jobbing builder for a while – though not a very successful one. He turned to fraud – and he wasn't too good at that either. The first time he was caught, he was put on probation. The second time he served two years.' Paniatowski paused. 'For his third offence, he was given a six stretch. He served his time in Durham Jail.'

Woodend was already ahead of her. 'Who were his known associates?' he demanded.

'He shared a cell with a man called Philip Swales. Does that name ring any bells with you?'

'Wilfred Dugdale was in Strangeways with a man called Swales!'

'The *same* man called Swales. I've checked. It's all starting to fit together, isn't it?'

It was! Woodend thought. It really bloody was!

'What kind of form has Swales got?' he asked.

'He's a thoroughly nasty piece of work. He's been involved in extortion, pimping and blackmail. And he's violent. He's got a string of convictions going back to childhood. But he's had no convictions for the last *sixteen* years. Don't you think that's significant, sir?'

'You're not sayin' that he's been clean all that time, are you?' Woodend asked.

'No, I'm not.'

'But you *are* sayin' that a habitual criminal like him has somehow managed to stay out of trouble since shortly after Taylor moved to Whitebridge?'

'Exactly.' Paniatowski opened the envelope and passed a photograph across to him. 'That's Swales.'

Woodend looked down at the face which was staring aggressively into the camera. Swales had tight, pinched features and hard eyes.

'I know this bugger,' he said.

'The picture's over twenty years old,' Paniatowski cautioned him.

'Doesn't matter,' Woodend said firmly. 'I saw him just the other night. In the Vic – my local. He was drinkin' with Terry Taylor. He reminded me of one of those spivs we used to see just after the war – long before your time – an' I thought then that they made an odd couple.'

'What were they talking about?' Paniatowski asked.

'I don't know, but it got very heated. Terry Taylor eventually stormed out of the pub – but not before he told this Philip Swales feller that he didn't like bein' threatened.'

Woodend walked over to the lounge window. With the onset of another chilling night, condensation had formed on the glass.

'Here we've got Dugdale,' he said, making a large 'D' with his finger, 'an' here –' making a 'T' several inches away from it – 'we've got Taylor. An' right in the middle we've got Philip Swales, who served time inside with both of them. What we *still* haven't got is any explanation of what actually went on that mornin' at Dugdale's Farm. An' that's not our only problem. We still don't know who the victims were, either.'

'Don't we?' Paniatowski asked.

'Are you sayin' you do?'

Paniatowski nodded. 'The second set of prints you asked me to take – the ones from the corpse – have come up trumps as well. They belong to a man called Harry Judd.'

'An' he's done time an' all?'

'Oh yes, he has.'

'With Taylor, Swales or Dugdale?'

Paniatowski shook her head regretfully. 'He was nothing but a petty criminal – not in their class at all. He's served several stretches over the years, but none of them in the same place or at the same time as the others.'

Woodend looked at the initials he'd made in the condensation on the window-pane again. They were already starting to dribble away and lose their distinctiveness.

'So there's nothin' to connect Judd with the other three?' he said despondently.

'Not a bloody thing,' Paniatowski confirmed.

Twenty-Four

There had only been a light drizzle when Woodend and Paniatowski had left Whitebridge at just after six in the evening, but by the time they had reached the main road into Manchester the skies had opened, the windscreen wipers on the MGA were swishing back and forth dementedly, and the traffic had slowed down to a crawl.

'I suppose it could be worse,' the sergeant said gloomily. 'At least it's not snowing.'

But the weather was the least of their problems at that moment, Woodend thought.

He lit up a cigarette. 'You're absolutely sure there's no connection between the dead man, Harry Judd, an' the others involved in this case?' he asked, more out of hope than expectation.

'None that I could find,' Paniatowski said, as she signalled to overtake a lorry. 'And believe me, knowing how much we needed some sort of link, I looked hard enough.'

'Harry Judd comes from Manchester, an' so does Philip Swales,' Woodend pointed out.

'That's true enough, sir. But, like I said, they're different kinds of villains completely. Swales is a really vicious bastard – they used to call him "Razor" Swales in the old days.'

'An' Judd's just a petty criminal.'

'His crimes never amounted to anything more serious than cat burglary. So whatever kind of racket Terry Taylor's

192

involved in, I can't see him finding a place in it for Judd.'

She was probably right, Woodend thought. But *something* had to explain Judd's presence at Dugdale's Farm.

And something had to explain his phone call which had promised that reporter, Bennett, the biggest story of his life – because from what BBC man had said of his caller's voice, that had almost certainly been Judd, too.

They turned off the arterial road and plunged deep into the suburbs. On either side of them were well-maintained semi-detached homes.

'How much further?' Woodend asked impatiently.

'It'll be a while yet.'

'You said Judd lived with his sister?'

'Not exactly. For most of the time over the last twenty years, his address has been some jail or another. But for the brief periods he's been on the outside, he's *stayed* with his sister, Mrs Doris Hargreaves.'

'Has she got any form?'

'Yes, but just like her brother, it's only for small-time stuff. Petty crime seems to be the family speciality.'

'So what's she been nicked for? Shop-liftin'?'

'And street-walking – though that was a number of years ago, when she was much younger.'

'So she was on the game, was she?' Woodend said – and wondered, though he couldn't quite say why, if that could possibly have any significance.

They had left the suburban roads behind them. The streets were narrower now, and the neat semis had been replaced by row upon row of crumbling terraced houses. Few of the street lamps in this area seemed to work, and the pavements were deserted. It was only in the obviously run-down pubs – of which there appeared to be one on every corner – that there were any signs of life.

This was not a district to be out alone in after dark,

193

Woodend thought. If Moorland Village was some people's idea of heaven, then this could only be an image of the other place.

Paniatowski pulled the MGA up to the kerb. 'That's it,' she said. 'Number Thirty-six, Tufton Road.'

They got out of the car, and walked up to the house. The dark-brown paint on the front door was peeling. The window to the left of it was covered with ragged net curtains, and the light inside shone only dimly through the thick layers of dirt that clung to the glass.

'Given the choice of stayin' in prison or comin' home to this, I think I'd have stayed banged up,' Woodend said.

'Perhaps it might be better if you didn't come in with me, sir,' Monika Paniatowski suggested.

'Not come in with you? Why?'

'Because this isn't our patch, and while my right to be conducting an investigation in Manchester's jurisdiction is questionable at best, you shouldn't be here at all. If it ever got back to the brass in Whitebridge that—'

'It won't. I've never met this Mrs Hargreaves, but I can tell just from the state of the place she calls home that she's not one to say anythin' to *any* bobby when she doesn't absolutely have to.'

'Perhaps you're right,' Paniatowski agreed. 'But at least leave the talking up to me.'

'I'll do my best to,' Woodend promised.

Paniatowski rapped on the front door with her knuckles. From the corner of his eye Woodend saw the shabby net curtains flicker for a second, but no one came to answer the knock.

The sergeant knocked again – even more insistently this time. There was the sound of shuffling feet in the hallway, then the letter-box opened and someone called through it, 'What do you want?'

'Police,' Paniatowski said.

'Have you got any sort of identification on yer?'

'Yes, we've got identification,' Paniatowski answered. 'If you'll just open the door, I'll show it to you.'

There was a longish pause, then the woman said, 'Shove it through the letter-box.'

Paniatowski looked at Woodend for guidance, and when the Chief Inspector nodded, she slid her warrant card through the box.

Another pause. 'It says here you're from Whitebridge,' Mrs Hargreaves shouted through the door.

'So we are,' Monika Paniatowski replied. 'But we're working with the local bobbies.'

'Why haven't they come round themselves?'

Paniatowski gave the kind of heavy theatrical sigh that would have made even a bad ham actor blush. 'I suppose I could go back to the station and pick up a couple of the local lads, if that would make you any happier . . .'

'Yeah, do that.'

'But if you think they're going to feel exactly chuffed about being dragged out of their nice warm canteen on a filthy night like this, then you've got another thing coming. If they haven't got anything against you when they arrive, I expect they'll manage to think of some sort of charge while they're here.' She paused, to let the idea sink in. 'So why not be sensible and open the door, Mrs Hargreaves?' she continued. 'We won't keep you for more than a few minutes.'

There was the sound of the latch being reluctantly drawn back, then the door swung open and they got their first look at Mrs Hargreaves. The police record Paniatowski had read said the woman was forty-two, but she could have passed for at least twenty years older. She was around five foot one, with frizzy, bleached hair, bloodshot eyes and a slack mouth. The skin on her cheeks and above her lip was faintly discoloured.

Bruising, Woodend thought. Not too recent, but definitely bruising.

Paniatowski held out her hand. 'Could I have my warrant card back, please?'

Mrs Hargreaves gave it to her, then placed her hands aggressively on her hips. 'What do you want?' she demanded.

'Just a little chat,' Paniatowski replied. 'Do you mind if we come inside, out of the cold and wet?'

And in her best police-officer manner, she was moving into the passageway even as she spoke.

'I haven't done nothin',' Mrs Hargreaves protested.

'Of course you haven't, luv,' Paniatowski said reassuringly. 'That's the door to the lounge, is it? We'll go in there, shall we?'

She opened the living-room door at the same moment as Woodend closed the front door behind him. Though they had no right to be there, they were now firmly inside the house.

The 'lounge' looked as if it belonged on a council rubbish tip. The furniture was old and neglected, the carpet was stained and littered with greasy pieces of newspaper which had once contained fish and chips. The air stank of cigarettes and unwashed clothes. Only the large television, which dominated one corner of the room, looked new and cared for.

Without waiting to be invited, Paniatowski sat down on the threadbare sofa. 'Why don't you take a seat yourself, Mrs Hargreaves?' she suggested.

The frizzy-haired woman looked confusedly from Paniatowski to Woodend, and then back again. 'Just who's in charge here?' she asked.

'I'll be conducting the interview,' Paniatowski said firmly. '*Do* sit down, Mrs Hargreaves. You're making me tired, just looking at you standing there.'

The woman sank reluctantly into a rickety armchair. 'You said this wouldn't take long.'

'It won't,' Paniatowski promised. 'Now then, Mrs Hargreaves, what we're here to talk about is your brother, Harry.'

The frizzy-haired woman snorted contemptuously. 'Oh, him! Waste of time, he is. Mam always said he would never amount to anythin'.'

Whereas *you* have really come up in the world, Paniatowski thought.

But aloud, all she said was: 'When was the last time that you saw your brother?'

'Last Saturday, it was. The day they let him out of the nick.'

And the day *before* he was found at Dugdale's Farm with his face blown away!

'Was there any particular reason for his visit?' Paniatowski asked. 'Was he planning to stay with you?'

'He was not! I told him after the last time they released him that I was tired of him spongin' off me. So he already knew, when he came out this time, that he wouldn't be welcome.'

'So why *did* he come? Was it to pick something up from here? A suitcase, perhaps?'

'He came to pick *Enid* up.'

'And Enid would be . . . ?'

'Don't you know nothin'? Enid's his daughter.'

The idea that Judd even had a daughter came as a complete surprise to Woodend, but then, unlike Paniatowski, he hadn't had the luxury of studying the man's file.

'I thought his daughter had lived with her mother ever since her parents separated,' the sergeant said.

Mrs Hargreaves shook her head disdainfully. 'You really should keep your records up to date,' she said. 'Enid's mother – like the slag that she is – buggered off with the rent man years ago.'

'And so Harry's been bringing her up himself?'

'He does when he can – which isn't very often. Thinks the world of her, he does. Our Enid can't do nothin' wrong as far as he's concerned. An' whatever happens, he'll always take care of her. Except that he *can't* take care of her when he's doin' time, can he? So who do you think's landed with the job? Her soft Auntie Doris, of course!'

'How old is Enid?' Woodend asked.

'She's fifteen.'

'Does she have blonde hair?'

'Yeah.'

'An' how tall is she? About five feet?'

'Why are you askin' all these questions about Enid?' Mrs Hargreaves said. 'I thought you'd come to talk about Harry.'

'About five feet tall?' Woodend repeated, commandingly. 'Slim figure, but not *too* slim?'

'Yeah, that'd about fit her,' Mrs Hargreaves agreed sullenly.

'So Harry took her away with him, did he?'

'Er . . . yes . . . that's right.'

'Where did she get the clothes from?' Paniatowski asked.

'What clothes?' Mrs Hargreaves countered.

'The silk blouse, the skirt with the Italian label and the hand-stitched shoes. Did you buy them for her?'

'Do I *look* cracked in the head?'

'So where did they come from?'

'H . . . Harry must have bought 'em for her.'

'They were this year's fashions,' Paniatowski said, all the understanding and reassurance she'd shown earlier now completely absent from her tone.

'So?'

'Your brother was inside at the start of the season. And even if he hadn't been, where would a loser like him have found the money?' She paused again. 'Or have I missed something? Have they suddenly started paying out a small fortune for stitching mailbags in prison?'

Mrs Hargreaves' eyes narrowed with ever-increasing suspicion. 'What's this about? Has Enid been arrested?'

'Now why would you even begin to think a thing like that?' Paniatowski wondered.

'Well, what with the questions you keep askin''—'

'The clothes, Doris!' Paniatowski shouted. 'Where the bloody hell did she get the clothes from?'

'I don't know.'

'I have enough of this,' Woodend said, his exasperation only half faked. 'Arrest her, Sergeant. She'll talk soon enough, after she's been in the cells for a few hours.'

'There's no need for that, sir,' Paniatowski told him, slipping back effortlessly into her gentle earlier approach. 'You'll tell us what we want to know, won't you, Doris?'

'Yer'll . . . if I tell you truth, yer'll only get the wrong idea,' Mrs Hargreaves said weakly.

'It's here – or at the station,' Woodend threatened.

Doris Hargreaves sighed. 'How do you *think* kids who live in places like this get the money to buy fancy clothes?'

'Doing something bent,' Paniatowski guessed.

'I tried to control her,' Mrs Hargreaves whined, 'but yer know what kids are like these days.'

'What was she doing?' Paniatowski asked. 'Shop-lifting?'

'You're a bit of dab hand at that yourself, aren't you, Doris?' Woodend demanded. 'What did you do – spend a few hours teachin' her all the tricks of the trade?'

'No, I . . . she didn't steal nothin'.'

'So where did she get the money from?'

'She was . . . you know . . . she was doin' the . . . well, the *other* thing I got nicked for.'

'She was on the game?' Paniatowski asked, her voice filled with incredulity. 'Is that what you're saying?'

'That's right,' Mrs Hargreaves agreed. 'She was on the game.'

Twenty-Five

O nly a minute had passed since Mrs Hargeaves' revelation that her niece had practised prostitution. Yet in that brief sixty seconds, Woodend's mind had performed mental gymnastics – swinging on ropes of speculation across a whole panorama, vaulting over wooden horses of theory – only to end up slamming into a brick wall of facts which seemed to contradict everything his instincts told him.

He'd had no idea who the dead girl found at Dugdale's farm was when he'd first entered the room, but within a few minutes he'd convinced himself that she simply had to be Enid Judd. And now that no longer seemed possible. The girl at the farm had died a virgin, and Enid – if her aunt was to be believed – had been far from that. But perhaps – just perhaps – the aunt was wrong about the girl.

'You're *sure* she was on the game?' he asked.

'Not exactly *on* it.'

'An' what the bloody hell is that supposed to mean?'

'Well, she wasn't what you'd call a "professional". She didn't do it all the time – only when she wanted a few bob. An' she didn't charge half as much as she could have got if she'd wanted to.'

'What a cosy scene it must have made,' Paniatowski said.

'What are yer talkin' about?'

'I can just see it. You and little Enid sitting in front of a glowing coal fire, while she tells you about all the men she's slept with that day.'

'We don't have no coal fires in this street. We're on gas,' Doris Hargreaves said uncomfortably. 'At least, we are when we've not been cut off. Anyway, it wasn't like that.'

'Like what?'

'Cosy chats about the men she'd slept with.'

'But she did tell you *something* about it?'

'Yeah. She mentioned it.'

'She might have been lying,' Paniatowski suggested.

'Why should she have done that?'

'To shock you.'

'Shock me? What do yer mean?'

Doris Hargreaves had no idea what Paniatowski was talking about, Woodend thought. And why should she? In her world, there was nothing *shocking* about girls going on the game. She would probably have been surprised if Enid *hadn't* followed in her footsteps.

'You're sure she wasn't making it all up?' Paniatowski persisted.

The frizzy-haired woman shook her head. 'I know some of her customers.' She sighed regretfully. 'A couple of them even used to be mine.'

It should all have fitted together so neatly, Woodend thought.

Judd comes out of prison and picks up his daughter on Saturday, and the very next morning he and a blonde girl matching Enid's description are found dead in a lonely Lancashire farmhouse. Logic dictated it *had* to be her. And yet flying in the face of that logic, there was the medical evidence that clearly stated that . . .

His mind travelled back to that Sunday morning – to the farmhouse living room where two people lay horrendously murdered.

He saw Doc Pierson standing there, just as he had stood at the scene of numerous other slayings in his time. Yet somehow the doctor had seemed different that day – far from his usual positive, helpful self.

For openers, there'd been his estimate of the time of death. He'd put it at much earlier than the hands on the smashed wristwatch indicated, and when the discrepancy had been pointed out to him, he'd apologized for the mistake and blamed it on his hangover.

And Woodend had believed him at the time – because the man had looked so rough. But now he was no longer sure that it had been the amount of alcohol in Pierson's system that had been responsible for the slip.

The Chief Inspector squeezed his eyes tightly closed, and re-lived the moment when Pierson had finished examining the girl's body and had straightened up again. He should have been inured to the sight of blood and gore. But he hadn't been! He'd looked really shaken!

And what was it he had said?

'*It should never have happened, Charlie. It simply should never have happened!*'

Almost as if he'd known the victim personally!

Almost as if he knew why she'd been killed!

Woodend glanced across at Paniatowski, and saw she'd reached the same conclusion he had – that if the second victim really was Enid Judd, then Battersby and Chief Superintendent Ainsworth had not been the only ones who'd been tampering with the evidence.

'Do you know a man called Philip Swales?' he asked Doris Hargreaves.

'Never heard of him!' the woman replied – far too quickly, far too emphatically.

Woodend shook his head sadly. 'I really am tryin' to do all I can to keep you out of jail, you know, Doris. But you're not doin' much to help yourself, now are you?'

Doris Hargreaves bit her lower lip. 'Look, yer've got to understand it had nothin' to do with me.'

'What hadn't?'

'Phil Swales came round here one day – about six months ago, it must have been – an' said he wanted to talk to Enid. Well, I knew what he was up to o' course – I remembered him from the old days—'

'When you were on the game yourself?'

'I was no more a professional then than our Enid is now,' the frizzy-haired woman said, with injured dignity.

'But that's when you knew him?'

'Yeah.'

'An' you worked for him?'

Mrs Hargreaves shrugged. 'Not exactly worked *for* him. But he helped me out a bit. I mean, a girl's got to have some protection, hasn't she? It's rough out on them streets.'

'So when he came round, you knew exactly what he was up to, didn't you? You knew he was offerin' to pimp for her?'

Another shrug. 'I couldn't have stopped her doin' what she wanted to, even if I'd tried. Anyway, it's her life, ain't it?'

'An' she agreed to work for Swales?'

'Yeah, I suppose so.'

'You *suppose* so? Stop pissin' me about! Did she agree to work for him or didn't she?'

'She agreed to work for him,' Mrs Hargreaves admitted.

'An' *where* did she agree to work for him? Around here?'

'That's right.'

'You're lyin'!' Woodend snapped. 'She couldn't earn enough round a shit hole like this to make it worth Swales' while pimpin' for her.'

'He . . . he took her away,' Mrs Hargreaves stammered. 'He said he was goin' to set her up in a nice flat somewhere.'

'An' you didn't try to stop him?'

Sally Spencer

'What could *I* have done?'

'You could have gone to the police.'

Mrs Hargreaves gave a hollow laugh, which rapidly turned into a heavy smoker's cough.

'Do you really think the police would be interested?' she asked. 'Dozens of girls go the same way as our Enid did every year – an' the bobbies don't give a toss. Besides . . .'

'Besides what?'

'You don't know Phil Swales like I do. He can turn real nasty when he wants to. I'd have been a bloody fool to have got on the wrong side of him.'

'Plus, you'd have lost your finder's fee,' Woodend said harshly.

'My what?'

'He gave you money, didn't he?'

'He might have slipped me a few quid – but it was nothin' like what Enid will be earnin'.'

'Let's get back to your brother,' Woodend said. 'What did you tell him when he came lookin' for Enid, an' found she wasn't here?'

'I told him she'd run away.'

'But he didn't believe you, did he?'

Mrs Hargreaves shook her head.

'Was he the one who gave you the bruises?'

'Yeah, it was him.'

'An' after he'd knocked you about for a bit, you told him all about what Swales had done?'

'I didn't have no choice, did I? I mean, it's not as if any of this is my fault, you know.'

'How did your brother get here?'

'I'm not followin' yer?'

'Did he walk? Did he come by bus? Did he arrive in the Lord Mayor's Coach?'

'No, he came in the old jalopy of his that one of his pals looks after while he's inside.'

204

'You don't happen to know the make an' model, do you?'

'Of course I know. I'm not stupid. It's a yeller Austin A40.'

He had the whole story now, Woodend thought – or most of it, anyway.

Judd had learned from his sister that Philip Swales had taken his beloved daughter away, and he had probably spent the rest of the day trying to find Swales. Then, late on Saturday night – or perhaps even early on Sunday morning – someone must have told him about Dugdale's Farm.

He'd got into his battered A40 and headed for Whitebridge. And while he was on the road, he must have been turning the whole terrible situation over in his mind. At first, his only thought had been to rescue his Enid. But as he got closer to the farm, he would have begun to realize that simply getting her back was not enough for him – and that what he really wanted was to take revenge on Swales and all the other men who had wronged his daughter.

But then he would have seen his problem. He was afraid of Swales. And he was afraid of the men Swales would be working for – rich, powerful men who would view him as no more than a troublesome insect. And they were right about him, he would have admitted to himself. He was strictly small fry. He could never bring them to justice on his own.

So he had pulled the A40 over by a public phone box, and called the most important man his limited experience and imagination could comprehend – a reporter from BBC Radio Manchester, who he had no doubt listened to from the narrow confines of his cell.

When Bennett had picked up his phone, Judd had told him that there was a big story waiting for him out at the farm. But the story he'd expected Bennett to cover hadn't been murder – it had been child prostitution.

'Have you heard enough, sir?' Paniatowski asked.

'More than enough.'

'Just a minute,' Mrs Hargreaves said. 'I've been sittin' here answerin' your questions for you, an' now I want to know what this is all about.'

'It's a little late for you to start takin' an interest, isn't it?' Woodend asked.

'What do you mean?'

'Your niece won't be botherin' you any more.'

'Won't she?'

'No. Nor your brother, either. They're both dead. They've been murdered,' Woodend said, as brutally as he could. 'But I wouldn't worry about it too much if I was you, Mrs Hargreaves. After all, it's not *your* fault, is it?'

Twenty-Six

The rain was hammering mercilessly against the windscreen of the MGA, with a fury that was making Woodend and Paniatowski's journey back to Whitebridge almost painfully slow.

But at least the rain was holding up work on the Moorland Village site, Woodend thought – at least it was preventing Taylor from tampering with the evidence. And then a sudden sickening insight flashed across his brain, and he felt his earlier optimism melt away as he realized that Taylor did not *have* to tamper with the evidence at all – that he only needed to sit and wait.

'We're buggered,' he groaned.

'What do you mean, sir?' Monika asked.

'I mean exactly what I say. We're buggered. We've got nothin' we can use. Not a bloody sausage.'

'We've learned a hell of a lot today.'

'We've learned almost the *whole story* today. The problem is, we can't actually prove *any* of it.'

'That's not true. We can prove that Taylor's been to prison twice and that he shared a cell with Swales, who also shared a cell, in another prison, with Dugdale. When we make that public knowledge—'

'We'll damage Terry Taylor's social standin' in the community, for at least a week. An' then what will happen?'

'I don't know.'

'After a while, a lot of people will start to form a different

207

opinion of him entirely. So he's an ex-con, they'll say. So what? He's managed to find the strength of character to put his past behind him, an' make good. He should be admired, not condemned.'

'Then there's the question of tampering with the evidence,' Paniatowski argued.

'What tamperin' with the evidence? The wrong fingerprints got submitted for examination. That was a mistake, an' mistakes do happen. An' even if we could prove it wasn't a mistake at all, the only man we can link it to is DC Battersby – an' he's dead.'

'The medical evidence, then,' Paniatowski said, a hint of desperation creeping into her voice. 'A fresh autopsy on Enid Judd would soon reveal—'

'I know what it would reveal,' Woodend interrupted. 'But how do we get a fresh autopsy carried out? Doc Pierson's highly respected in Whitebridge – an' if he says the girl was a virgin when she died, who's goin' to doubt him? We didn't even start to doubt it ourselves until half an hour ago. Even if we could persuade another doctor to check on Pierson's findin's, Ainsworth would be bound to oppose it – an' Ainsworth's the boss.'

'We could go over his head.'

'With what? Bloody hell, Monika, we can't even prove the dead girl's *Enid Judd* – an' we're as sure of that as we are of our own names. So what would come of us tryin' to stir things up by goin' over Ainsworth's head? The entire force would think we'd gone doolally with desperation. That wouldn't really hurt me. Well, what *could* hurt me now, more than I'm hurt already? I'm that close to jail I can already smell the boiled cabbage. But it could hurt you – an' I'm not prepared to see you thrown on the scrap heap for no good reason.'

They had already passed the sign for Whitebridge, and in another five minutes they would reach the city centre.

After what they'd learned that evening, it should have been a triumphant homecoming. Instead they felt like two dogs slinking back with their tails between their legs.

'If only we could dig up that bloody Austin A40 . . .' Paniatowski said despondently.

'But we can't, can we? We've no grounds whatsoever for invadin' a private buildin' site.'

'But when Terry Taylor digs it up – when one of our lads spots it on public view . . .'

'Then, based on the reports of a similar car bein' seen near the scene of the crime, we could do somethin'. But it might be months before he digs it up. Or he might *never* dig it up at all.'

'Never dig it up!' Paniatowski gasped. 'But he has to!'

'No, he doesn't,' Woodend said. 'An' it was when I realized that depressin' bloody fact myself that I knew we were well an' truly buggered.'

'It's a building site. There's bound to be excavations.'

'What do you think made Taylor choose to bury the A40 exactly where he did?'

'I don't know.'

'Well, I think I do. I haven't seen the plans for Moorland Village, but I'm willin' to bet that he didn't bury it where there's goin' to be houses. He'll have chosen a spot where he's goin' to put in a car park. Or a tennis court. Or some other bloody thing where they don't have to dig down far before they start layin' concrete. You see where I'm leadin' with this, lass?'

Paniatowski nodded. 'As soon as the weather clears up a little, he'll have obliterated all signs that there ever was a hole there.'

'Exactly. An' with that, our last chance will have gone. A yellow Austin A40 was seen near Dugdale's Farm. So what? Dugdale has disappeared, as well as a little lass from

Manchester called Enid Judd. Again, so what? These things happen. Judd an' an unknown female were killed by an old farmer who had a history of violence, an' had probably gone round the twist through livin' out on the moors all by himself. End of story. Taylor gets away with it. DCS Ainsworth an' Doc Pierson get away with *helpin'* him to get away with it . . .'

'And you're ruined,' Paniatowski said quietly. 'You're ruined, and I have to continue working in a police force which I know is rotten to the core.'

'Aye, that's a pretty fair summary,' Woodend agreed.

'We've just got time for a quick one in the Royal Oak, if you fancy it,' Paniatowski said, without much enthusiasm.

But failure was not something Woodend felt inclined to share at that moment.

'No, if you don't mind, I think I'll go straight home,' he said.

'Is that wise?' Paniatowski asked anxiously.

'Why wouldn't it be?'

'You've been living in my flat for the last two days because you were worried about what Taylor might do to you.'

'If he saw me as a threat, he'd do whatever was necessary to get rid of me,' Woodend said. 'But he'll only have to look at my face to see I'm no danger to anybody any more. Besides . . .'

'Besides what?'

'Nothin', lass.'

'Besides what?' Paniatowski insisted.

'You can't pin the two murders he's already involved in on him, but if he killed again, it'd give you another shot at puttin' the rope round his neck.'

'Jesus, I don't like hearing you talk like that.'

'I'm not exactly thrilled to hear it myself. But, let's face it, lass, I've got so little to look forward to that I might as well be dead.'

'Why . . . why don't you come back to my flat, and we can . . .' Paniatowski began, before suddenly trailing off.

'An' we can what?' Woodend asked.

'Nothing.'

'Nothin'?'

'Have a drink. Watch a bit of television together.'

'No thanks,' Woodend said. 'I'd be better off in my own house.'

They were passing the police headquarters. Lights were blazing from the basement windows, and under their harsh glare were perhaps a dozen officers, labouring hard at tasks which one of the highest-ranking police officers in Whitebridge was determined to see would lead them absolutely nowhere.

They're goin' to get away with it, Woodend thought.

And Paniatowski's windscreen wipers, swishing back and forth in their battle against the rain, seemed to echo his words and add a little touch of mockery of their own.

Goin' to get away with it . . . goin' to get away with it . . . goin' to get away with it . . .

'Unless . . .' Woodend said suddenly.

'Unless what, sir?'

'Unless we can *panic* them. Unless we can persuade Terry Taylor or DCS Ainsworth – or preferably both of them – that they're not quite as secure as they thought they were.'

'And how the hell are we going to do that?'

'By hittin' them when they least expect it. By gettin' them to *act* before they've really had time to *think*.'

Monika Paniatowski chuckled. 'I knew if you thought about it for a while, you'd come up with a clever plan.'

'Sorry to disappoint you, lass, but it's not a *clever* plan,' Woodend said. 'With clever plans, the people behind them have some control over what's goin' on. What we'll be doin' is makin' a big hole in the dam an' hopin' the water comes pourin' out in just the way that we want it to. But there's absolutely no guarantee that it will.'

Twenty-Seven

They had learned so much the previous evening that it seemed an age since he had last stood in Monika's living room – watching the sun set and seeing his own career sinking with it. It *seemed* an age, but it was no more than a few hours, and soon the sun would rise again, edging the dark clouds which were now drifting across the moon with a golden edge of hope. He wished he could share that hope, but his own dark clouds of doubt made it almost impossible for him to believe that a new day really was dawning in the investigation into the murders at Dugdale's Farm.

Woodend turned away from the window. Monika Pania-towski was stretched out on the sofa, in a deep sleep. She was a very attractive woman, he thought. Perhaps even a beautiful one. Yet at that moment he found it hard to think of her as anything but an innocent, trusting child.

He lit up a cigarette. Did he have the right to allow her to take the risks this operation would entail? he wondered. And *why* was he asking her to take them, anyway? For the sake of the dead girl they had found in the farmhouse? Or for his sake – for the sake of his precious career? He prayed he was doing it for the girl – although he knew that he would never be really sure.

He went to the kitchen, made two cups of strong, black coffee and took them back into the lounge.

'Time to wake up, Monika!' he said, thinking that he

sounded more like a jovial uncle on Christmas morning than a chief inspector who was asking one of his subordinates to put her job on the line.

Paniatowski rolled over, groaned, then opened her eyes and saw him standing there.

'Have I been asleep?' she asked.

'Just for a while,' Woodend said softly.

'And how long's "a while"?'

'Three or four hours.'

Monika groaned again, and shook her head in an attempt to clear the sleep from it.

'I'm sorry, sir. I meant to stay awake, to keep you company.'

'Don't worry about it. I managed to grab a couple of hours kip myself,' Woodend lied.

Monika swung her legs off the sofa and reached for the coffee. 'I'll just knock this back, then I'll be ready to make that call.'

'That call.'

The words echoed around Woodend's mind. How casual they sounded – how utterly insignificant. But they weren't insignificant at all – the acceptance of them was the vital first step in an operation during the course of which a hundred things could go wrong.

Paniatowski drained her cup, and lit the first cigarette of what she fully expected to be a very long morning.

'Right, let's get started,' she said, trying to sound brisk and thoroughly businesslike.

'You don't have to do this, Monika,' Woodend cautioned her. 'There's still time to back out.'

Paniatowski walked over to the small table on which her telephone sat. 'There's an extension phone in the bedroom,' she said, ignoring his warning. 'You can listen in from there, if you want to.'

Woodend walked into the bedroom, picked up the receiver,

and clamped it to his ear. Monika was already connected, and he found himself counting the rings.

One . . . two . . . three . . . four . . . five . . . six . . .

It was on the tenth ring that the phone was picked up, and a sleepy, irritated voice said, 'Who the hell is this?'

'It's me, sir. Paniatowski.'

'Do you realize what time of day it is, Sergeant Paniatowski?' DCC Ainsworth demanded.

'Yes, sir, I do. And I'm sorry to disturb you like this, but I didn't have much choice.'

'Not much choice?'

'The thing is, there's been a big break in the Dugdale's Farm case, and I can't seem to reach DI Harris.'

There was a silence at the other end of the line, and Woodend could almost picture Ainsworth trying to work out the proper way to respond.

'Big break? What kind of big break?' the Deputy Chief Constable said finally.

'I've identified the victims, sir.'

'Jesus Christ Almighty!' Ainsworth said, then added – belatedly – 'Who do you think they are?'

'I don't *think*, sir – I know. The man's name was Harry Judd. He was a villain, but strictly small-time. The girl was his daughter, Enid.'

'You're sure of this?'

'Like I said, I'm absolutely certain of it, sir.'

There were another few seconds silence while Ainsworth sweated on the other end of the line, and Paniatowski – keeping her nerve admirably – sat back and let him drown in it.

'This . . . this is really excellent news,' Ainsworth said unconvincingly. 'Well done.'

'There's more.'

'More?' the DCC said fearfully, after perhaps as much as ten seconds had passed.

'I know who killed them, as well, sir.'

'I don't see how you could possibly—'

'It was a man called Philip Swales.'

'Swales!'

'You sound as if you know the man, sir.'

'No, I . . . it just struck me as a rather unusual name.'

'And I think we'll have all the evidence we need if we can find the dead man's car.'

'His car?'

'That's right, sir. A yellow Austin A40. Our only problem is, I haven't quite established where it is yet.'

'What do you mean – you haven't *quite* established where it is?' Ainsworth asked.

'I suppose I mean that I've no idea at the moment,' Paniatowski lied. She paused, to give Ainsworth the time to develop a little false hope, then added, 'But I do know it's still in the area, and based on the same sources of information I used to identify the victims and the killer, I expect to be able to pinpoint its exact location sometime this afternoon.'

'Be more specific,' Ainsworth said. 'What are these sources of information you're talking about?'

'To tell you the truth, it's all a bit complicated to explain over the phone,' Paniatowski said. 'Couldn't we meet somewhere, and talk it through?'

Woodend counted slowly to six before the DCC spoke again.

'I'll meet you down at headquarters, Sergeant Paniatowski,' Ainsworth said. 'Shall we say around half past nine?'

'That would be fine, sir.'

'Don't try to ring DI Harris again before you talk to me. I want to evaluate the evidence myself before I decide whether to present it to him.'

'Understood, sir.

'And Sergeant . . .'

'Yes, sir?'

'After waking me up at this godawful time of the morning, you'd better make damn sure you've got solid evidence to back up your claims – or I'll make you pay for it in ways you wouldn't believe.'

'I've no worries there, sir,' Paniatowski told him. 'My evidence is as solid as a rock, sir.'

The line went dead. Woodend checked his watch. It was just after half past six.

They had another cup of coffee, and two more cigarettes. Both of them looked longingly at the whisky bottle that was standing invitingly on the table, but neither made a move for it.

At a quarter to seven, Woodend said, 'You'd better go and get the search warrant sworn out by the magistrate, Monika. I'm sorry it has to be you. I'd do it myself if I could.'

'I've no objection to doing it,' Paniatowski replied. 'I'm just not sure we're taking it to the right person.'

'Have you got somethin' against Polly Johnson?'

Paniatowski looked embarrassed. 'No,' she admitted. 'It's just that she's a woman.'

'So?'

'Given that we're on such shaky legal ground to start with, I think I'd rather deal with a man.'

Woodend heard himself chuckle – and was surprised that he still could. 'What you're really sayin' is that with a man you can use your feminine wiles to wrap him round your little finger, but you're not so confident you can get a woman to co-operate.'

'I wouldn't have put it quite like that,' Paniatowski said uncomfortably.

'But it's what you meant.'

'I suppose so.'

'Let me tell you a little story,' Woodend said. 'They put

up a council estate next to Polly Johnson's house last year. Some of her neighbours objected, claimin' it would bring down the tone of the area. Polly herself didn't really mind. In fact, she thought it might do those same neighbours good to see how the other half lives at close quarters. What she *did* object to was them loppin' off half her beloved garden for the project, when they could just as easily have expanded in the other direction instead. She tried to fight it, but the builder said that was the way that it had to be done, an' the council backed him. An' the builder was . . . ?'

'T. A. Taylor and Associates!'

'That's right,' Woodend agreed. 'An' that's why you should have no difficulty gettin' your search warrant from Polly Johnson.'

It was ten minutes since Monika Paniatowski had returned, brandishing the warrant Polly Johnson JP had been more than willing to sign. Now the hands of the lounge clock pointed to a quarter to eight.

Woodend lit a cigarette, then realized he already had two more burning in the ashtray.

'It's not goin' to happen, Monika,' he said despondently. 'We gave it our best shot, but it's simply not goin' to happen.'

'It'll happen. I know it will,' Paniatowski replied in a tone of voice that fell short of matching the confidence of her words.

'If Ainsworth an' Taylor were goin' to do what we need them to do, they'd have already started.'

'I'm not due to meet Mr Ainsworth for another hour and three-quarters,' Paniatowski said, half-heartedly. 'There's plenty of time yet.'

No, there wasn't, Woodend thought.

They'd called his bluff, and even though he could reconstruct what had happened out at Dugdale's Farm almost minute by minute, there was no way he'd ever be able to bring the guilty parties to book for it.

The phone rang, and Paniatowski sprang out of her chair in her eagerness to answer it.

'Yes it's me,' she said. 'Yes . . . He has? . . . I see. Keep in touch.'

She replaced the phone on its cradle.

'Who was that?' Woodend asked.

'DC Hardcastle. He says that Terry Taylor has just left his house.'

The news should have cheered Woodend up – but it didn't.

'Didn't you hear what I said?' Paniatowski asked. 'He's just left his house!'

'The fact he's gone out doesn't mean a thing,' Woodend replied. 'It's nearly eight o'clock now. Lots of folk are leavin' their houses by eight o'clock. Taylor might be just settin' off for an early mornin' round of golf.'

'In this weather? That doesn't seem likely.'

'You don't know golfers, Sergeant. They'll play through fire an' brimstone if there's no other choice.'

'But they always like to dress appropriately, whatever the weather, don't they?'

'What's that supposed to mean?'

'If Terry Taylor had been meaning to play a round of golf, wouldn't he have been wearing his golfing tweeds?'

'I suppose so. Wasn't he?'

'No, he wasn't.'

She was teasing him, Woodend realized. She was happy enough – confident enough – to be bloody teasing him!

'So what *was* Taylor wearin'?' he asked.

Paniatowski grinned. 'He was wearing overalls,' she said.

Twenty-Eight

They'd argued about how many officers to use in the operation. Woodend had said four, Paniatowski had insisted on eight. And Paniatowski had been right, Woodend thought, as the convoy of cars made its way across the bleak moors towards the Moorland Village. When dealing with a violent criminal like Philip Swales, it would have been foolish to go in anything less than mob-handed. And yet . . . and yet he wished that he could have found a way to keep all the others out of it, so that if the swoop came up with nothing, he – and only he – would have to face the consequences of that failure.

They were half a mile from the Village when they heard the whine of heavy machinery drifting across the moorland.

'That's one worry out of the way,' Paniatowski said.

'What?' Woodend said, startled out of his musings.

'With all that racket going on, they'll never hear us coming.'

She sounds bright and hopeful, Woodend thought. He wished he could share in her optimism, but the cloud of impending doom that had been hanging over him since before Paniatowski woke up was refusing to drift away.

They had reached the site. The lead vehicle, driven by Hardcastle, parked near to the big double gates. The second car fanned out to the right, and the third to the left.

'Do they all know what they've got to do?' Woodend asked, as Paniatowski brought her MGA to a halt.

The sergeant nodded. 'We go in first, and Hardcastle and Duxbury follow us.'

'An' the other units?'

'As we agreed, one stays where it is, and the other goes around the back of the site, in case the targets try to get out that way.'

It was a good plan, Woodend thought – a good plan being executed by good men. But he was still not happy.

'It's not too late to call it off,' he said.

'Call it off? Now?' Paniatowski exclaimed. 'Just when we've got them exactly where we want them?'

'Just when we *think* – when we *hope* – we've got them exactly where we want them,' Woodend corrected her. 'But what if we haven't? I'm not sure I'm willing to risk sacrificing you an' the rest of the team.'

'You won't be. It'll only be me.'

'What?'

'I've told the lads the plan has the full backing of DCC Ainsworth.'

'An' did they believe you?'

'Of course not. But they can say they did – and that's enough to put them in the clear.'

Woodend felt a lump come to his throat. 'I really appreciate this, Monika,' he said.

'Bollocks to that! You'd have done the same for me, wouldn't you?'

'Yes, but . . .'

'Well, there you are, then.'

Hardcastle and Duxbury got out of their vehicle and walked over to the gates. Hardcastle grasped hold of the left one, and pulled. It shook – but did not open. He ran his eyes quickly up and down the gate, then turned towards the MGA and mouthed the word, 'Padlock'.

Paniatowski made a snipping gesture with her fingers, and Hardcastle nodded that he understood.

The big detective constable walked back to his car, and took a pair of wire-cutters out of the boot. He returned to the gates, sized up the job in hand, then began cutting a hole in the chain-link fence. From inside the building site, the mechanical digger gave one last howl, and then fell silent.

Get on with it, man! Woodend urged silently from the passenger seat of the MGA. Bloody-well get on with it!

Hardcastle pulled a rough oblong of wire mesh free from the fence, leant through the gap he'd cut, and fixed his cutters on the padlock on the other side of the gate.

There was the sound of another heavy vehicle – possibly a crane – starting up inside the building site.

'Won't be long now,' Paniatowski said.

No, Woodend thought, it wouldn't. It shouldn't take more than another three or four minutes – at the most – to find out if he really was as good a detective as he thought he was.

Hardcastle's arm emerged from the gap in the wire, then he and Duxbury took hold of one gate each, and swung them open.

'Ready, sir?' Paniatowski asked.

'As ready as I'll ever be,' Woodend replied.

Paniatowski slammed the MGA into gear, and the car shot forward towards the open gateway. Hardcastle's vehicle fell in behind it. The operation – for better or worse – was entering its final phase.

Once through the gates, the MGA made a sharp turn, its tyres screeching as it skidded past the site office – and past the four furious Dobermanns which were chained to the rail in front of it.

Bouncing up and down on the rough track, the MGA roared past the show house with its genuine hardwood doors and real brass fittings. Buckets of slush were being thrown up, and the windscreen wipers gave a dull rubber moan as they did their best to combat them.

Paniatowski kept her foot down on the pedal as they passed the completed shells of the first row of houses, then wrenched the steering wheel to make a sharp right turn. The virgin section of the building site was now ahead of them – the couple of acres of muddied grass that lay between the last building and the fence. And right in the middle of it – at roughly the point where he had found the sliver of yellow paint – was just the tableau that Woodend had been praying he would see.

The mechanical digger was closest to them, with a large mound of earth piled up next it. Beyond that there was a heavy crane. Three cars were parked near to the crane – Taylor's Jaguar, Ainsworth's Volvo, and the garishly red Mercedes Benz which Woodend had seen parked outside the Victoria Hotel on the night Taylor had had the heated argument with Philip Swales.

But it was the lorry he was most relieved to see – the lorry with a battered, yellow Austin A40 sitting on the back!

They were less than twenty yards from the large hole in the ground now – close enough for Woodend to see Taylor was sitting in the cab of the crane, and that Ainsworth and another man were standing by the cars.

Paniatowski slammed on the MGA's brakes, and skidded to a halt near the Jaguar so suddenly that DC Hardcastle, who had been right behind, had to swerve to avoid tail-ending her.

The sergeant looked at the yellow A40, and allowed a broad grin to spread across her face. 'Caught the bastards with their pants right down around their ankles, haven't we!' she said gleefully.

But as Woodend climbed out of the passenger seat he saw the Deputy Chief Constable striding furiously and confidently towards the MGA – and realized that it was going to be nothing like as easy as Monika seemed to think.

Ainsworth drew level with them and, looking straight through Woodend, turned his anger on Paniatowski.

'What the bloody hell's going on, Sergeant?' the DCC demanded.

'I've got a search warrant here, sir,' Paniatowski replied, offering him the precious piece of paper.

Ainsworth brushed the warrant angrily aside without even taking a proper look at it. 'Who authorized this warrant?' he asked.

'Mrs Johnson, sir.'

'I'm not talking about which of Whitebridge's magistrates actually put their name to it. What I want to know is which of your superiors swore it out. Was it DI Harris?'

'No, sir.'

'Then who?'

'I did it on my own initiative.'

'On *his* initiative, you mean!' Ainsworth said, glaring briefly at Woodend. 'You had no right to request a warrant without getting it cleared through me, or someone else in authority, first.'

'Maybe I didn't,' Paniatowski agreed. 'but that still doesn't invalidate it as a legal document.'

Ainsworth shook his head dolefully. 'I always thought you were a smart bobby, Sergeant Paniatowski. But it seems as if I was wrong, doesn't it? You haven't even got the brains of a rat on a sinking ship – because Charlie Woodend's already well below the waterline and you're *still* clinging on to him. Well, let me tell you, this misjudged loyalty's going to cost you dear, Sergeant. You may not have fully realized it yet, but unless you start playing this by the rules – by *my* rules – you're finished in the force.'

The short speech had had its intended effect, and Paniatowski shifted her weight uncertainly from her left foot to her right, and then back again.

'Would you like to explain what you're doin' out here at this time of the mornin', sir?' Woodend asked.

'And in case you're wondering why *I'm* here, Sergeant,' Ainsworth said, ignoring the Chief Inspector completely, 'I'm here because, shortly after I spoke to you about the Austin A40 you were so eager to find, I got an anonymous telephone call telling me where I could find it.'

'What about the others?' Paniatowski asked, trying her hardest to keep her voice steady. 'Why are they here?'

'Mr Taylor is here because this is his site, and because he knows how to operate the heavy equipment we needed to use to dig the car out,' Ainsworth said. 'And as for Mr Swales,' he indicated the thin-faced man who had not moved an inch during the whole discussion, 'he is one of Mr Taylor's associates, and we brought him along to act as a witness to whatever we found.'

'Why did you bring along a man I'd already told you was a suspect in my investigation?' Paniatowski asked shakily.

'*Your* investigation?' Ainsworth asked. 'I wasn't aware that you had an investigation of your own. And as to bringing a murder suspect along with me, I really have no idea what you're talking about.'

'I told you when I called that I thought Philip Swales was the man we were looking for. You said you'd never heard of him.'

'I did no such thing, Sergeant. I've met Mr Swales socially on several occasions and—'

'Did you know he's got a record? That he's a violent criminal?'

'—and if you *had* mentioned his name to me – which you certainly did not – then I would have told you that although he's had certain problems in the past, he is now a thoroughly respectable businessman.'

This wasn't how things should be going, Woodend thought. It didn't even come close.

Ainsworth had been caught red-handed, trying to remove the evidence of a serious crime. By now he should have been so panicked that he would be doing all he could to shift most of the blame on to Swales and Taylor. Instead, he had not only kept his nerve, but seemed to be getting more confident by the minute.

And he was not alone in that. Philip Swales, standing a few feet away from him, was watching the whole confrontation with little more than the interest of a mildly curious passer-by. And even Terry Taylor, who had climbed down from the crane and was now walking towards them, showed none of the concern he should have been displaying.

There was nothing incriminating in the A40! Woodend thought, with a sinking feeling in the pit of his stomach.

Or if there *was* something, the conspirators had all realized that it was not enough – nothing *like* enough – to tie them in with the double murder at Dugdale's Farm!

Terry Taylor had reached the edge of the circle, and came to a stop. Woodend looked on, powerless to do anything, as the builder searched Ainsworth's face for some hint as to how he was expected to react to the situation.

'I was just explaining to my rather over-enthusiastic sergeant here that I rang you the moment I got the anonymous call about the Austin being buried here on your site, Terry,' Ainsworth said, giving him all the lead he needed. 'About what time would you say you received that call?'

'I suppose it must have been around twenty to eight – or perhaps five minutes later than that,' Taylor said, falling in easily with Ainsworth's line. 'As you can imagine, it came as something of a shock to me.'

'Let's stop playin' games, shall we, Mr Taylor?' Woodend asked.

'Games?' Taylor repeated.

'You weren't shocked at all. An' you didn't need any call from anybody to learn where the Austin was. You've known all along. You *had* to know, because only you – or one of the two security men you employ – could have buried it in the first place.'

Ainsworth shot Taylor a glance that warned him not to say any more, but the builder now appeared to be so sure of himself that he allowed a bemused smile to appear on his face.

'I had to know the car was buried here, because there were only three of us who could have buried it?' he said. 'Now that *is* a very interesting theory, Chief Inspector. Can I ask what you base it on?'

'On the four bloody big Dobermanns you've got chained up at the entrance to the site.'

Taylor laughed. 'Ah, you've been questioning them, have you? I'm surprised you could understand them. I thought the only language they spoke was some kind of doggie German.'

'You're a funny man, an' I'm sure you'll be a real hit at the prison concert parties. Because you *are* goin' to prison, you know,' Woodend said, with more conviction than he felt.

'On the evidence of four foreign canines?'

'Aye, if you like. When the site's got people workin' on it, the dogs are kept chained up. But when it's closed, they're let loose to roam as they please. I've seen them myself.'

'So?'

'The dogs won't allow just *anybody* to come in an' chain them up again. It has to be somebody they've been trained to obey. And that's what happened on Sunday, when the car was buried – somebody they'd been trained to obey came on to the site an' chained them up. So who was it, Mr Taylor? You? Or one of the dog handlers whose wages you pay?'

Taylor should have crumbled – but he didn't. 'Perhaps it was someone whose wages I *used* to pay,' he suggested.

227

'Come again?'

'During the time I've owned the dogs, I've employed five different handlers. Two of them still work for me, but the rest have moved on. It could quite easily have been one of those other three who came to the site on Sunday.'

It was plausible, Woodend thought – it was all too *bloody* plausible.

'What if it turns out that the three men who *used* to work for you all have alibis for Sunday mornin'?' he asked.

Taylor shrugged. 'I don't know,' he admitted. 'I'm a builder. I have no knowledge of how police investigations work. If they do turn out to have alibis, perhaps you'll want to question me again – but I have an alibi, too.'

I bet you bloody do, Woodend thought. An' I bet the two handlers you still employ have alibis, an' all. God knows, you've had long enough to set somethin' up for them.

'Where will I find these three ex-dog handlers of yours, Mr Taylor?' he asked.

'I have absolutely no idea,' the builder told him. 'They worked for me – and now they don't. They could be in Australia, or even Timbuktu, for all I know. I really have no interest in them any more.'

Woodend glanced quickly over his shoulder at Hardcastle and Duxbury. The two detective constables were standing by their car listening to the whole exchange – and registering the defeat they were already beginning to feel on their faces.

And they were right to feel defeated, the Chief Inspector told himself. He had completely lost control of the situation – and everybody there knew it!

He looked up at the yellow A40 on the back of the lorry and saw, not a car, but his last chance to make anything stick.

'Search the Austin, Monika,' he said.

'I forbid you to take orders from a man who has been

228

suspended from duty and is currently under investigation for his criminal activities,' Ainsworth snapped at Paniatowski.

'I'm not taking orders from Mr Woodend,' Paniatowski replied. 'But since I've gone to all the trouble of getting the warrant sworn out, I might as well search the car now that I'm here. If that's all right with you, sir.'

'And what if it's *not* all right with me?' Ainsworth countered.

Paniatowski hesitated for a second, as if she were considering her options. And perhaps she really *was*, Woodend thought.

'I think I'm *still* going to have to search it,' the sergeant said finally.

The DCC shrugged. 'Go ahead, if that's what you want. After all, it's your career that is on the line.'

He shouldn't have given in anything like so easily, Woodend thought miserably. Given the position he was in, the DCC should have fought against the idea of a search every inch of the way. And the fact that he hadn't bothered – didn't even seem to really care – could only mean one thing. He was willing to let them go through the ritual of a search because he knew that they would find *nothing*.

Twenty-Nine

Paniatowski walked over to the open lorry, placed her right foot on the top of one of the rear tyres, and pulled herself up on to the tailboard.

She's not goin' to find anythin', Woodend told himself. She's not goin' to find a bloody thing!

The sergeant dusted off her hands, opened the driver's door of the A40, and peered inside.

'The front's empty, but there's a lot of stuff on the back seat,' she said, over her shoulder.

'Stuff? What kind of stuff?'

Paniatowski pulled the driver's seat forward, and leant further into the car. For perhaps thirty seconds, she rummaged through the contents of the back seat. As she emerged from the A40, she took a deep breath, sucking the air in greedily.

'There's a couple of whips, some leather corsets, and a stack of dirty magazines,' she said. 'And two stained bed sheets,' she added, looking down at her hands in disgust.

It was as bad as Woodend had ever imagined it could be. Some of the material was probably illegal, but that, in itself, was not enough to tie it to the murders. Christ, it wasn't even enough to tie it in with Dugdale's Farm!

What a fool he'd been, Woodend thought bitterly. He'd managed to convince himself that by taking sudden, dramatic action, he'd rush Taylor and Ainsworth into making a mistake. Now he saw the situation as it really was. It had been desperation rather than his usual judgement that had guided him, and the only person who'd been rushed into a wrong move had been him. He'd taken his gamble at entirely the wrong moment. He should have waited. He should have bloody waited!

Paniatowski was still standing on the back of the lorry, uncertain of what more he expected of her.

'Check the boot, Monika,' he said.

'Think carefully about what your next move should be, Sergeant!' Ainsworth warned.

'I have, sir,' Paniatowski told him. 'Since I'm here, I think I might as well check the boot.'

Paniatowski stepped carefully round the side of the car, clicked the boot open, and immediately pulled a face.

'What's the matter?' Woodend asked.

'It stinks.'

'What of?'

'Strong disinfectant, I think. It smells as if someone's poured a gallon of the stuff in here.'

But excessive use of disinfectant was no crime, was it?

'Is there anything else in the boot?' Woodend asked.

'More filth – a few more magazines, couple of leather masks – but nowhere near as much stuff as there is on the back seat.'

Why had they stored nearly all the pornographic material on the back seat? Woodend wondered. Wouldn't most people have automatically put it in the boot?

But it was pointless asking such questions now. He might have a car with Taylor's and Ainsworth's prints on it, but they could easily explain that away.

'*Of course it's got my prints on it,*' he could almost hear Ainsworth saying. '*I helped disinter it.*'

'*We have reason to believe some of the prints were made when you were burying the car,*' his interrogator would reply weakly.

231

'*That's impossible, since I had nothing to do with burying it,*' Ainsworth would reply.

And there would be no way of proving that he was lying.

Possibly they would find Dugdale's prints on the car, too – but Dugdale had disappeared, so that would get them precisely nowhere.

He may as well face the truth, Woodend thought. The game had been played through to its end – and he had lost.

He became aware that Ainsworth had been studying him closely – no doubt charting his thought processes and observing the changes on his face as the case he thought he'd built up disintegrated into nothingness. Now, satisfied that total collapse was on hand, the Deputy Chief Constable turned his attention back to Paniatowski.

'Consider yourself suspended, Sergeant Paniatowski,' he said harshly. 'And as for you two,' he continued, turning towards Hardcastle and Dugdale, 'don't think you're getting away from this scot-free. I'll see the pair of you – and anybody else I find out was involved – up before a disciplinary board.'

'They were just obeying my orders,' Paniatowski protested.

'Then they should have known better. Now get the hell out of here – the whole pack of you! Oh, and Duxbury,' he added maliciously, 'be sure to give my best wishes to your son – the school Sportsman of the Year.'

'What about the A40, sir?' Paniatowski asked.

'Mr Taylor and I will take it down to police headquarters for forensic examination – just as we always intended to.'

Just as they'd always intended to!

Bullshit! Woodend thought. Their plan had been to either bury the car somewhere else, or destroy it completely. Now they *would* have to take it down to headquarters, but before they did that, they'd go over it with a fine-toothed comb, to make completely sure that there was not even a shred of evidence to connect it with the murders.

But then, if they'd been going to destroy it, why swill all that disinfectant around in the boot, he wondered? That just didn't make sense at all.

'Why are you still here?' Ainsworth asked. 'Don't you recognize an order when you hear one?'

Hardcastle and Duxbury looked first at each other, and then, expectantly, at Woodend. When he nodded his head to indicate that they should obey – what else was there left for them to do? – they turned and began to move lethargically back towards their car.

I've let them down, the Chief Inspector thought. I've let them down – and they'll be paying for it for the rest of their careers.

Monika Paniatowski would be out of a job, and he himself would go to prison for a long, long time. The only thing he could find behind the dark cloud that had loomed on his horizon all morning was an even darker one.

It was as Hardcastle was reaching for the car door handle that a small miracle occurred. It manifested itself in the form of a sudden smile on DDC Ainsworth's face, and though there was perhaps nothing truly miraculous about it all, it seemed to Woodend to be heaven-sent. Because it was not the smile of triumph that the Chief Inspector would have expected to appear! It was a smile of relief – a smile that said Ainsworth thought he had got away with it, but *only just*. A smile that told Woodend that there was still evidence lying around, if only he had the wit to work out what it was!

'Wait a minute, lads,' the Chief Inspector called out to Hardcastle and Duxbury. 'Sergeant Paniatowski hasn't finished her search yet.'

Paniatowski, having climbed down off the lorry and now back on the ground, looked at him with amazement.

And who could blame her?

'What do you mean, she's not finished the search?' Ainsworth asked, now – finally – speaking to him directly. 'She's already examined the interior of the Austin thoroughly. Do you want her to take the engine to pieces next?'

'The warrant covers everything on the site,' Woodend said.

'So what else would you like her to examine? The site office? The concrete mixers?'

'No. There wouldn't really be much point in that, sir. But she would like to search your Volvo – as well as the vehicles which belong to Mr Taylor and Mr Swales.'

A look of fear and uncertainty flickered briefly across Ainsworth's face – then it was gone, to be replaced by the arrogant expression of a man who acknowledged that he might have had a few set-backs, but knew that he still held most of the winning cards.

'Sergeant Paniatowski will search nothing further,' Ainsworth said, speaking to Hardcastle and Duxbury, as well as to Woodend. 'In case you didn't hear me before, Sergeant Paniatowski has been suspended.'

There was a still a way out, Woodend thought, but it was a way which was open solely to Monika – if only she had the bottle to carry it through.

'Look at me, Sergeant Paniatowski,' Ainsworth said. 'Look at me, and listen very carefully to what I have to say. Things are already bad enough for you – don't make them any worse.'

But Paniatowski did *not* look at him. Instead, her uncertain, questioning eyes were gazing at Woodend.

'Do it, Monika,' Woodend's eyes said in return. 'It's the only chance we've got left. Grab it while you can.'

Paniatowski squared her shoulders, and turned back to Ainsworth. 'With all due respect, sir, I'm not sure that you still have the necessary authority to suspend me,' she said.

'What the devil are you talking about?'

Paniatowski gulped, as if she knew exactly what she wanted to say, but just couldn't seem to get the words out.

'Do it!' Woodend urged her silently. 'Do it now!'

The sergeant took a deep breath. 'Richard James Ainsworth, I am arresting you on the charge of conspiracy, after the fact, in the murders of Harold Judd and Enid Judd,' she said in a rush. 'You are not obliged to say anything, but anything you do say may be taken down and used in evidence against you.'

'This is insane,' Ainsworth protested.

Paniatowski held out a shaky hand. 'If you'd just like to give me the keys to your car, sir.'

'I'll do no such thing.'

'Please don't make me use force, sir,' Paniatowski said, dredging up courage from the very bottom of her reserves. 'That would really be terribly undignified.'

Ainsworth patted his pockets perfunctorily. 'Don't seem to have the keys on me,' he said.

'That's not true! You must have them. You couldn't have driven here without them.'

'Oh, I had them then, but I don't seem to have them now.'

'I don't believe you.'

'Don't you?' Ainsworth asked. 'So what are you going to do about it?'

'I . . .' Paniatowski began.

'A body search?' Ainsworth suggested. 'You can't do it yourself, you know – because you're a woman. So you'll have to order either Hardcastle or Duxbury to do it, won't you? And do you really believe either of them will obey you? Do you really believe – even for a second – that a mere *detective constable* would have the nerve to search a *Deputy Chief* Constable?'

He probably knew the words were a mistake the moment

235

they were out of his mouth, Woodend thought. And if he didn't then, the look on the face of DC Duxbury – who should have been *Sergeant* Duxbury by now – would have been enough make it clear.

Duxbury took two steps forward. 'I'll do it,' he said. 'I'll search him if you tell me to, Sergeant.'

'An' I'll help him – if he needs any help,' Hardcastle added, moving forward to join his partner.

It was then that Philip Swales decided the moment had come to move. He had been leaning against his Mercedes, a mere spectator to the drama unfolding before him, but now he made a break for it, suddenly beginning to sprint towards the chain-link fence like a fox which has got his first sniff of the hounds.

He did not get far. Hardcastle's time on the rugby pitch had taught him to mark his man, and he brought the pimp down with an impressive flying tackle.

Paniatowski looked on as Hardcastle and Duxbury pulled Swales to his feet and handcuffed him, then turned her attention back to Ainsworth.

'If a hard case like Philip Swales knows when the game's up, don't you think it's about time you admitted it yourself, sir?' she asked, with a new confidence in her voice. 'Why don't you give me the keys?'

Ainsworth sighed, then put his hand in one of the pockets he had patted down earlier and pulled his keys out. Paniatowski nodded to Woodend, and the two of them walked over to the Volvo.

'I hope you've got it right *this* time, sir,' Paniatowski whispered, as she inserted the key in the boot lock.

'You're not the only one,' Woodend agreed.

The key clicked in the lock. 'Here goes nothing,' Paniatowski said, opening the boot.

The smell of disinfectant was overpowering. Now Woodend understood why it had been used so liberally in the boot of the A40. It hadn't been the car itself they'd wanted to disinfect – it was the package they intended to transfer from there to the Volvo.

It was a long, sausage-shaped package, wrapped up in an old blanket. Woodend took hold of the corner of the blanket and peeled it back to find himself looking at the head of a white-haired man in his middle sixties. The disinfectant had not quite succeeded in masking the smell of rotting flesh, and even without the maggots crawling on his skin, the man would still have looked very dead indeed.

Woodend stepped back, looked across at Ainsworth, and pointed to the boot. 'I think you might have just a little difficulty explainin' *this* away, sir,' he said. 'It is Farmer Dugdale, I presume.'

Ainsworth nodded. 'Yes,' he admitted. 'That's Wilfred Dugdale.'

Thirty

As Woodend walked down the corridor, he was aware that the eyes of other officers were following him. And why wouldn't they? He was Lazarus returned from the dead, Napoleon landing in France after his escape from Elbe, the man who had fought against the odds and – this time, at least – had beaten the system. He was also, he admitted to himself, what he had always been before any of this had happened – a maverick. Perhaps even, in some people's eyes, a bit of a freak.

He came to a halt in front of Interview Room Number Two – the room in which he himself had been grilled by the humourless DCI Evans and malicious DCC Ainsworth. He wondered whether he should go inside – wondered whether he even *wanted* to.

As if I really have any choice! he thought, turning the handle and pushing the door open. As if young Enid Judd – although dead – wasn't still compelling him to be there.

There were three people already in the room – DI Harris and DS Paniatowski sitting at one end of the table, DCC Ainsworth at the other.

Woodend only gave the Deputy Chief Constable a brief glance, but it was enough to see that the man seemed to have aged twenty years in the previous hour or so.

Ainsworth glared at him. 'Why are you here, Chief Inspector? Have you come to gloat?'

Woodend shook his head. 'You should know me better than that. This is what I do – not what I enjoy.'

'Will you be taking over the questioning now, sir?' DI Harris asked, with a trace of relief in his voice.

'No,' Woodend told him. 'Officially, I'm still under suspension. But the Chief Constable has asked me if I wouldn't mind monitorin' the progress of the investigation.'

'So even *he's* abandoned me, has he?' Ainsworth asked.

'Did you expect anythin' else?' Woodend wondered.

'No, I suppose not.'

Nor should he have. Ainsworth might have been high on the Chief Constable's crony list for a long time, but unlike Monika Paniatowski, Henry Marlowe was one rat who *did* know when it was time to desert a sinking ship.

'*I'm sorry about what Ainsworth's put you through, Charlie,*' the Chief Constable had said to Woodend, not half an hour earlier. '*He seems to have duped us both, doesn't he?*'

And come the next morning, the story would have drifted even further from the truth. By then, Marlowe would be letting it be known that he had suspected Dick Ainsworth all along, and had only cut Woodend loose to enable him to conduct the kind of investigation that could not go through the official channels.

The Chief Inspector picked up a spare chair, took it over to the corner of the room, and straddled it. 'Carry on as if I'm not here.'

Harris nodded a reluctant acknowledgement. 'You were telling us that you were only peripheral to this case, Mr Ainsworth,' he said.

'The whole thing was Taylor and Swales' idea from the start,' the DCC said, in a dull, flat voice.

'What whole thing?'

'The Pleasure Palace.'

'That's what they called Dugdale's Farm?'

239

'Yes.'

'And why did they call it that?'

'You know why.'

'Tell us anyway. We need it on the record,' Paniatowski said, taking over the questioning.

Ainsworth sighed. 'The Pleasure Palace was where middle-aged men went to meet young women.'

'In other words, it was a brothel?'

'If you must put such a crude, unimaginative label on it – if your self-righteousness really feels the need – then, yes, I suppose that you could call it a brothel.'

There was not just one Ainsworth in the room, Woodend told himself. There were a number of different Ainsworths, who were constantly coming and going. And the changes – this slipping out of one character and into another – were reflected in the man's face. His eyes were filled with defiance one moment, and a dull acceptance of his fate the next. His mouth continually altered its shape, as if he were unable to decide whether he was playing a part in a tragedy – or only in a black comedy. His whole demeanour shifted between the extremes of a child begging for acceptance, and a superior being who did no more than tolerate these lesser mortals as they went about their pathetic business.

It was nothing Woodend hadn't seen before. Rich man or poor man, genius or idiot, they all came to resemble each other once they were sitting in that particular chair, he thought.

'Did this brothel operate every night?' Paniatowski asked.

'No,' Ainsworth replied. 'It was mainly a weekend thing – though it always did good business on bank holidays as well.'

'And why did Taylor and Swales choose to locate this brothel of theirs in a moorland farmhouse?'

'Isn't that obvious?'

'Tell me anyway.'

'Because there was no danger of prying eyes in a place that's so isolated. And because Dugdale had done time in Strangeways with Swales, so Swales and Taylor knew they could trust him.'

'What went on at this Pleasure Palace?'

'You want me to spell it out for you?'

'If you wouldn't mind.'

'*Everything* went on, Sergeant. Whatever your taste, Swales would find a way to cater for it.'

'And did they charge for this service?'

'Oh yes. We'd all have been suspicious about the place if they hadn't. But the charges were more than reasonable – because it wasn't really money they were interested in.'

'So what *were* they after?'

'Influence, of course. But they played it cleverly. And they were very patient. None of us guessed what was really going on for the first couple of years the Pleasure Palace was running, but once they'd got enough important people snared up in their web, they . . . they . . .'

'They started to blackmail their customers?'

'It was rarely as crude as that.'

'Rarely?'

'It happened – but not often. It wasn't necessary. Say, for example, that you were a member of the council planning committee, and you were considering Terry Taylor's tender for a contract – you'd have been a fool not to give him your support, wouldn't you?'

'And if he wanted information about the other bids before he put his own in?'

'Someone would give it to him.'

'What about your own role in all this?'

'Until the day of the murders, all I ever did was turn a blind eye.'

'And make certain that the rest of the Central Lancs force was turning a blind eye, as well?'

'Yes, that too,' Ainsworth agreed. 'If I didn't protect them, why should they bother to protect me?' He experienced another shift of mood, and looked Monika Paniatowski pleadingly in the eyes. 'You have to understand that I'm as much a victim as anyone else.'

'Did DC Battersby go to the Pleasure Palace?' the sergeant asked, completely unmoved.

Ainsworth snorted. 'Of course not! Battersby was a mere police constable – far too insignificant socially ever to have been invited. Terry Taylor had another hold over him – his gambling debts.'

'And Dr Pierson?'

'Yes, he was a member of what we liked to think of as the club.'

'What was *his* weakness?'

'Does it really matter?'

'Just for the record.'

'He likes boys. Very young boys.'

'So when Taylor asked him to falsify his post-mortem findings – to say that Enid Judd was a virgin, which she clearly wasn't – he agreed to do it.'

'What choice did he have?' Ainsworth asked. 'You have to understand that the killings were a complete accident. Nobody *wanted* them to happen. Not even Phil Swales.'

'Let's move on to the events leading up to the morning of the murders, shall we?' Paniatowski suggested. 'Was there a big party the night before?'

'No. Sometimes Swales would bring up half a dozen girls, but that night there was only Lola.'

'Lola?'

'That's what the girl – Enid – called herself.'

'So who else was there – apart from Dugdale, Swales and the girl?'

'A few of Whitebridge's more prominent citizens.'

'What were the names?'

Ainsworth shook his head. 'I'll tell you everything else you want to know, but I won't tell you that.'

'But since you obviously do know who they were, presumably you were there yourself?'

'Yes, I . . . I was there.'

'What time did the party break up?'

'It was around midnight when most of the guests left.'

'But Swales and the girl stayed on?'

Ainsworth nodded. 'He had some business to do with Taylor the following morning. Teddy had said he'd pick Swales up from the farm, because the Merc was in dock until Monday. Swales could have had someone else drive out and pick up the girl, but I suppose he wanted her to share his bed.'

'Did *you* sleep with Enid?' Woodend asked – knowing that as a monitor he should say nothing, yet being unable to restrain himself.

'Yes,' Ainsworth admitted.

'She was only fifteen, for God's sake!'

'You have to try and understand what the Pleasure Palace was like,' Ainsworth told him. 'It . . . it was a different world, where the normal rules just didn't apply. When we were there, it felt as if we could do anything we wanted to, and nobody would really get hurt.' He looked down at his hands. 'And though we all knew that every time we went there we were putting ourselves more and more in Taylor's power, we still couldn't stop going. I think we must have been addicted to the place.'

'You make me puke!' Woodend said angrily.

Paniatowski shot him a warning look. 'What happened on Sunday morning?' she asked Ainsworth.

'I wasn't there at the beginning, so I can only tell you what they told me later.'

243

'Understood.'

'They heard the car drive up, and then they saw Judd through the living-room window. His turning up like that came as a complete surprise to Swales – he thought the man was still in jail.'

'And he panicked?'

Ainsworth shook his head again. 'Swales is not the kind of man to panic. At first he thought that Judd could be bought off with a few pounds – and when it became obvious that that wasn't going to work, he thought he could be *frightened* off.'

'What made him change his mind?'

'Judd did. He was screaming at the top of his voice about how much he loved his daughter, and how he was going to expose the whole operation. He said there was a reporter on his way to the farm at that very moment.'

'And that's when Swales decided to kill him?'

'Yes.'

'And his daughter, too?'

'She'd just seen him murder her father. He couldn't very well let her live after that, could he?'

'He shot them in the face to disguise their identity?'

'Yes. He thought he'd have a much better chance of covering his tracks that way.'

'And then he rang you?'

'No. He rang Taylor.'

'And *Taylor* rang you?'

'Yes.'

'Which is how you came to be the first policeman to arrive at the scene of the crime?'

'Correct. I knew I ran the risk of drawing attention to myself, but I wanted to make sure they hadn't left any obvious evidence around.'

'Like tyre tracks?'

'Exactly. DCI Woodend was right about – there were

244

tracks in the snow that the A40 had left. I drove over them.'

'Swales and Dugdale had gone by the time you arrived?'

'Yes.'

'So what happened next?'

'This is hearsay again.'

'Noted.'

'The A40 wasn't in very good condition, and it broke down about a mile from Moorland Village. While he was trying to get it started again, Swales turned on the car radio. He thought it might help to distract Dugdale. That's when they heard the BBC already broadcasting details of the murders.'

'And *that* made them panic?'

'It certainly made *Dugdale* panic. The report didn't actually say that he was the main suspect, but it certainly suggested it. He told Swales that he wanted to turn back and give himself up. He said he didn't see why he should take the blame for the murders, when it was Swales who'd actually committed them.'

'So Swales killed him, too?'

'That's right. He broke his neck.'

'Let's get back to your part in all this,' Paniatowski said. 'Did you go straight from Dugdale's Farm to Moorland Village?'

'Yes. Taylor and Swales were already there by then, of course.'

'And Dugdale?'

'And Dugdale's body . . . yes. Swales had already put it in the boot of the Austin. He was going to drive off and dump it somewhere.'

'So why didn't he?'

'I advised against it. I knew that by then DCI Woodend would be setting up roadblocks. Even if the Austin wasn't actually searched, there was still the danger that some bright young bobby might take note of its number, and since the car belonged to Judd, it would have pointed the investigation in his direction.'

'Which was the last thing you wanted?'

Ainsworth nodded, and turned towards Woodend.

'I don't like you, Charlie,' he said. 'I never have. But you're a bloody good bobby. I knew if you made the connection with Judd, you'd piece the rest of it together. I wanted to do all I could to stop that happening – and, just to make double sure, I jumped on the first opportunity I had to throw you off the case.'

Harris coughed awkwardly. 'And put me in charge of it instead,' he said, speaking his first words in what seemed like a very long time.

'And put you in charge of it instead,' Ainsworth agreed. 'Let's face it, Harris, you're not exactly Sherlock Holmes, now are you?'

'You're a real bastard!' Harris said.

'You see what I mean?' Ainsworth asked Paniatowski. 'Harris has been working for me for ten years, and only now has he uncovered that basic fact about me.'

'Whose idea was it to fit Mr Woodend up on the bribery charges?' Paniatowski asked.

'It was Taylor's. I didn't even know about it until the whole thing was a *fait accompli*.'

'Taylor told me it was your idea,' Woodend said.

'He was lying.'

'But whoever's idea it was, you exploited it to the full, didn't you?' Paniatowski said.

'What else could I have done?' Ainsworth asked, almost back to pleading again. 'It was Chief Inspector Evans who actually "uncovered" the "evidence" Taylor had planted. What was I supposed to do when he presented it to me? Tell him I knew it had been faked? How could I have, without admitting I knew who'd done it – and *why* it had been done?' He turned to Woodend again. 'However much I may have disliked you personally, I would never have fitted one of my own people up. I still have a little self-respect and professional pride left.'

'Self-respect!' Woodend repeated incredulously. 'You sleep with a girl who's little more than a kid, you keep the lid on the biggest corruption scandal this town has *ever* known, and you cover up a triple murder. And you can still talk about *self-respect*?'

'Sir . . .' Paniatowski said worriedly.

Woodend rose suddenly to his feet, and for a few heart-stopping seconds it seemed as if he were about fling himself across the table and grab Ainsworth by the throat. Then the moment passed and, as much to his own surprise as everyone else's, he found himself walking to the door.

He paused on the threshold, and turned to face Ainsworth for one last time. 'I've got grave doubts about capital punishment,' he said. 'But if what you'd done was a hangin' offence, I'd put the noose around your neck an' pull the lever myself. Aye, an' polish off a good fried breakfast straight after it.'

As he stepped out into the corridor, he could feel the bile rising in his throat. He had known more than his share of horrendous murders. He had seen the desperation that circumstances could drive otherwise ordinary, decent people to. But in all that time – through all those cases – he had never felt quite like this.

He strode rapidly towards the lavatory – totally unaware that there were other people on the corridor who he was forcing to step quickly out of his way.

The girl who had died up at Dugdale's Farm had probably known more about sex than he ever would, he thought. But in so many ways, she had been a complete innocent – a child caught up in adults' games, who had paid for it with her life when those games had gone wrong.

247

He pushed open the lavatory door and went straight into one of the stalls. He only just made it in time. The moment he was standing in front of the bowl, a searing pain shot across his stomach, and he bent over to spew out all the sickness that had been building up inside him.

Thirty-One

T he lads on the team had earned the right to a heavy drinking session at their boss's expense, and that was just what the lads had got. Now, as the hands of the clock behind the bar moved inexorably towards closing time, only Woodend and Paniatowski – and an army of empty glasses – remained.

'I think we're both a bit drunk,' Paniatowski said, only slightly slurring her words.

'After all we've supped, we'd better be – or I'm suin' that bloody brewery,' Woodend replied.

Paniatowski fumbled awkwardly with her cigarette packet for a few seconds, then seemed to decide that if it took *that* much effort, she didn't need a smoke after all.

'You remember the drive back from Manchester?' she asked.

'Yes.'

'You thought we'd never get to Taylor. You were so depressed that you said it might be a good thing in the long run if he murdered you, because at least then we'd be able to get him for something.'

'I know.'

'Yes, but what you *don't* know is that right after that I was almost on the point of asking you if you wanted to take me to bed.'

'Why?'

Paniatowski shrugged awkwardly. 'I'm not quite sure.

I think I thought it might make you feel better. I think I thought it might make *me* feel better, too.'

'So why did you only *almost* ask me?'

'Big question.'

'An' what's the big answer?'

'I think it was because I knew there was always the slight chance we'd crack this case, and that if we did, we'd end up sitting here, just like we are now.'

'So?'

'If we had slept together, we *wouldn't* be sitting here just like we are now. Things would have been different, and I'm not sure I would have been happy with that – because I like the way things are between us.'

'So do I,' Woodend told her.

'Would you have?' Paniatowski asked.

'Would I have what?'

'If I'd offered to go to bed with you, would you have said yes?'

'I'd like to think I'd have said no. I'd like to think it, but we'll never know for sure, will we?'

'No,' Paniatowski agreed solemnly. 'We won't. So what happens now?'

'At a guess I'd say that in five minutes time Ethel will call last orders, an' I'll go an' look for a taxi.'

'I didn't mean that. I meant, what will happen to the Whitebridge police?'

'Dick Ainsworth will go to jail, DCS Whittle will be kicked upstairs to fill his shoes, an' we'll get a new DCS to replace him who'll probably turn out to be a bigger bastard than any of them.'

'That new DCS could be you,' Paniatowski suggested.

'Nay, lass. Not in a million years.'

'*Why* not?'

'Because apart from the fact that everybody knows I'm temperamentally unsuited to sittin' on my arse an' orderin'

250

other people about all day, there's a new black mark against my name.'

'What are you talking about?'

'I've brought down one of our own. Worse, it's the second time I've done it. Once could be seen as a mistake. Twice looks like it's becomin' a habit.'

'But Ainsworth was rotten to the core!'

'Aye, he was,' Woodend agreed. 'An' for a few months, everybody'll remember that. Then the memory of what Ainsworth's done will fade, just as the memory of the man himself will. An' all that will be left is the uncomfortable thought in the minds of the people I'm workin' with that Charlie Woodend broke ranks twice, and might just go for his treble. It won't make my job any easier. Yours neither – for that matter – since you were almost as involved in the whole nasty business as I was myself.'

'Thanks for that,' Paniatowski said. 'You've really cheered me up.'

'Only tellin' you how things are, lass,' Woodend said.

The lights flashed, and the landlady called out, 'Time, gentlemen, please!' in one of those shrill, grating voices that only pub landladies seem able to produce.

Woodend rose to his feet. 'There's a taxi rank just round the corner,' he said. 'I'd better get there before all the other drunks turn up.'

'Mrs Woodend's still away, isn't she?' Paniatowski asked.

'Aye. She's not due back until the day after tomorrow.'

'So you've no actual *need* to go home now?'

'What are you gettin' at?'

Paniatowski hesitated for a second. 'That offer I nearly made on the drive from Manchester? It might be back on the table.'

Woodend shook his head. 'I appreciate the compliment, lass, I really do, but . . .'

251

Paniatowski smiled weakly. 'I expected that answer. The only reason I brought the whole thing up again was so that you could be sure in your own mind that you'd have turned me down the last time.'

Woodend smiled back. 'Well, I knew *that*,' he said. 'What did you think? That I'd taken you seriously?'

'No, of course not.'

Woodend patted her softly on the head. 'I'll see you in the mornin', Monika.'

'Yes, sir. See you in the morning.'

She watched him as he crossed the room, opened the door, and stepped out into the night. Only when she was sure that he had finally gone did she turn to the bar and signal for a last vodka before they threw the towels over the pumps.